WAS SHE
OR
WASN'T SHE?

"But I don't look the way I used to."

"Don't be ridiculous. You obviously aren't a restoree," Harlan said sharply. Sara felt tension return to his body. "There isn't a mark on you."

"That's just it . . . there isn't. I've lost three scars. I had a long gash on my arm where I . . ."

Her voice trailed off as she saw his face. The mixture of horror, distaste, disbelief, anger—and, strangely, hatred— stunned her.
Now she knew something was really wrong . . . but she didn't know how bad things had become!

"*Restoree* is SF at its best . . ."
—KLIATT

RESTOREE

Anne McCaffrey

A Del Rey Book

BALLANTINE BOOKS • NEW YORK

To
"My Favorite Relations"
G. N. McElroy

A Del Rey Book
Published by Ballantine Books

ISBN 0-345-27674-4

Manufactured in the United States of America

First Edition: September 1967
Fourth Printing: May 1978

Cover art by The Brothers Hildebrandt

CHAPTER ONE

THE ONLY WARNING OF DANGER I had was a disgusting wave of dead sea-creature stench. For a moment, it overwhelmed the humid, baked-pavement smell that permeated the relatively cooler air of Central Park that hot July evening. One minute I was turning off the pathway to the Zoo in search of a spot that might have a breeze from the lake and the next I was fainting with terror.

I have one other impression of that final second before all horror overcame me: of a huge dirigible-shaped form looming lightless. I remember that only because I thought to myself that someone was going to catch hell for flying so low over the city. Then the black bulk of the thing seemed to compress the stinking air through my skull, robbing me of breath and sanity with its aura of alien terror.

Of the next long interlude, which I am informed was a period of withdrawal from a reality too disrupting to contemplate, I remember only isolated incoherencies. It is composed of horrifying fragments, do-si-do-ing in a random partnering of all nightmare symbols, tinted with unlikely colors, accompanied by fetid odors, by intense heat and shivering cold and worst of all, nerve-memories of excruciating pain. I remember, and forget as quickly as possible, dismembered pieces of the human body; the pattern of severed blood vessels, sawn bones, the patterns of the fine lines on wrinkled skin. And throat-searing screams. And a voice, dinning into the ears of my mind, repeating with endless, stomach-churning patience, collections of syllables I strained desperately to sort into comprehensible phrases.

Red, yellow, blue beads rolled, parabolically, evading a needle and its umbilical string. A spoon dipped into a blue bowl, into a red bowl; a spoon dipped into a red bowl, into a blue bowl, until my body was forced into the mold

5

of a spoon and itself was dipped into the bowl, my greatly enlarged mouth the bowl of that spoon. Plaits of human hair swayed toward oddly shaped sheets of pale white leather. The gentle voice with the iron insistence of the dedicated droned on and on until each repetition seemed to trampoline into the gray matter of my mind.

Then, after eons of this inescapable routine, I began to clutch at snatches seen normally and rationally; a face on a sea of white which stretched limitlessly beyond my blinkered perception. I would be aware of bending over this face. I kept trying to make the face resemble someone I knew: one of the junior account men who invaded the source library of the advertising agency where I worked; one of the anonymous faces on the buses I rode from my 48th Street cold-water flat.

At other times, I would find a tray of food held in front of me and associate myself as the carrier. This troubled me even more because of all things, I hated serving food. In college I had paid for my board working as a waitress and sometimes a cook in private families, resenting the necessary exigencies of a junior female member of a large family. It seemed to me my earliest recollections were of setting or clearing the table and serving food. But the feeling of the entire scene here had an alien quality to it, despite the fact my coherent vision was limited. The tray and dishes had a different touch and the smell of the food was unfamiliar.

The next identifiable sensation was that of the warmth of sun on my shoulders and the caress of wind, of green light in my eyes. I heard screams that can only be heard and not described, but they might have been from earlier sections of the nightmare. I had the feeling on my hands of the slippery softness of soapy water. Then the face on the vast expanse of white would reappear. I gradually became aware of an unfailing order in the procedure of my dreams. Face, food, water, sunshine, face, food, water, dark. The repetition was endless and I was passive to it, prompted by the droning voice, no longer gentle, but equally insistent.

Slowly, not just that face on a sea of white but

peripheral details took form and coherency. The face
would belong to a man, an ugly man with vacant eyes,
black hair, sallow pitted skin. The fact that he bore not
one morsel of resemblance to any of my brothers or any
of the overbright young men at the agency gave me distinct pleasure. His face was on a pillow which was on a
bed of hospital height. And always I was in the position of
looking down, not being on a level, with him. Had he
been bending over me, I might just have been alarmed
that all the tales of rampant white slavery in New York
City drilled into me by my provincial parents were indeed
true. My first conscious query was why was I not the
patient since, obviously, something was very wrong with
me.

The mere sensation of sun warmth gradually expanded
to include oddly shaped trees with willowy, waving
fronds, and with the feel of the wind was the cool
fragrance of floral odors.

The ground no longer hovered somewhere beyond my
comprehension but was suddenly squarely under my feet.
I was standing on a walk, bordered with blooms I never
remembered seeing before. The trays I carried contained
individual colored dishes with foods that smelled appetiz-
ingly and I fed them to the face in the sea of white.

I cannot judge the length of this semiconscious state. I
was a passive observer, comparing the anomalies with
personal recollections and finding no parallels. I was, however, not the least bit alarmed by all that, which should
have alarmed me, as I am normally very curious, in a
discreet way.

I do know that the transition into full consciousness was
brutally abrupt. As if the focus of my mind, so long
blurred, had suddenly been returned to balance. As if a
kaleidoscope had astonishingly settled into a familiar de-
sign instead of random, meaningless patterns.

Out of the jumble, my grateful eyes reviewed an entire
panorama of sloping bluish lawns, felicitously set with
flowering shrubs and populated by couples strolling casually down the paths. Each woman wore a gown the exact
cut and color of the blue one I wore. Each man had a

blue tunic and a coat gruesomely reminiscent of a
straitjacket. Beyond the bluish swath, lay little cottages of
white stone, with wide windows, barred by white columns
at narrow regular intervals. Directly in front of my face
was a shimmering opacity I recognized, by some agency,
as a fence and dangerous to me.

I was not, however, one of a couple. I was in a group
of eight people, strolling the walks, and the other seven
were men. Only one, the man directly to my left, wore the
strange jacket.

A voice, issuing from the left side of the man in the
jacket, spoke an irritating combination of comprehensible
words and jumbled syllables.

"And so . . . he is as well as can be expected. Certainly
his physical appearance has improved. Notice the firm
tone to his flesh, the clear color of his complexion."

"Then you do have hopes?" asked an urgent, wistful
younger voice. Its owner I could see without noticeably
turning my head. He was a young man, tall and slender,
with a sensitive, pale-gold tired face dominated by deeply
circled eyes. He was dressed in a simple but rich fashion.
His concerned attention was on the man whose harness
controls I now found myself holding.

"Hopes, yes . . . [another incomprehensible spate of
words. It seemed to me I was hearing another language in
which I could not yet think] . . . we have had so few
successes with this sort of. . . . Our skill does not include
mental breakdowns . . . the strains and concerns of affairs
in your behalf and for his country . . . but you may be
sure we are taking the very best care of him until that
time. Monsorlit's . . ."

This was not the reassurance the young man wanted.
He sighed resignedly, placing a gentle hand on my charge's
shoulder. It was the lightest of gestures, but it stopped
the man stolidly in his tracks. In the vacuousness of the
face, there was no comprehension of the action, no reaction, no sign whatever of intelligence.

"Harlan, Harlan," the youth cried in bitter distress, his
eyes brimming with tears, "how could this have happened
to *you?*"

"Come, Sir Ferrill," commanded a stern voice with no vestige of sympathy in its hardness. "You know that emotional stress can bring about another one of your attacks. You have little enough strength as it is."

The speaker fetched round in my sight. Immediately I saw his face, I disliked him. I considered myself scarcely a proper judge in this newly rational state of mind, but the instinct to hate him was as sharp as the fleshy face of the man was bland. His eyes, close together on either side of a large nose, were disturbingly cold, calculating and wary. His full sensuous lips sealed tightly over his teeth and his heavy jaw was implacable. His heavyset figure was ponderous, not just fleshy or muscular but unwieldy.

"Your solicitude for my health is touching, Gorlot, but I will judge which emotions I can afford," snapped the young man with such regality the implacable man demurred.

The youth continued to speak, ignoring this Gorlot.

"Since that is his condition, I must leave Harlan here," he said to a corpulent, moon-faced individual who bowed with oily obsequity at each phrase. "But . . . if I am not informed the moment an improvement is noticed . . ." and the youth left the threat in mid-air with the authority of one who is used to complete obedience.

The unctuous man bowed again to the back of the youth who turned and walked with brisk steps down another path. The smile on the fat man's face did not indicate obedience to the injunction. Nor did the knowing look this Gorlot exchanged with him. The others in the party walked into my line of vision and followed the youth and Gorlot.

When they were out of hearing, the fat man turned to me with a sneer and snapped a command, "To the house," and I, obviously from some well-rehearsed practice in that dim past from which I had so recently emerged, turned myself and my charge around and took a path toward a little cottage among the trees.

At the door stood an armed attendant, a brutish, coarse-looking person who spoke as we approached but spoke as one who knows he isn't heard.

"Back in your cage, most high, noble and exalted Regent." He threw open the door he had just unlocked. With a brutal shove he pushed my charge into the house. With an equally brutal and obscene caress, he pushed me inside and snapped the door lock.

The patient lay crumpled over the chair into which he had been pushed. I wondered how I would be able to get him to his feet, for he was tall and big-boned. But, as I put one hand under his arm, he took it as a signal and almost unaided got to his feet. His shins were bleeding slightly, but there was no sign of expression in the vacant eyes.

"Poor man," I muttered to myself, "which of us has been the madder?"

"Take off harness," blared a voice from the ceiling, startling me breathless. I spotted the grillwork that housed the speaker. "Take off harness," the voice repeated, slowly, distinctly, as to a child or . . . a childlike mind.

I did as I was told.

"Take off harness," the voice repeated four more times even as I had completed the task. "If I've said that once, I've said it a million times," the voice grumbled in a lower and more normal tone.

"You'd gripe in a priest's cave, you would," came a half-muffled reply. "By the Seven Brothers, you won't find me complaining. This life suits me fine. Plenty of food, nothing much to do except lock doors and . . . unlock any pretty legs I want."

"You like that, you Milbait," was the sneering reply.

"Ahhh, that's your main problem in life, Balon, you have to have a struggle to please you. Not me."

"Who do you think you are, telling me what my problem is? Monsorlit?" Balon growled. His voice altered again as he issued another command. "Seat patient."

I scuffled with the chair, picked it up, half pushing the man into it.

"Get tray at wall slot. Get tray at wall slot."

I located the wall slot and the tray on which were two sets of dishes, one red and one blue.

"Feed patient blue food. Feed patient blue food."

My patient ate with a half-animal intensity, snapping at each bite as the spoon touched his lips, gulping it down half-chewed.

"Eat red food. Eat red food," was the next order. "Damned if I care if the dummies eat or not. They give me Milshivers."

"You'd care all right if you had to feed all of Gleto's drugged prizes yourself. Then I'd never hear the end of your blasting. Your trouble is, you don't know a prime cave when you see it. Me, I like it fine. Those dummies do all our work. This is better pay than patrolling, too. Not that I'd patrol with the half-blown reliners they call squadron leaders these days. And not with a war on Tane. Who wants hand-to-hand combat? And it's better than running illegals. You can never tell nowadays when Gorlot's going to have to make more commitments and who wants to end up with a needle? Or tied to the local Mil Rock?"

"Balon," shouted a new voice in the background I recognized as Gleto's. "You've been at Lamar again. Leave him alone. Just luck I looked in at him on my way to greet Ferrill. You keep your hands off him."

"If you knew what the Milrouser had done to me, you wouldn't . . ." began the grumbler passionately.

"I don't care if he blocked your cave," Gleto said angrily, "you cut him up once more and you'll join him."

"Eat red food. Eat red food," Balon snarled into the speaker system.

There were no more incidental remarks over the speaker that day, but it was a constant source of odd, vulgar dialogues between much the same personnel during the next week.

Although I never understood their topical references until much later, my understanding of the language increased immensely . . . if limited to a very rough vernacular. I knew there was a war going on between these people and the inhabitants of another planet, Tane. I knew that the army unit, the Patrol, was considered to be run by incompetents and that the casualties were high. That there was a

sudden epidemic of insanity that caused the guards no end
of secret amusement.

I had been told by Balon to return the tray after I had
eaten the red food. I was then told to be seated in the
other chair of the room without any further commands for
what seemed a long time. My private meditations were
uninterrupted until the green sun had sunk from sight and
a twin-moonlit night well darkened.

As the greening twilight increased to the point of low
visibility, I was briefly startled to see the lights in the four
corners of the room come on. It was not overly bright for
me to assume that a central agency turned on all the
functions of the cottage, remotely controlling the order of
the days with no need for personal contact. This isolation
was merciful to me as I sorted out truth from fancy in
newly regained sanity.

Perhaps, on another day, if I hadn't heard the coarse
interchange, I might have innocently announced my rationality. The wise decision to remain silent was strength-
ened each day by the grotesque conversations I overheard.
It was lucky, too, that there was not a single diversion in
that barely furnished room so that my activity, outside of
the care of my patient, was restricted to looking out the
window or sitting looking at my vacant-eyed companion.
Any other industry would have immediately communi-
cated my change to the guard on his random rounds.

I learned early that the speaker system was two-way. A
chance, overloud comment on my part fetched the guard
instantly. To him I presented the same vacant stare that
inhabited the face of my charge. He looked at me suspiciously, caressed me in a vulgar fashion that shocked me
motionless and departed with a shrug of his shoulders.
After that I lived with another dread, that one of them
might select me for his pleasure.

It was a good thing, too, that there was no visual check
installed in the cottage or I should have been apprehended
the very next morning of my rationality as I stood in front
of the window and made my most amazing discovery.

For the body I inhabited bore few resemblances to the
one I distinctly remembered possessing. It was the same

height, same chestnut hair, but it was a slim, graceful figure I saw, not my former awkward self. And my skin was a warm golden color. All over. In contour my face was similar, but now my blue eyes stared at, to me, a totally transformed face. My incredulous fingers softly caressed the new, marvelously congruous nose. No longer was I crucified by that horrible hooked monstrosity bequeathed me with hereditary injustice from some New England zealot. This new nose, all golden, fine-grained skin, was straight, short and charming. I stroked it, reveling in the tactile sensation that proved it was really part of me and there was no more of it than I could see in the window reflection. How many, many agonies that horrid nose had given me. How often I had railed at the injustice of parents who produced child after indiscriminate child and had no money to provide more than the basic needs and none to remedy cruel genetic jokes.

Had they been at least sympathetic, I would not have left home. But they couldn't even understand why I wanted to save money for plastic surgery. Only Jewish girls felt it necessary to have nose bobs. The fact that I looked Semitic with such a nose didn't bear on that problem.

"You are as God made you, Sara, and you've much to commend you to any decent self-respecting man."

"But nothing to commend myself to *me*," I remembered saying, "and I don't see any decent self-respecting men pounding a path to my door."

They couldn't argue that, certainly, for not even my brothers could be blackmailed or pressured into getting me dates. But they could and did argue against my going to New York although I had a written job offer, a good one with an advertising firm, confirmed and secured.

"Why the library right here in Seaford has offered you a very nice position," my father had argued.

"Seaford? I might as well rot in the end of the world," I had cried. "I'm twenty-one and I'm leaving home. If I cook another meal for anyone, it'll be for myself and not for six field-hand appetites that don't know decent food from pigs' swill." I had glared at my brothers, busy shoveling food into their mouths. "If I iron anything, it'll be my own clothing, not shirts and shirts and shirts."

"The girl's ill," my mother had declared as if this explained my unexpected outburst.

"All that education," my father had retorted sourly. He had resented my insistence on college, to the point where I had had to work constantly to support myself: making ends meet only because library majors got state support.

"I'm not ill. I'm sick, but not of education. I'm sick of Seaford and everyone in it."

"But everyone knows you here, hon," Seth, the brother next oldest to me, said soothingly. He alone came nearest to appreciating my despair. He had needed glasses desperately as a young boy and his now permanently damaged eyes were weak, watering and subject to continual inflammations.

"And *no one* wants me," I had cried from the bitterness of my soul. "At twenty-one, I have never even had a date."

"I'm leaving, Mother," I had repeated quietly and to end conversation had started to clear the table. And I did leave, taking my suitcase from the back porch on my way out the kitchen door to catch the night bus to Wilmington and the train to New York City.

But now, here on some strange planet, God only knows how many light-years from Seaford, Delaware, I had my new nose. I giggled. If I ever got back home, I could use my savings for a trip to Europe. Only I was abroad already.

I stroked my nose again and then the smooth, golden-skinned arms where a dark hairy growth had once added to the list of my physical embarrassments.

Further examination proved that three prominent scars, the rewards of trying to play tomboy to my older brothers, were gone from my body. Of my disfiguring marks, only the double gash on my right instep where I had stepped on a bottle wading remained. But the corns on my toes from shoes too short for growing feet were gone.

I was utterly delighted, mystified and grateful to, if appalled by, the strange agency that had caused this transformation. I was all my most glowing dreams had once evoked. Not beautiful but pretty, healthy looking with my golden tan (only it wasn't a tan, I discovered), properly curved—and precious little advantage could I see of it, locked in one room with a mindless idiot.

The air of danger and despair that hung over the pleasant gardens and bare cottages could not be mistaken. When outsiders walked among us, the guards were tensely alert. The lack of treatments of any kind, the tenor of the conversations I overheard on the loudspeakers, contrasted strangely with the luxurious surroundings and the physical appearance girls and patients were made to maintain. The other women who paraded with their charges were pretty, perfect in their prettiness with almost frightening similarity. Their expressions were only slightly more intelligent than those of their patients. A case of the dolt caring for the idiotic in a moronic paradise.

I learned the reason for the simple harness that had to be strapped on my man before each promenade in the garden. A small, needled vial containing a tan, viscous fluid was aimed at the right arm through the padding that kept both arms bound to the sides. A jerk on the reins exerted a pressure that drove the needle into the arm.

I saw one man run berserk, yelling, dragging the girl who, in her stupidity, still clutched the reins. He halted abruptly, screaming in agony, and dropped rigid to the ground. The performance thoroughly frightened me and I regarded the big man I cared for with alarm. I knew of no such precautions should a seizure overtake a patient in the cottage. One night, though, I did hear the sudden crescendo of hysterical laughter, shrieks and a final shrill cry from a neighboring cottage. I did see the limp, bloody figure of a girl carried out. Another pretty, blue-robed woman took her place by the next exercise hour, vacantly parading her glassy-eyed charge. I took to staring at my ugly man at all times, hoping to forestall such an occurrence in my cottage. I knew every line on his face, every pitted scar, every twitch of his muscles. At one point, I started with every deep breath he took.

My patient received his first professional visit eight days

after my recovery. Three men came in; a white-coated technician pushed in a small treatment cart and immediately left; the fat-faced man called Gleto came in and a man whose appearance was an odd contrast to Gleto's.

Gleto ordered me to stand in one corner and vacantly I moved after what I considered an appropriate time for moronic comprehension. I stood, however, so that I could see everything that went on and the third man held my attention most.

He was not tall, just my height, and carried himself stiffly erect. His movements were all as precise as a Scots guardsman, no motion was wasted. His skin seemed to be drawn tightly across his skull and each straight black hair on his head was precisely combed into place. His nose was high-bridged and thin; his lips were thin, his eyes of a nondescript shade were penetrating and intense, set deeply into his skull. There was no expression on his face nor were there any lines that indicated he had ever had any expression. A colder personality I never met nor a more impressive one. In dress, manner, color, motion, speech, he was a machine of efficiency, not a human being.

He made a rapid and thorough examination of the patient, skimming the first page of the stiff chart on the treatment wagon without missing a word. Looking up, he said:

"I see no need whatever of increasing the dosage now. The injection every two weeks plus the oral amounts in his food are ample to subdue his personality," and he implied that his valuable time had been wasted.

"I'm taking no chances," Gleto replied accusingly, "and you haven't been here in two months. You know how powerful Harlan is physically," and the heavy, fat eyelids flickered with unctuous insolence, "since it took three injections to hold him under the first week."

The cold man looked at Gleto. "And you will no doubt recall from whose laboratories cerol originated and who is most familiar with its properties. I am no more eager for his recovery than you. It would interrupt my research at a time when success is a matter of weeks away." The thin, precise eyebrows raised imperceptibly and the cold man reached for the chart again, flipping over a few rigid sheets before his thin finger jabbed at a notation.

With no expression he now indicated displeasure.

"Where is the weekly absorption count? If you are stupid enough to ignore the simple precaution of an absorption count, naturally you are stupid enough to sit quivering with fright that Harlan might recover. I thought I had made the necessity of those checks adequately clear to your technicians."

Gleto attempted to pass this off.

"Do not evade the issue, Gleto," came the implacable voice. "The absorption count has not been taken for four weeks. One is to be taken immediately and retaken every other week. When I have perfected a simple check, I do not intend to waste time coming here just to remind you to use it."

"I don't have the technicians to . . ."

"What about that . . . fellow outside?"

Gleto snorted at the suggestion.

"I thought so. You've spent only enough of your wealth to maintain an outward appearance of efficiency and shiver in your bed at night because your avarice prevents you from hiring sufficient personnel to run this *place* properly."

Gleto looked at him suspiciously and then twisted his lip into a sneer.

"You don't fool me, Monsorlit; absorption rates, ha! That's just an excuse to get more of your dummies off your hands."

Monsorlit turned his eyes from the chart he had started to reread to gaze at the fat man. The room became still, broken only by the breathing of the patient, until the sneer left Gleto's face and he began to shift his bulk restlessly.

"Your assessment of the situation is erroneous and I mistakenly credited you with more medical acumen than you possess. And I correct your term 'dummy' to 'mental defective.' " Monsorlit's voice without changing pitch gave the effect of a shouted disgust for Gleto. "Since your perception is limited by its effect on your cash pouch, I will send, with my compliments, a repossessed technician who can perform this simple but necessary test. He will come each fifth day. I will have one ready for such tasks in four weeks. In the meantime," Monsorlit took a lancet and ampul and deftly took a blood sample from the ugly man.

Gleto recovered his poise and affected a knowing smile.

"Your generosity, indeed," he scoffed.

"The technician's instructions will be limited to Harlan, as he is the only one with whom I am concerned," Monsorlit continued, taking up a filled syringe, testing it and then plunging it into the patient's vein. The man's body became rigid with muscular tension, quivered as if trying to release itself from the grip of the drug and finally relaxed. Sweat beaded his brow and rolled unheeded to the pillow.

"If he's here, why can't he do Trenor's nine as well," Gleto insisted angrily.

Monsorlit stood up, wiped his hands precisely with an antiseptic solution.

"As I said, my only concern is Harlan. If you wish to hire the services of the technician for the others, you may check with the business director for the rates."

Gleto's face turned an apoplectic purple and he controlled himself with effort.

"That's how you market your dummies. Oh, you're clever, Monsorlit, but one day . . ."

Monsorlit eyed him dispassionately.

"One day my techniques will replace this . . . this," his gesture indicated the gardens and cottages, "unprofessional arrangement. There will be no need for it. Men may come to my hospital, broken in body or mind, and leave whole and sane."

Gleto's little eyes widened with a touch of horror.

"They aren't dummies then; you've been restoring again. That's your deal with Gorlot. I thought your safe-from-Milness had taken a tumble." Gleto laughed derisively now. "How long do you think it'll be before Council finds out! And gasses you and your vegetables!" Gleto stopped with a sudden thought and gasped, looking at me in terror. "Is this one a restoree? Are all these dummies restorees? Are you unloading the dead-alive on me?" he screeched, advancing on Monsorlit.

"Does she act like a restoree?" the physician asked calmly. "No, she acts exactly as she is, a moron from my Mental Defectives Clinic, repossessed through shock techniques of enough intelligence to perform the monotonous and routine duties of your establishment just as others from my Clinic pick fruits and vegetables in the farmlands of Motlina and South Cant. Don't think you're the only miser to take advantage of this type of limited perception personnel in these times of worker rebellions and rising prices. And don't think you do me a favor when you use them. The only favor is to your fat self and your fattening purse." Monsorlit accurately judged the fat man's capacity for insult and took up another subject.

"The technician will be sent here for Harlan's absorption rates and, because of his limited intelligence, will be unable to grasp the necessity for performing any other tests. Trenor will, for all his imperfections, take a jaundiced view toward your neglect of his nine reluctant patients. The decision is up to you and I believe your loss would be the greatest."

Monsorlit left the room, motioning to the technician to collect the cart.

Gleto stared after the precise figure, pouting angrily, and when the technician nervously tipped over several bottles on the table, his fat fist clubbed the man viciously. Satisfied, he hitched his tunic into a more comfortable crease over his shoulders and stalked out. I stood staring in front of me while the cart was wheeled out and for some minutes after the lock snapped into place. The tension of the scene between Gleto and Monsorlit was cold and heavy in the room and I was cold and scared.

CHAPTER TWO

THE UGLY MAN WHOM THEY called Harlan lay twitching occasionally. I had considered it misfortune enough that he should have fallen over the edge of sanity in the prime of life. Now I knew him to be an unwilling drugged victim of some scheme, my pity was tinged with outraged righteousness. I looked more closely at the face, hoping to find in it some vestige of intelligence I had missed, some reassurance of personality to fit in with the entirely different role in which he was cast.

His gray eyes, their pupils dilated to the edge of the iris, stared with their customary vacuity at the ceiling. I saw now that the ugly face did have an innate strength and that immobility did not rob his long, heavily boned frame of its look of power. I wondered if a vibrant personality overcame the basic ugliness of features. Perhaps a smile. I fashioned one on the lax lips, but it was too much a mockery for me to judge the spontaneous effect.

I had noticed during my care of him the scars on his person: the new tissues were smooth, no gaping pulls to indicate stitches, not even on the raggedy gash across one cheek. The tip of one index finger was missing. He was a battered and bedamned fellow.

As I pitied him, I pitied myself, for my sympathy now tied me to him more effectively than any possible dedication to a mental cripple. I was stung with an impulse to batter down the door and run, run, run away from the fear, the implications of evil, the vulgarity of the guards and the massive frustrating boredom. I wanted to leave all this unfamiliarity, and somehow, although logic indicated I was nowhere near my own world, find my way home.

After I had settled him for the night, it occurred to me that if he were sane, he could help. And perhaps, he could be made sane. Monsorlit had spoken of doses in his food.

If I could withhold his food long enough, he might partially recover, at least enough to help me.

There was one drawback. If I didn't feed him, his hunger would betray me. And I would go hungry if I fed him all my food. I decided, in the final analysis, that I had no choice but to try this idea. I certainly didn't know the planet and he did.

The next morning I fed him most of my food, and just a little of his own, eating the remainder of mine and some of his to sustain me. I felt strangely disoriented all day and had difficulty in forcing myself to move. The next day this feeling had increased so noticeably that I ate none of his food and gave him none. I got very hungry.

By the fifth day, I was ravenous and he was so restless during the night I had to block the speaker grill with a pillow. He was hungry, too, and bit savagely at the spoon, so that I gave him even the little I had reserved for myself, eating only enough of the blue food to stop the roaring within me.

That night, he spoke in his sleep and I lay rigid with terror that the pillow had not sufficiently muffled the sound. Every moment I expected the guard to come striding in.

During breakfast on the sixth day, his eyes blinked and he tried desperately to focus them. He was struggling so hard, mouthing sounds in an effort to speak, that I was torn between the desire to hear and the necessity of keeping him quiet.

Such hope as swelled in my heart for his return to sanity was rudely disappointed during our morning walk. He did not seem to grasp my furtive, whispered explanations. His eyes still blinking furiously to focus were as vacuous as ever. At dinner, he ate more normally, chewing with intense concentration. The night was a continual struggle for me, against the sleep I desperately craved, against his moaning which I had to muffle against my shoulder. The next morning, he actually seemed to see me and I smiled encouragingly, hopefully, patting his hand reassuringly. The witlessness had left his expression and he looked at me, deeply puzzled, struggling to form a question when the guard walked in on one of his sporadic visits. Rigid with horror, I stared at the man I had almost rescued, my one chance to leave this horrible place suddenly torn from me as success was so near.

The guard barely glanced at me. Furiously he jerked his finger at the red bowls and then, shouting a litany of "Blue bowl for the patient. Blue bowl for the patient," he struck me again and again with his whip. I shrieked in pain and fear and cringed back from the flailing whip, trying to climb under the bed, away from the searing lash.

"This imbecile piece of idiocy is color-blind all of a sudden," he yelled at the loudspeaker. "Blue bowl for the patient. Blue bowl for the patient," he shouted, emphasizing his phrases with lashes for me until his rage was spent and I lay weeping, sore and bleeding, half under the bed.

Gleto arrived in minutes and examined the patient, giving him an injection and watching as I was made to feed Harlan from the blue bowls. Gleto added his blows to my painful back, grinning sadistically at my yelps. I cowered back against the wall as far from him as I could get.

"What bowl do you feed the patient from?" he demanded, advancing on me. "Red bowl?"

I shook my head violently.

"Blue bowl?"

I nodded violently.

"Blue bowl, blue bowl, blue, blue, blue," he roared, punctuating each word with an open-handed slap on whatever part of my twisting body it met.

"Blue, blue, blue," I shrieked back, covering my face with my arms and keeping my back to the wall.

"That'll take care of her," Gleto grunted with satisfaction and, to my weeping relief, he and the guard left.

Although some of the weals on my back and legs were bleeding, a warm soaking in the shower was all the treatment I had. That night, uncomfortable to the point where no position gave me relief or the solace of sleep, I lay awake. Several times, Harlan's heavy limbs overlapped me and made me cry out involuntarily. The speaker chortled back with delight at my discomfort. I resolved not to give them additional satisfaction and stifled my moans.

Mulling over my "bravery," I realized that I had actually escaped very lightly. The guards and Gleto were so secure in their assumption of my idiocy, they never once had questioned a deliberate attempt on my part to feed the prisoner the wrong food. They also assumed that I had made the mistake only once. They had not examined Harlan closely, but the administration of the drug had drawn him back into his witlessness. No technician, though, had come to take an absorption count. I had not yet lost my chance to escape nor to free Harlan from his stupor.

I was not lucky enough to continue my experiment with Harlan as immediately as I had resolved. A guard was present at every feeding for the next four days. Four longer days I never endured, filled with constant cuffs that added new bruises to barely healed ones and new obscenities to a list my limited experience had never wildly imagined.

As soon as I was sure they had decided I had learned my lesson, I started again. Nothing could have induced me to acquiesce now. That brief, if interrupted, respite from the drugged food contributed to Harlan's quicker recovery. By the fourth day, he responded to my insistent urgings for silence. On the fifth day, he spoke for the first time on the morning walk. I saw the deliberate effort he made to keep his voice low. It was difficult for him to enunciate. He had to repeat the simplest phrase with frustrating ineptness.

"They beat you," he managed to say finally, his eyes focusing on the bruises on my face and arms. I clutched at him and nearly wept for the unexpected comfort of his first rational words. A deep feeling of gratitude, joy, respect and love flooded me. I had been too long denied a normal society. The bruises abruptly lost their aches and I straightened shoulders I had curved against the tenderness of my back.

"How long?" he struggled to say, "am I here?"

"I don't know. I have no way of telling."

The approach of the guard curtailed conversation for a while.

"Way escape?"

"I don't know."

"You must," he insisted.

I steered him toward the menacing opacity of the force screen fence and he nodded imperceptibly in understanding.

"There has to be a way," he asserted. "The date?" and I could only shake my head as his look reproached me for my ignorance. He couldn't know I had never been taught to tell the time of his world nor understand the names of days and months.

We were herded back to the cottage and the guard, while I shuddered apprehensively, kicked Harlan into the room as he always did. I ducked by as quickly as I could as much to escape the lascivious touch of the guard as to caution Harlan against violence and warn him about the ceiling speaker. He was staring at it as I hurried to him, his lips moving, his eyes snapping as the therapy of anger cleared his mind of the last hold of the drug.

He examined his jacket with care and discovered the needle and its paralytic fluid. With bare nails we managed to pry it out of the stiff fabric. He held it in his hand thoughtfully for the prize it was, looking speculatively at the door. He grinned suddenly, not at all nicely, and secreted the vial in the belt of his loose tunic.

I indicated that we would have to sit down, would have to follow the orders of the speaker assiduously, panto-mined the pillow over the grillwork and nighttime. He nodded comprehension, sighing with impatience.

So we sat, facing each other. He looked above my head, deep in thought, his big hands flexing and stroking the arm of the chair as we waited.

Now his face was alive with the spirit of him, he was no longer an ugly person. His deep-set eyes sparkled and his mobile face showed some of the changes within him his thoughts provoked. Occasionally he would glance at me, curiously, smiling to reassure me. Once or twice, after some thought struck him, he inhaled as if to speak, caught himself and compressed his lips impatiently.

The arrival of dinner was a very welcome diversion. He reached for the blue bowl and I all but snatched it out of his hands. I hurriedly dumped it in the commode and showed him that it could not be eaten.

With a quizzical expression he regarded the one small portion of dinner that remained, shrugged his shoulders and divided it in two. Bowing with mock ceremony, he handed me my spoon with a flourish that made me want to laugh. We ate slowly to make our stomachs think they were being fed. I have since looked back on that bizarre first meal with Harlan as one of the happiest moments of my life.

To have found a friend, again, to be companionable with another human!

The next day, at lunchtime, we had an awful moment. As Harlan was about to dump the blue bowl with obvious relish, I heard the lock turn. Harlan needed no prompting to assume a stupid expression. I began, slowly, to feed him from the blue bowl. The guard watched this performance, fingering his whip. I trusted he interpreted my trembling as fear of a beating rather than terror at discovery. He left and the lock clicked us into privacy.

Harlan rose swiftly and, by the simple expedient of thrusting a finger down his throat, expelled the drugged food.

That first night, lying beside him on our mutual bed after the muffling pillow had been crammed against the grillwork was another of my special memories. I was keenly aware of his warm strength beside me. Before I had had no thoughts at all about the propriety of sleeping next to an inert moron, but a vibrant personality rested beside me now and I was acutely conscious of myself and him.

Harlan recovered control of his tongue, but he was puzzled at my own still-halting speech and my inability to understand parts of his questions.

His perplexity made me nervous in a half-fearful way as if by the mere accident of not speaking clearly, I had committed some wrong. Defensively and with some involved explanations of my presence, I managed to make it clear that I knew I came from another solar system. His doubt was so apparent that I sketched the Sun and its planets by fingernail into the bedsheet. It held the impression long enough for him to grasp my meaning.

Immediately his expression became wary and veiled. He strained to see me clearly in the moonlight and shook his head impatiently at the limitations of that glow. We were lying side by side when he suddenly leaned away from his close inspection. He took my hands in his, stroking my wrists with hard thumbs. He sat up and did the same thing to my ankles, then my hairline. His confusion persisted and, against my soundless protest, he turned back my dress to run light, impersonal fingers over the rest of my body as though I had been someone dead. This reassured whatever worried him. But his body remained tense and his expression was no longer as open and friendly as before.

He asked me almost too casually how I got here.

"I don't know. But you do believe me ... that I'm not from this world?"

He shrugged.

"My sun has nine planets, my world only one moon; my sun is golden, not green," I persisted urgently. "And the reason I have trouble understanding you is that you speak so fast and use words I don't know. It isn't because I'm stupid ... or insane."

His withdrawal made me frantic that I might lose the precious companionship I had so recently won. He must understand me so he would take me with him. I could see he had every intention of escaping as soon as he could. I had no doubts he would succeed or die in the attempt. Death to me was preferable to the alternative of remaining in this ghastly place.

"I can't remember how I got here," I wailed softly. "I just don't know. I was walking in a park at night on my own planet and something big and black hovered over me. The rest is all mixed up in the most horrible, horrible nightmares."

"Describe them," he demanded in a cold, tight voice that scared me.

The words rolled out. The weight of the grotesque scenes and experiences, walled up in my subconscious, poured out, as if voicing them would erase the remembered horror and terror. I don't recall what I did say and what I couldn't bring myself to say until I realized that I was trembling violently and he was holding me close against him. At first, I thought he was trying to muffle my voice, but then I heard his voice soft with low reassurances and his hands were very gentle.

"Be quiet now. I do believe you. I do. There's only one way you could have got here. No, no. I don't doubt now a thing you've said. But that you are sane and . . . well, it's a miracle."

There was incredulous wonder in his tone. He looked at me again, excitedly. The only thing I cared about was that he was no longer withdrawn and cold, and that he did believe me.

"You know how I got here?"

"Let's say," he demurred candidly, "I know how you must have got to this solar system. But how you reached Lothar and this place, I can't even hazard a guess. The only possible explanation . . ."

"You mean your people have interstellar travel and brought me here as a slave," I interrupted, thinking with a sudden rush of hope that I would be able to get back to Earth. Though what Earth held for me was too mundane after this experience.

He hesitated, considering his next words. Then, settling me into a comfortable position against his shoulder, his lips above my ear, he explained.

"My people didn't bring you here. I'm reasonably sure of that. We do have interstellar travel, but I cannot believe my race has penetrated to your section of space. Before I took so conveniently ill," and his voice was sardonic, "no new exploration was contemplated." He snorted with remembered exasperation. "I am reasonably sure, however, that your planet has been invaded by the curse, and paradoxically, the salvation of our Lothar. We call them the Mil. They're a race of cellular giants which havē had interstellar flight since the beginning of our recorded history, some two thousand years ago. To be precise, they *are* the beginning of our recorded history. We are, bluntly, their cattle, their fodder. That's all right, take it easy," he said reassuringly.

His similes forced me to admit to myself what I had desperately tried to hide; that the disassembled pieces of anatomy that twisted and turned through my nightmares were horrifyingly like the joints on hooks in a meat market.

"They have periodically raided this system for centuries. When we finally penetrated one of their depots here on Lothar, [I realized he was using the historic 'we'] we began the long struggle to free ourselves and our planet of this terrible scourge. We turned their own weapons on them and then had to learn how to use them properly and repair them. Kind of progress in reverse. Now, we have not only been able to keep them off Lothar, but also out of this immediate sector of space. Our losses are still heavy in every encounter, as it is difficult to best an enemy with armaments similar to your own. Our big advantage is our own physical structure. However, rarely do any of our ships and patrolmen fall victims of the Mil.

"I don't know how far they range, but I suppose we have forced them to find new sources of supply. Your planet, for one. Easy now. I forget it's difficult for you to accept such a terrible fate for your people. We've lived with it all our lives."

"But, if these . . ."

"Mil, although at one time we called them 'God,'" Harlan remarked, grimly humorous.

". . . these Mil captured me on a raid on Earth, how did I get here? On your planet?"

Harlan frowned. "I would like to believe that our Patrol intercepted the ship you were on and captured it. But . . ." and he stopped as if he could see the fallacies in the theory and they disturbed him. "It must be way past Eclipse; or is it? If it is, I've been here a long time.

Haven't you got *any* idea of how long you've been here?"

"I can only recall the last few weeks clearly. Yet it seems as if I've been here forever. I guess I was in shock or something," I ended lamely. "I certainly was surprised to find I was a nurse for someone else."

"All the more reason to get out of here as soon as possible. My head is clear now and my reflexes feel normal. It's been like swimming through sand. Still," and he looked at me speculatively again, shaking his head, "I don't understand how you managed to remain ..." he hesitated and supplied another word, ". . . untouched."

"Untouched? Oh, but I don't look the way I used to," I assured him, my hand rubbing my nose.

"Don't be ridiculous. You obviously aren't a restoree," he said sharply. I felt tension return to his body and coldness to his voice. "There isn't a mark on you."

"No, that's just it. There isn't," I replied. "I've lost three scars," and I pointed to the areas involved, "and someone took pity on my ..." my hand touching my nose.

"Scars? Missing?" he interrupted in a hoarse whisper.

"Yes," I prattled on. "I had a long gash on my arm where I got caught on a picket fence ..." and my voice trailed off as I saw his face. The mixture of horror, distaste, disbelief, anger and, strangely, hatred, stunned me.

He grabbed my wrists in an angry grip and rubbed them, tracing the junction of hand and arm with fingers that hurt with their prodding. He felt around my ears, pulling my hair back roughly.

"What's the matter?" I pleaded, my delight congealing.

He shook his head, hard, as someone whose neck muscles have contracted spasmodically.

"I don't know, Sara. It's just hard to believe," he replied enigmatically. "Yet you would not have been able to think things through the way you have if ... We've got to get out of here. We have got to get out!" he said passionately.

With a fluid stride, he crossed the room and yanked the pillow from the grill. He settled back in the bed, patting my arm reassuringly, as if he realized how worried I was by his reactions.

It was a long time before sleep came to either of us. I remember feeling his fingers on my wrist again just as I drifted into unconsciousness.

CHAPTER THREE

DURING HIS SLEEPLESSNESS, HARLAN HAD made the only plan of escape our mutual limited knowledge of the asylum afforded. To pass the force screen, we must overpower the guard in the cottage by means of the drug vial we had pried from the straitjacket. Harlan would wear the uniform, I would daub myself with blood, Harlan having assured me that the blood would be donated by the guard. We would try to pass out the gate of this section of the asylum as if I had been attacked by my patient. From there on, we must improvise. If it came to sheer strength, the powerfully built Harlan would prevail. However, neither of us could foresee what preparation might have been made for escapes.

We also had no choice. Each day might bring the arrival of the technician to take Harlan's absorption rate and we were too sure of the results of that test. I also couldn't tell when the next intravenous injection would be administered. With it, I would have to start all over again, denying Harlan the drugged food, waiting for his return to sanity.

Whatever qualms or fears I might have normally entertained were overruled. Harlan's anxiety and frustration intensified my own desire to be out of this mad place. And, too, not once did Harlan intimate he felt he had a better chance of escaping by himself although I was sure he did. He had included my release in his calculations and brushed aside my one half-hearted attempt at sacrifice.

Every day Harlan's recovery had been jeopardized by the random appearances of the guard. This one day, when we were nervously primed for our escape, he was conspicuous by his absence. Harlan had to exert a tremendous control over his impatience and I was constantly forced to remind him during the exercise period to stop charging up the paths, to school his expression into the proper witlessness. He endured these corrections far better than I should have. All in all, by evening both our tempers were frayed by the unrewarded waiting.

As soon as the lights were out, Harlan, releasing some of his frustration in the action, rammed the pillow against the speaker and began to pace around the room in a frenzied way.

His pacing grew as unendurable to me as a fingernail scraped across slate.

"Last night," I began hesitantly, not knowing what I wanted to say but knowing that any conversation was better than this taut silence, "last night, I told you who I was and how I got here. Who are you besides Harlan and how did you get in here? Who drugged you? Why?"

He paused in mid-stride, frowning as my questions brought him out of his thoughts. He gave a sort of snort, smiled and, after another moment's silence, began to talk. He had a pleasant voice when he kept it low, but it had the burr of the military bark and a metallic quality. Gradually, as he talked, he stopped pacing, and then sat down, watching me as he spoke with a disconcerting attention.

"You certainly do deserve some explanations, if only for all the meals you gave up," he said, gripping my shoulder as a gesture of his continued gratitude.

"Before I came here, I was Regent of this planet for my eldest brother's son, Ferrill."

"I thought the guard had called you Regent, but it didn't make any sense then."

Harlan grimaced. "That guard . . . It's the custom here on Lothar for the Commander of the Perimeter Patrol to assume the duties of Regent if the heir to the Warlordship is underage when he becomes a candidate."

"Why couldn't you be Warlord if you were brother to the . . ."

"No, that doesn't follow," Harlan replied blandly. "I should say, Fathor was my half-brother. We had the same father, but Fathor's mother was the first wife and his progeny inherit. Besides, I've other plans for my time once Ferrill is of age. Like finding your planet. I like finding new planets. I like exploring." A boyish grin lit his features. "I've had luck in that direction already. Found two new ones, fraternal planets around the star we call Tane, my fourth year on Patrol."

I gathered this involved more than just searching a section of space until you found stars with satellites. I murmured proper things, only he frowned.

"They've been more trouble than they're worth . . . almost," he continued. "The inhabitants are humanoid, but the gentlest, dumbest people imaginable. They make some of our associates here look like Council members. They've got two of the most beautiful planets, crawling with game animals; Lothar doesn't have too many anymore. Their oceans are full of edible fish; their lands, which the Tanes don't even bother to cultivate, would support millions of us. They've got mineral resources that make the mind swim when you think how many ships, instruments and fuel it means in terms of our fight against the Mil. And those innocent creatures roam from one place to another like pleasant dreamers."

"Haven't the Mil bothered them?"

"Evidently not. They don't have even an elementary sense of caution or suspicion. They would have fled from our expeditionary ships if they had encountered the Mil. Most of our fleet has been recruited from or designed after Mil ships."

"Why are the Tanes trouble then? Can't you just colonize or mine or . . ."

Harlan leaned forward, balancing his elbows on knees and slapping one palm into the other to emphasize a statement. Or, which was disconcerting, he would point his tipless finger at me.

"I don't know about your world, but here on Lothar we're crowded. So crowded that every inch of land is either cultivated or catacombed with mines, cities and factories. We run to big families, sort of law of supply and demand. But the Mil don't harvest us anymore, so every new child crowds his family that much more. There aren't enough jobs to go around nowadays nor is there enough food as there used to be. We don't need so many men in active Patrol, but yet we have to train every young man against the day we're big enough and strong enough to follow the Mil back to their own planet and wipe them off its face."

"So," I interrupted, "everyone who isn't well off wants a share of one of the Tane planets and to hell with the Tanes."

He nodded agreement. "Only it isn't just those that aren't well situated. It's the big landowners, the big industrialists and the big scientists who want priority and mean to get it. And they've got all kinds of reasons."

"I'll bet," and I refrained from giving him a brief account of the American Indian. "And I imagine no one cares what happens to the Tane."

My perspicacity pleased him.

"Council had accepted a plan to allow colonization first for farmers, because our crying need is food. But farmers are conservative and those younger sons, willing to go, those without patrons in Council, are being intimidated or beaten up unless they belong to a certain guild. And the people who lead that guild will buy up the land once the farmers settle on it and that will be the end of individual agricultural expansion. Or, take the small mining outfits. Only a few have dared to apply for permission to work the Tanes. Why? They've found their homes ruined, their credit is suddenly destroyed, or their equipment is wrecked just before takeoff."

"But surely you're trying to find out who's behind it?"

"It is one group," Harlan said wearily. "I'd found that much out before this happened to me. There is one man, or a few men, who were guiding the attacks on my colonists. But what baffles me is: why? I mean, for what reason. You see, Lothar has always had just one purpose since we first shook off the yoke of superstition and managed to repel the Mil from landing on our planet. We mean to destroy the Mil completely. Our whole psychology, our whole history, has been directed toward that aim."

"Perhaps after . . . how long did you say . . . two thousand years, this purpose is wearing a little thin," I suggested with the Crusades in mind.

"It couldn't," he said without qualification. "Not when the Mil are always so close." He frowned. "You see, actually it's only in the last one hundred and fifty years that we've kept them entirely away from our planet. And we couldn't have done that without Ertoi and Glan."

"Who?"

"Inhabitants of another nearby star. You can see them from here," he said blandly. He pointed out the window to a pulsating red blink that was the primary of the system.

"Ertoi and Glan take care of that entire section of space. We've been able to push our Perimeter Patrol four light-years beyond our own system. Since then, we have adequate protection against a concerted attack. The first time," he said with justifiable pride, "we lost all but two ships of our entire combined fleets, but no Mil landed on our three planets."

"Well, who do you think is the traitor?"

"My second-in-command, a fellow by the name of Gorlot." Harlan's eyes narrowed speculatively. "I'm not sure. It couldn't be that . . . No. They know we're not ready to go after the Mil yet unless that new weapon . . ." and he trailed off tantalizingly. "This Gorlot's a throwback. Uncivilized. He lives only for battle and he's a master strategist. Pulled off some extraordinary maneuvers three Eclipses ago. That's why I seconded his appointment when Gartly retired. But he's no good as a peacetime officer and the Perimeter has been very peaceful. He belongs back in the days of the first Harlan with the Seventeen Sons when it was all we could do to find caves deep enough to escape the Mil. He'd be the proper man to send out to the Mil but . . . That hothead forgets that no Lotharian has the guts," he threw in, "besides himself, because he did it one day on a wager, to walk into a Mil ship until it's been completely decontaminated. The smell of those things is enough to set a tough squadron leader raving. Until the Alliance with Ertoi and Glan, we had to wait until the Mil decomposed inside their ships before we

could refit them. Fortunately, the Ertoi and Glan aren't
hampered by such childish terrors.

"I wonder," and Harlan drew back into his thoughts for
a long time. His conclusions did not settle his mind, for he
growled with impatience and resumed his pacing, cursing
Gorlot, cursing his own stupidity for falling into the trap
of the asylum.

"I've got to get out of here and back to Lothara," he
cried in a groan, clenching and unclenching his fists behind his back as he paced.

CHAPTER FOUR

SLEEP THAT NIGHT WAS NOT restful. It was peopled with formless obscenities and charged with fear and anger, frustration and hopelessness. I was alone in the bed when I awoke. Startled I turned in panic and saw with relief that Harlan was up and pacing, his face black with worry and fatigue.

At breakfast there were none of the pleasant pantomimes we affected about the division and consumption of our scanty ration. Harlan ate quickly, glowering.

The walk in the garden that morning was sheer relief. The four bare walls of the cottage had grown smaller with every passing minute. Harlan had draped his jacket loosely on him so that a strong outward pressure would free him. We had agreed to delay returning to our cottage until the guard was forced to round us up. This assured us of a chance of overcoming him once we got to the cottage. So we dawdled at the far end of the grounds on the outside paths following the line of the force screen. We were at the high end, midway between two posts when it happened.

One of the patients went berserk. He threw himself at the screen, dragging his unwilling companion with him. Together they went up into a torch of blue flame, burning fast and hotly with only the echo of screams of unutterable agony to mark their death.

Even as I stared with paralyzed horror at these human torches, Harlan had reacted to the opportunity. Flinging off the jacket, he grabbed me by the shoulder and together we hurtled into the faltering screen. I thought I, too, would be consumed in flame. The pain and shock that coursed through my body was too intense for me even to scream a protest. Then, once past the weakened barrier, only an endurable ache and burning sensation remained. The burning was quite legitimate because our clothing had been reduced in an instant to scorched tatters. Even the heavily padded jacket was singed brown. Harlan, however, gave me no time to pause and take stock. Grabbing my hand, he pulled me through the land moat around the force screen and into the grain field with its high waving grasses.

"Have you no idea, Sara, where this asylum is?"

"None," I cried, feeling the pull of the sharp grass tendrils against my sensitized flesh. The fence had always blotted out the environs of the asylum.

"Farm, farm, farm," Harlan panted. He was tall enough to see over the rolling fields that stretched out in all directions from the institution. He glanced up at the sun, squinting, but it was too near the zenith to be much help. He halted briefly, sniffing the slight breeze.

"Sea!" he declared and abruptly turned off to the right, guiding me with a firm hand under my elbow.

"Can't we just find a road? It would lead us somewhere," I gasped, struggling to keep my feet under me at the pace he set.

"Road!" he flung at me contemptuously and trotted up the rise in front of us. He kept glancing back over his shoulder. I didn't dare look back. It was all I could do to keep up with him.

We ran through the fields until I had such a grabbing in my side, I could not run farther. He sensed, rather than inquired, about my condition and let me collapse in the shelter of the tall grain at the next rise. Keeping himself sheltered by the grain, he looked out in all directions, again sniffing the breeze.

"We may have a little time before we'll be turned up missing, Sara," he said, dropping down beside me. "They'll have their hands full, rounding up the patients. They may not even take a head count right away. They've gotten lax and overconfident. However, the situation of the asylum itself, located right in the middle of farmlands, makes an air search ridiculously easy." He stopped and grabbed up a handful of straw. "Of course. We've got part of our camouflage right here." He laughed and started stuffing straw into his tunic so that the stalks stuck straight up behind his back and out across his shoulders. I followed his lead and, when my tunic parted over one shoulder, plastered myself hastily with the soft moist earth.

"Good girl," Harlan said and smeared his own skin with dirt where it showed whitely through. We looked like scarecrows after a week's rain when we had finished.

"Now, we will make for the sea. The moment you hear any noise at all, drop flat in the furrows," and he pointed out the cultivation ridges. "The grain is tall enough and thick enough that we may not be visible when they're going to look for running figures. And, they won't expect me to make for the sea," he added cryptically.

He held out his hand to me and, taking a deep breath, I rose and we started out again.

We had scarcely gone the length of that field when I heard something other than our laboring breath. Before I could react on my own, my face was in the dirt, Harlan's body overlapping mine.

Had the searchers been on foot, passing near us, I'm certain the sound of my heart would have given us away. The chirrop, chirrrop of a plane car neared, passed over us, retreated and cautiously we rose, checking to make sure another was not hovering. Running low we made it to the top of the next field. Even I could see that the land was sloping down gradually. The smell of the sea, tart and crisp, was strong enough for me to scent as I held my sweating face up to cool in the wind.

I'm not sure I was grateful for the times we had to lie face down in the moist black soil, waiting till the searchers passed over us. I got my wind back each time, true, but the terror of waiting, unable to risk a glance above, was more breath-snatching than the exertion of flight. Six times we dropped, each time a little nearer to where the land dropped off to the sea. And then, there was the sea before us, a hundred feet down the high straight precipice on which we stood.

My courage sank, for here, at the cliff edge, which seemed to curve for miles in each direction, the fields of tall grain ended. Fifty yards between sea and field was

covered with only low straggling bush, inadequate cover
for us walking strawstacks.

Harlan caught my despairing appraisal and squeezed
my hand reassuringly.

"There are ways down to the beaches."

"And then what?" I gasped, indicating the pounding
surf.

"The tide will be going out soon and we can go swiftly
on the sand, taking cover under the cliffs if necessary.
Much better for us. Come, now we strike northeast. These
cliffs tell me exactly where we are."

But he didn't bother to tell me, either because he knew
it wouldn't matter or because he forgot I wouldn't know.
As it happened, we were in South Cant.

He had held on to the padded jacket all through our
flight in the fields. Now, as he removed the straw from his
own clothes, he realized my nakedness. Ripping off two of
the dangling tapes with which to secure his tattered tunic
round his waist, he gave me the jacket. Quickly I threw it
on, tying the remains of my dress around my waist.

"Good, the dirt is still useful," he grinned and, taking
my hand, we set off again.

Harlan was too good a leader to tire us both to the
point where we would be unable to make a final dash. We
rested at intervals and a bit longer when we chanced on a
stream not far from where we made our descent to the sea
beach. As he had predicted, by the time we did find a way
down, the tide was retreating from the bronze sands. The
cool strand was refreshing to our weary feet.

My flimsy sandals, adequate for treading garden paths,
gave way all too quickly on the abrasive surface of the
beach. Walking on the damp coarse sands turned into
torture for me once the sandals gave out and the soft skin
on my feet was abraded with each step. I was wondering
how long I could continue this way when I was brought
up sharply against Harlan's rigid body. There was no need
for him to caution me to silence. I could see the boat as it
stood out from the cove we faced. I could see the men as
they clustered around their fire, hear their voices as they
argued. Worst of all, I could smell the food they were

cooking for their supper. Now hunger overruled the other
discomforts and the fact that I had missed what lunch
there was to eat made the lack of dinner torture.

Harlan pulled me back into the sheltering shadows of
the cliff. Had we continued on much farther, even the
gathering darkness would not have hidden us from a
chance look by the fishermen.

"Can you swim?" and when I nodded, "To that?" he
asked, pointing to the boat.

"Yes," I agreed although I was not the least bit confi-
dent. I was so tired and my feet hurt and my stomach
ached and I was very annoyed with everything for going
so wrong so long. I didn't consider how extremely lucky
we had been so far. At least not with the smell of food in
my nostrils after a prolonged fast. I comforted myself with
the thought that I wouldn't have to *walk* to the boat.

I didn't count on the icy water nor the sting of salt in
the multitude of scratches and abrasions that scored my
body. Nor did Harlan allow me time to ease into the water
as I preferred doing on family outings at Rehoboth. Harlan pulled me inexorably deeper.

"Don't swim overarm yet," he hissed at me and a wave
caught me full face. His arms supported me while I
coughed the water out. "You can swim?" he asked.

"Yes, yes," I assured him, stung by his skepticism and I
struck out toward the boat with a vigorous breaststroke.

As if he still doubted my ability, Harlan matched his
pace to mine, only he guided me out to sea, rather than on
an oblique line toward the boat from the shore. I caught
his purpose, to approach the boat from the seaside, although it added many yards to the original distance.

If the sea stung my cuts, its coldness supplied me with a
false feeling of exhilaration. I tried to speed up, to prove
to Harlan I was competent, but he warned me not to
extend myself. He was right, of course, because as we
turned toward the boat finally, my weariness returned
doubled. It was so difficult to get my arms out of the
water, hard to keep my legs moving.

"Sara, not far now," Harlan's voice said encouragingly.
His face was a white blob over my right shoulder as I

swam and ahead of us the boat was a solid blackness, its single mast silhouetted against the dying light of the twilight sky. Thrashing frantically, I lunged at the stern line, missing, going under, writhing upward, grabbing out in panic. Harlan's hand found mine and guided it to the security of the rope.

"Rest," he whispered and cautiously swam round the boat. I could hear him, a barely discernible rippling, as I gulped for breath.

"No one aboard," he confirmed. "But they took the smallboat ashore." For some reason this disappointed him. "Oh, well, in that case it'll take them a long time to spread the alarm."

"Maybe they'd be friendly," I hazarded, looking up at the sheer slippery side of the ship and wondering how I was ever going to make it into the cockpit.

Harlan answered my suggestion with a snort. He lunged up out of the water, caught at the gunwale, his body a whiteness against the dark boat. He got both hands secured and then I heard him inhale as he gathered his strength to pull himself up.

How selfish can you get, I derided myself, he's just as hungry, just as tired, just as sore as you are and worried to boot.

I heard him swear softly, a note of pain in his voice. I could hear him padding somewhere on board and then his face appeared above me.

"Grab this," he whispered and a heavy soft rope dangled in my face.

I looped it around my wrists, thankful I shouldn't have to make the climb unaided. Kicking myself out of the water, I felt Harlan pull me. As soon as I could reach the side, I grabbed for it, resolved to use as little of Harlan's energy as possible. Once safely on board, I felt drained of any power to move and I was numb with the chill of the cool evening.

"Here, get this on," he urged and pressed a handful of clothing on me. The garments smelled of sweat, stale and sour, and were sticky with salt. But I struggled into an old sweater and found it covered me halfway to the knees. I rolled up the sleeves and wished it covered me to the ankles.

"I suppose it's too much to ask if you've sailed a boat," Harlan said in a low voice.

"Yes, but only as a crew member, long ago."

He gripped my shoulder with rough gratitude. "You never cease to supply my need."

I struggled to a sitting position, wondering what he meant exactly, and looked around. As nearly as I could gauge in the light, the boat was about thirty-five feet long, sloop-rigged, the sail now neatly furled on the boom, the jibsail not even out. The boat was obviously a workship; I could see piles of nets and woven baskets. There seemed to be a small cabin and it was here that Harlan had found sweaters.

"It's a shame but I've got to cut the anchor. Too much time and noise to lift it out of the water," Harlan told me. I could see the gleam of a knife blade in his hand.

"It'll save time if I cut and you hoist the sail," I told him and taking the knife, crept forward. My hands seemed strengthless as I sawed away at the heavy anchor line, thankful it wasn't chain. I heard Harlan heaving at the sail and it seemed like noise enough to rouse the dead. It did rouse the men on the beach. I sawed faster.

"Hurry, Sara," I heard Harlan call and wondered why he still kept his voice low if the men had heard the creak of the sail.

I felt the line and there was only one strand still uncut. Frantically, I hacked away and, just as I felt the pull of the ship against the wind in its sail, the anchor line parted.

"Grab the tiller and head for the sea," Harlan cried, still struggling to lift the cumbersome sail. I guess in the dim light it was difficult to see what he was doing. And he was tired, but he made heavy work with the sheet.

Tripping over deck-stored gear, I scrambled astern and found the unfamiliar tiller handle.

If for only this one adventure, my tomboy days paid rich dividends. I had run with Harlan, swum with him and now I was able to crew for him. And, undoubtedly I

cautioned myself with the memory of sour disappoint-
ments, when the Yacht Club Dance on this world came
round, it wouldn't be Sara who was waltzed by the ship's
captain.

Harlan was cursing as he tried to make fast the sheet. I
caught at the trailing line as the boom threatened to knock
him overboard. I trimmed sail and steered for the open
sea.

The men on shore now had realized what had happened
and were shouting threats across the water as Harlan
joined me.

"It's another miracle that you can sail," he muttered to
me. "I can't."

"You can't?" I gasped, appalled at the situation. "Why
not?" I demanded, as the responsibility now resting on me
became apparent to my tired brain. He couldn't possibly
imagine that I could sail this bloody boat on an unknown
sea to a port I'd never seen.

"Too busy," he grinned. "You're doing all right."

That explained his ambiguous comments and his awkwardness with the sail.

"Now, yes," I practically screamed at him, "but if you
knew you couldn't sail, why in heaven's name did you
steal the boat?"

"I'd've figured it out, but I'm glad you already know
how," he repeated complacently.

The volume of his audacity was frightening.

"That's comforting to know," I said acidly. "Sailing an
open sea is easy even for an idiot Regent. And I imagine
you probably would have figured it out before you piled
up on a beach or reefs. At least you have the advantage, I
assume, of some familiarity with the coastline of this
world. I don't. I don't *know* your goddamned world!"

"My what world?" he asked as I had interjected an
English cussword.

"What do you want me to do now?" I cried, tears of
fear, frustration and fatigue starting down my face.

"Steer for the open sea," he said blandly.

"And then what? I don't even know how big your seas
are, what the tides are like! You've got two bloody moons

to complicate that minor detail of sailing. How do you expect me to . . ."

He put his arm around me, settling down beside me. His very presence and magnificent self-confidence helped calm my hysteria.

"The Finger Sea on which we sail," he began calmly, "is deep, no reefs or shoals except along the eastern edge. We will sail due east across it toward Astolla. It will probably take all night, so we would face the reefs in daylight when nothing is as overwhelming as it is at night. I do know navigation, Sara. And since you can handle the mechanics of sailing, we'll be all right. My purpose in heading east is to reach the home of an old friend of mine." He chuckled to himself. "We fought so the last time we met, I'm sure no one will think to check at Gartly's for me."

"If you fought, why would he welcome you?" I demanded, worrying not so much about what happened when we arrived as to how we would manage to arrive in the first place.

"Gartly is part of my loyal opposition, that's all. He has no love for Gorlot at all or any of that cave. None at all," and Harlan mused on some private memories, his face sober.

The wind freshened and the ship moved at a willing clip. The wind was also cold and I began to shiver.

"First, there must be some food aboard. I could eat a brant," Harlan said. "And there had better be more clothing, too."

He found both. The coarse bread and strong cheese filled my stomach and with rough cloth pants to keep me warm, my fearfulness dissipated. The ship was simple to handle, even for one person, the lines being winched astern so a lone steersman could handle the sheets from the cockpit on a long haul.

"How long a sail is it?" I asked Harlan when he settled down beside me again after another thorough prowl about the ship.

He shrugged.

"I have only a spaceman's idea of distance. A mere half hour or so by planecar."

I groaned. "I wish you really knew what you had let us in for," I said, depression overwhelming me.

"I do what I must," he said sternly. "And I must get to Gartly."

No apologies was I ever to get from Harlan. And naturally I found myself accepting his inexorable logic that we would get where we wanted to go, novices though we were, because we *had* to.

The sheer audacity of his idea was what saved us, I think, from discovery. For we sailed all that night with a good stiff following breeze. Harlan insisted on taking a trick to allow me to rest although I was reluctant to leave a complete tyro in charge of the ship. He assured me that if the wind would change—my one worry because sailing with a good following wind is child's play—he would wake me. He kept his word, waking me at dawn when the breeze dropped off. He also pointed with smug complacency at the distant outline of mountains on the horizon.

He had used a hand line and caught us breakfast. Once I had mastered the cooking stove, we ate hot food until we were stuffed. With land at least in sight and a full stomach for only the second time in several weeks, my depression disappeared.

"We were farther up the coast than I thought," he remarked. "Let's get close enough so I can figure out where we are."

I shook my head over his blithe unconcern. He laughed at me and then peered at the rising sun.

"That is," he amended, "if we get any wind."

"That'll be a long paddle," I remarked, trying not to be too sour.

"Pessimist," he teased. "Yesterday at this time, we were securely locked up in Gleto's amusing retreat with not a chance in a hundred of getting out. You make the most of the opportunities the gods grant and you'll win out," Harlan said with fine good humor. "Did I not have you as a nurse? Did you not have the wit to understand what was being done to me? Can you say that we have not succeeded in escaping?"

"Those men had all night to get somewhere to report their ship stolen," I reminded him.

"True enough," he replied, unruffled. "But they don't know *who* stole. One man? Several? There are plenty of bandsmen prowling. Nor, if they were simple fishermen, are they likely to give wind of it to Gorlot's people. I had meant to take the smallboat which they might easily believe had been improperly tied. But . . ." and he shrugged. "But this gets me closer quicker to help. Then, too, how long will it take Gleto to summon up enough courage to inform Gorlot I'm missing?" he chuckled nastily.

"He'll delay as long as he can," I replied, feeling a little reassured by that one fact.

"And, as it is known I have never sailed, the last place anyone will look for Harlan is on the sea."

"It's going to be a long row," I repeated, looking anxiously at the limp sail and the glassy water.

"We can while the time away," he suggested in such an altered tone of voice I glanced around sharply at him.

Before I had realized what he had in mind, he had pulled me into his arms. Startled and completely surprised, I clutched involuntarily at his shoulders for balance and was being kissed expertly and thoroughly. What thoughts my emotions gave room for were chaotic. I was as split into the various facets of my personality as if I had been literally blown apart.

The girl with the beaknose had never been kissed except as a party joke or absentmindedly by departing brothers. The unwanted girl who had stolen longing looks at shamelessly necking couples in Central Park had no firsthand experience with returning a kiss. His forceful invasion of my lips met neither resistance nor response. The stranger, by some crazy agency dumped on a strange planet, could and did not want to antagonize her one friend. And the sister who had overheard her brothers' candid comments on girls was all too certain the direction such beginnings would take. And I, all of me, didn't want him to stop kissing because of the way my heart pounded and my body ached for the feeling of his hands. Yet I didn't know what to do.

I could sense the change almost as soon as it began. Harlan lifted his head and looked at me slightly puzzled.

"And what's wrong with me?" he asked.

I realized he was asking me if *he* were the cause of my inability to respond.

"Nothing, it's just . . ."

"Don't they kiss on your planet?" he asked with a boyish incredulity.

"Yes, but I never did," I said inanely, my hand going to my nose.

That did it. I could see his face change again, that closing-out look I hated. Although I was still in his arms, against his chest, he had withdrawn.

"Please, Harlan, don't go away from me like that," I pleaded.

His look softened and he took my hand, his thumb absently rubbing my wrist.

"Then you are untouched?" he asked kindly, as if this were not exactly a privileged state on his world.

I could only nod, knowing I must be blushing at his frankness. I was torn with a horrifyingly unmaidenlike desire to encourage him, even if I didn't know how to go about it at all.

He chuckled at some inner thought and hugged me with affection but no passion, kissing me gently on the eyes.

"Then, my dear Sara, this is neither the time nor the place if such beginnings are to be auspicious. We both smell to the high heaven and . . ."

A sudden flapping, creaking, caught both our attentions and we hastily disengaged to duck as the untended boom, moved by the rising wind, missed knocking us overboard by a hair's breadth.

"Yes, this is neither the time nor the place," Harlan repeated, laughing boyishly as he lunged for the trailing line and I grabbed the swinging tiller.

Again I was torn by opposing desires: relief that I had been saved rude wakenings, and frustration because I had been aroused. I *wanted* Harlan. And when again would I be in a position alone with him when there was opportunity and time?

"Damn the wind," I muttered to myself as I eased the ship about.

The purple smudge on the horizon deepened into the green of treed slopes, fringed with boiling surf. I pointed out the inhospitable coastline.

"We can't land in that, Harlan," I protested.

"Let's sail southerly. The land breaks into the delta of the Astolla River past this range. Only we want to land before we get to Astolla itself." He squinted at the mountains. "Gartly lives above Astolla and that will be the hardest part of the trip."

He didn't qualify his comment, so I didn't realize then he meant that the danger of being encountered by someone who would recognize him was greater. I took him to mean the mountains and I groaned.

He turned to me, laughing. "All uphill, Sara, all uphill. Only," he noticed my feet, bruised and raw, "we'll have to do something about them."

"And this," I added, distastefully indicating my overlong sweater.

He rummaged in the cabin and came up with additional ill-smelling garments. Finding a bucket and a line, he heaved it overboard and to my amused astonishment, he started to sluice the clothing up and down in the clean seawater. He wrung them out neatly and spread them to dry on the deck.

"Our hosts were probably good fishermen but incredibly dirty," he commented when he had finished. "They'll dry quickly. Shall I take a turn?"

"I'm fine," I assured him and then I still was, what with the recent sleep and enough food and his approval.

He went forward and I saw him heave the bucket overboard again. This time it was himself he washed. I tried to keep the sail between me and glimpses of his strong golden body. It had been one thing to tend him as a moron, another to consider him as a lover.

I should not presume on his friendship later, I promised

myself. He was of too much consequence for someone like me and I'd be more than a fool to think I meant anything to him.

We sailed on for a long while, well into the sunny morning, until I was lethargic with the sun, hungry again and very tired. I was mesmerized by the masthead and the jibsprit which I kept pointed toward the ever nearing shore line. I was lost in fatigue and musings when suddenly Harlan's hand dropped to my shoulder.

Startled, I gasped and flinched as though I'd been struck.

"Is my touch offensive?" he asked, frowning.

"No, no," I hastily assured him. "I was worlds away."

He knelt down beside me and I noticed his bare chest was red with sun.

"You've got a burn."

"So have you," he retorted and I saw he had put on clean dry pants. He thrust a handful of dry clothing toward me. "These were the smallest and may fit better. Go on forward and wash some of the mud off, Sara."

I hesitated as I rose, as much from weariness and being in one position so long, as from the knowledge the sail did not conceal much from a determined watcher.

"If I look, I won't tell," he taunted, grinning wickedly.

Grabbing the clothes from him, I turned on my heel with as much dignity as I could and made my way to the bow. The pail was there and some soft, linenlike sheeting that he must have used as toweling. Traces remained of mud stains that hadn't come out with just a seawater rinsing.

It was very heartening to remove that filthy old sweater. And better still to get the rest of the mud off my body. My face stung in the salt bath, but when I was clean and dressed again, I did feel better. With decided pleasure I kicked the rags of my asylum tunic overboard and watched them sink below the surface.

"Now," said Harlan as I returned to the cockpit, "we must give you a plausible account of your existence in case you meet some awkward questioning. Gartly was my second-in-command and is an honorable man, but you, my dear Searcher," and his phrase puzzled me, "require some explanation, even to the most loyal comrade."

"Why not the truth?"

"Sara," and he turned my face so I looked at him fully, "you have no idea how you got to this planet?" When I shook my head negatively, he continued, "Then until I do find out, or you remember, the mere fact that you are *not* of this planet is very dangerous. As soon as I can, I shall start some adroit inquiries, but for you to come out and admit to an extraplanetary origin would mean your death without further explanation to you or from you."

"It'd be much easier to tell the truth. Then it wouldn't matter how many things I didn't know," I said plaintively.

His look silenced me. "I have taken that into consideration. I'd prefer to be able to send you up to my estates in North Lothar, but I may not be able to do that right away. Of course, the less you have to say about your past the better, but Gartly's of the Old Beliefs, and clan and cavesite mean much to him. Now listen. Jurasse is the next largest city to Lothara. It's northwest of the Finger Sea, deep in the mountains. Your father ... what was your father's name? Steven? No, make him Stane, a better Lotharan name. Your father Stane was a mining engineer. I'll put you on a professional level, my dear lady," and he grinned at me, "and as there are several hundred thousand miners and engineers in and out of Jurasse, there's scant way of checking."

"But he must have gone to college or university," I said.

"Un-i-ver-sity?" Harlan asked, puzzled.

"Advanced schooling, training in his specialty," I qualified.

Harlan shook his head quickly. "No. One learns on the job here. Stane is a fairly common name and we'll make you of Estril clan and Odern cavesite."

"What is the significance of clans and cavesites?" I asked grimly.

Harlan exhaled his breath and looked at me. Then he covered my hands with his big strong one. "I'll explain all that later. In the meantime, it is only important for you to know a clan name; the Estrils are conservative but known for their intense loyalty to their leaders, and the Odern is such an enormous old cave, hundreds of clans could refuge here."

"All right. Estril and Odern. Jurasse, next largest city, mining, northwest."

"Good girl. Your father died in a mine accident that happened just ... well, I *don't* know how long ago now, but it happened in the Tenth Month of the Single Eclipse. Just memorize it, Sara, no explanations. The same earth fault destroyed blocks of apartment buildings. So you can have lived at the sign of the Horns and no one will be able to run an accurate or quick check. Your important relative is your mother. What was your mother's name?"

"I wish you'd stop saying 'was.' For all I know, they are very much alive," I snapped.

"Not as far as you're concerned on Lothar," Harlan said with patient firmness.

"Maria."

"Make it Mara of the Thort clan, that's a South Cant group. Farmlands had some bad plague about thirty years ago, ... how old are you, Sara?"

"Twenty-four."

He smiled and started to say something, changing his subject even as he opened his mouth to speak. "Fine. Then all but your mother died in that plague, so you have no maternal family to worry about. This happens often enough and as the Clan Head may always be approached, no one is ever really orphaned. Between Jurasse and South Cant your accent can be accounted for. South Cant slurs and Jurasse is throaty."

"Mara of the Thorts from South Cant. No cavesite?"

"South Cant was not settled until caves were no longer a necessity."

"Where did I meet you?" I asked.

Harlan stared off into space, rubbing his mouth with his hand.

"That's the hard one, Sara. Particularly since I don't

know how long it's been since I was first drugged nor how or when you might have been brought here."

"Might there have been a group of old loyal cavemen who have fallen out with Gorlot and were suspicious of your collapse?"

"It's possible. Let me think on this. Once I get to Gartly, I can catch up on recent happenings. Then I'll fill in a logical background.

"Now," he said more briskly, "the last part of our journey presents the greatest hazard of discovery. If we are taken into custody, you can insist on silence until you have talked to a Clan Officer."

Earth-type spy stories and atrocities crowded into my mind.

"Won't they just kill me to keep me quiet and have done?"

"Kill a potential mother?" he demanded, his eyes flashing. "Unheard of." He looked at me. "Do they kill women who can bear children on your world?" he asked with trenchant scorn for such a wasteful culture.

I nodded slowly.

"Not on Lothar. Women are too important, even to Gorlot. No, your life is safe." He emphasized 'life.' "And I have made my claim on you already. Is that agreeable to you?"

His eyes locked with mine in an expression that warmed me to the pit of my stomach. I could only nod mutely. His hand again covered mine as he continued. "However, should I be taken and you can escape, no, no ... it is possible. And, Sara, you are to run if I tell you. Promise me that!" Again I nodded until his hand ceased his painful grip as he got my grudging consent. "All right, I am taken and you are free. Get to Lothara itself and to the 'Place of the Birds.' Ask for Jokan. Tell him, and only him, all that has happened. He is my brother."

"And how do I get there? Fly?"

"That's the quickest way," he said, taking me literally. "Oh. No money." He shook his head, gritted his teeth and swore with an eloquence that beggared what I had heard from the guards.

"We'll do it together, somehow, Sara. We've come this far in our search because my Sara can sail, and think and act," and he grinned at the face I made at him. "If we can win through to Gartly, we'll have money, a planecar and help. Then we can make further plans. The important thing is to make it to Gartly."

The way the surf broke so savagely against the shore line, even that modest ambition seemed unlikely. We were sailing a close-hauled tack now, and farther down the coast, I could see the mountains falling away to a plain. And at the farthest point, the glint of buildings in the sun.

"Let's beach the boat as soon as we can," Harlan urged, scanning the shore.

I glared at him.

"Pick your spot, pal."

"It's easy to see I spent my youth exploring the wrong planets," Harlan growled to himself as we sailed on and on.

I had noticed other sails, standing out to sea.

"Any chance they might be investigating us?" I asked him. He shook his head impatiently. I glanced out at the shore line anxiously and sighed.

"I haven't been to this part of Astolla in years, but it seems to me there *is* a beach. Gartly's one form of relaxation is fishing and . . ."

"Look," I cried, half-rising from the cockpit.

Directly ahead of us, half hidden by the sail's spread, was a planecar. Harlan catapulted into the cabin.

"You there in the fisherboat, " a voice, magnified artificially, roared down at me. The hovering craft swung round the ship. All I could think was they'd been able to see Harlan hiding in the cabin. "From where are you bound?"

"And what business is it of yours?" I demanded evasively, cursing because that was another thing Harlan had not bothered to brief me on.

"Answer when you're spoken to, woman," I was told rudely and I doubted Harlan's surety that women are not maltreated on Lothar.

"Come back when I can answer, you idiot," I said, throwing over the tiller on an unnecessary tack which made me obviously too busy with sheet and line to answer. It also cut off the plane's view of the cabin.

"Are you alone?" they persisted.

"Son of a Seventeenth Son, yes," I screamed at the top of my lungs, remembering a mild oath from the guards' dialogues.

The boom, swinging free, completely covered the cabin hatch although the plane was hovering suspiciously low on my stern. The ship had lost all way, sail flapping. I glanced up at the planecar as it swung forward. I saw the military uniforms on the occupants. I could even see the faces of the men and I didn't like them.

"You Milrousers, go bother someone else. I'm too busy. Get off my back," I yelled, shaking a fist at them.

The boat rolled in the surf and another look to port confirmed that my ruse was putting me in peril. Hastily I trimmed the sail and tried to get sea room between me and the jagged rocks of the shore. That I was in trouble now was too apparent to the airborne nuisances. The plane roared off with a speed startling to one used to wallowing helicopters.

"Harlan, get up here on the double," I called once the plane was safely away. "Harlan," for the tide had seized the boat, carrying us farther and farther inshore. "HARLAN!" I screamed just as the boat struck a submerged rock I had not even a moment's warning to avoid.

Harlan came on board just as the boom swung about and, as I rose in horror, it swept us both off the deck and into the sea.

I came up gasping, the heavy seaman's clothing weighing me down. But Harlan came up, too, not far from me.

"Are you all right?"

"I'm mad, clear through," I screamed at him. "Of all the stupid things to have happen . . ."

"Don't waste energy, swim," Harlan ordered as the little fishing boat, unguided, was lifted by the surge of the tide and cracked down onto the rocks. Planks, splinters, tackle, debris of all sort went flying in every direction as we swam out of the way. A flying piece of deck hit me heavily on the shoulder, but the thick sweater protected me enough so that all I got was the terrible initial buffet. Harlan disentangled himself from fouled line and we both struck out away from the flotsam on the water.

"I'm sorry," I told Harlan, swimming at my shoulder.

"I wouldn't be," he said good-naturedly. "It'll probably be easier to get ashore swimming than sailing."

We were about a hundred yards from the rocky beach and I could see that the haphazard rocks, a menace to a boat, were wide enough for a man's body to pass between them. One only had to hold one's course through them to make it safely in. Still, the tidal pull was now very strong and if we were smacked against one of those rocks, it'd be too bad. It was nervous business and we swept awfully close to the rough-skinned boulders. The uneven footing when we reached shallower water was worse going than the actual passage of the reef rocks. The footing was slippery and the tide tore at my feet. I slipped several times and then went completely down, skinning one leg so badly that Harlan had to support me the last five yards.

Quickly, when he saw the bleeding, he picked me up in his arms and carried me up the sand to the edge of the woods. He slit the trouser leg, baring the nasty gash the length of my shin. My whole leg ached from the jar of my fall as well as the lacerations. I felt very very tired.

"We must get farther into the woods before the plane-car comes back. The wreck will be noticed," Harlan said.

"Leave me here," I pleaded with him after one glance at the thick underbrush. "I'm so tired. I'll only slow you down."

"My dear lady, I have no intention of leaving you," he said angrily.

He tore the sleeve from my sweater and bandaged my leg. He was about to pick me up despite my protests when he froze, his eyes on the shore a little to the right of us.

I whirled and saw a figure sauntering along the rocky

beach, fishing gear draped all over him. The young man stopped when he saw us and then hurried forward.

"Can you give me a hand, stranger?" Harlan called. "We've lost our sloop and my lady is hurt."

I thought that his audacity would win out over the odds again. The young man was almost to us when he stopped short, his mouth open in surprised shock, his body dropping to a crouch as recognition dawned on him.

"Harlan?" he cried, half questioning, half stating the incredible fact.

It was too much for me and for the only time in my life I fainted.

CHAPTER FIVE

SOMETHING WAS BURNING MY THROAT and my leg was on fire and someone was choking me and I struck out wildly.

"Sara, Sara, it's all right," I heard Harlan say. Opening my eyes, I saw first trees all around us, then Harlan and then the concerned face of the young man from the beach. "We're safe, Sara. This is Cire, the youngest son of my old commandant, Gartly. It's all right."

"You're sure?" I asked stupidly, looking at Cire who seemed to me far too young to be as much help as Harlan's cheerful reassurance implied.

"Here, drink this." He held the metal bottle for me and it was more of the stimulant that had burned my throat. It was powerful and spread feeling through my arms and stomach, down to my vitals and my aching leg. I looked down and this had been bandaged with something white and far more comforting in appearance than the sleeve of my sweater. Cire's fishing jacket was wrapped around me, warm and far cleaner than anything else I had on.

"I don't want any more of that," I assured Harlan as he lifted the bottle to my lips again.

Harlan chuckled. "Patrol issue is noted for potency."

"How long have I been out? Of all the silly things to do."

"Yes, very silly of you," Harlan agreed amiably. Then both he and Cire laughed at my expression of shock. "That's better."

He got up.

"Now, Sara, we've got to move on. The planecar did come back and saw the wreck. What'll happen now I don't know. Cire says there's been no mention of my escape, so that planecar may only have been a routine flight. But the boat's registry number may come ashore with the wreckage. Then there'll surely be inquiries made.

Cire and I covered our tracks up from the beach to make them think there were no survivors ... or survivor. But I want to get out of Astolla entirely by the time an official investigation of the wreck is made."

I struggled to my feet.

"You don't like it, but it'll help," he added proffering the bottle. I looked at him and then at Cire and reluctantly steeled myself for another long swig.

"I'll be drunk in no time," I gasped.

"You'll be walking it off," Harlan retorted.

I'm not exactly sure "walk" is what I did. Harlan made me take considerable quantities of that brew once he felt me shivering through Cire's jacket. I remember not too clearly the events following the first long climb from the shore. I remember putting one foot in front of the other and talking about it. I remember complaining because I wanted to sit down and no one would let me. I remember being carried and then I remember fighting with someone because they wanted to put me on a planecar and I knew that was not right and I shouldn't get on a planecar and I couldn't get away from Them. The last thing I do remember is Harlan's voice, angry and arguing.

"By the Deep Cave, she's exhausted, that's all. Naturally she's talking gibberish. Here, give her to me a minute."

Someone was shaking me by the shoulders and I kept trying to get free. Then Harlan kissed me and I managed to focus on his face and realized he was the one holding me.

"Sara, Sara, *listen* to me. We're safe, we made it to Gartly's. Go to sleep now. It's all right to sleep now."

"Well, why didn't someone say so?" I remember saying bad-temperedly. I heard Harlan laugh and then I slid down, gratefully, into dark softness and warmth.

For me, time resumed after my legs stopped moving even in my dreams. I awoke in a comfortable bed in a pleasantly sunlit room with an indescribably appetizing odor tantalizing me. I sat right up in bed and looked around, trying to place my surroundings. The wide bed had had another occupant from the dents in the pillows beside mine. I decided I had better ignore speculations in that direction for the moment.

It might even be a female Gartly, I told myself, having remembered Harlan's final words to me. This pleasant blue room with its heavy wooden furnishings was the antithesis of the institutional asylum cottage.

A long soft gray robe was draped on the chair nearest the bed which turned my attention on the nightdress I wore. To my relief, it was utilitarian but feminine. Whatever was cooking made me ravenous. I put on the robe and looking around for a bathroom, stumbled over Harlan's fisher clothes.

"That settles that," I told myself, both irritated and pleased.

The delicious odor was irresistible and I hurried through the necessary, noticing in passing the mirror that I had picked up a nice tan, and that I had lost my eyebrows and singed my hair slightly shorter in passing the force screen barrier.

As I opened the bedroom door, I walked out into a hall, half open to the large room on the level below. Four men were sitting around a table cluttered with the debris of a meal. They had been talking solemnly and their voices died as first one, then another man became aware of my presence on the balcony. The oldest, gray-grizzled man glowered up at me fiercely and started to rise to his feet. I was about to take refuge in the bedroom when Harlan, laden with a plate of food and a mug, backed through a swinging door from the side of the house.

"Hi there, don't run, Sara," he laughed. "Come on down." He noticed Gartly's expression. "Gartly frowns to hide a tender heart and Jessl," he added, nodding to the man he was passing on his way to the table, "frowns from unfamiliarity with the light of day." He set his dishes down and, going to the foot of the stairs, waited for me to descend. He squeezed my hand reassuringly and led me to the table.

He was an entirely different person in his joviality, in the obvious affection toward two of the men, Jokan and Jessl. The Harlan I had known in the hospital, tense, frustrated, pensive, the apparently unconcerned Harlan of the sailboat, had transformed into this admirable stranger with whom I was not at ease.

The four men rose gravely in turn as Harlan introduced us, bowing formally, each bow as different as the character of the man. Gartly gave me a peremptory bow, his mind obviously on the business interrupted by my appearance. His blueing eyes passed over my face with the light dismissal of an older man for any younger person.

Jokan, and I remembered he was Harlan's brother, was nondescript in appearance, totally different from his brother. But his eyes, a sparklingly clear blue in his rough tanned face, had a vitality that detracted from the commonplaceness of his features. His bow was leisurely as he measured my face, my body, my legs and looking again into my eyes, his lips echoed the greeting in his brilliant eyes.

Jessl, a stocky, chesty man in his late thirties, was less courtly, checking me off in his mental catalogue as woman; intelligence unknown; and unnecessary. But it was he who held out my chair.

Cire smiled warmly at me. He resembled his father in face and outstripped him in size by half a foot but with undeveloped breadth. His bow was jerky, unpracticed, and he flushed boyishly, yanked out of the fascinating world of men to which he had so recently been admitted, by the arrival of a woman his senior in years.

"How's your leg this morning?" he asked considerately.

"I didn't even remember," I laughed, kicking my leg from the full robe.

"That's because you've slept nearly two days," Harlan laughed. "Cire, I appoint you chief server to the exiled court of Harlan and hope I left enough in the pot to fill a very generous plate for Sara. I've had five servings, my dear lady," and I heard Jokan draw his breath in sharply and Jessl turned around to look at me queerly, but Harlan continued briskly, "so I'm the guilty one if there isn't enough. You should, by rights, be even hungrier than I," and his lighthearted grin included an intimate reference to my abstinence for his sake.

Cire showed no reluctance to assume his honorary rank and went to get me food. Harlan took up the conversation he had left to refill his plate.

"Hindsight, my friends, is of no use. to us. We could sit here until the Mil come again before that would solve our problem. Don't think for a minute I haven't run from the caves of Jurasse to the Barren Plains for believing myself inviolate just because I was Regent. I've succeeded in making an absolute fool of myself and unless I'm careful about the next move, I shall compound that impression and lose any chance whatever of regaining the Regency.

"I've had a lot of good luck, lately," his hand touched mine in illustration, "and we'll hope it holds until Stannall can reinforce it. You're sure, Jokan, no one knows of your trip to Astolla?"

"I made the decision myself on the way to Jurasse and circled the Finger Sea," Jokan reassured him. He kept looking at me, however, not his brother.

Harlan regarded the meat on his fork speculatively, then carefully set the piece aside, leaning back in his chair.

"Now, Jessl has not been closely connected with me. Gartly and I had that quarrel about sector assignments," and Harlan's eyes twinkled at Gartly who harrumphed righteously. "They won't think of checking on any of you first. We've got to get Council in session to revoke Gorlot's temporary Regency. Ferrill can do it if we can reach him."

Jokan and Gartly immediately jumped in to elaborate on the young Warlord's rapid physical decline. No one had been allowed to see him recently, even such old friends as Gartly and his uncle, Jokan. Gorlot intercepted every attempt.

"I did get a few words with Maxil," Jokan added, "before that Milbait Samoth came breathing down my neck. I shall take great delight in kicking that fattail into so tight an orbit he's eating . . ."

"Jo," snapped Harlan, indicating me. Jokan glared at me for the curtailment of his invective.

I hadn't been paying too close attention because Cire had brought me the stew. I was eating with unladylike speed.

"Well," Jokan continued, "I was in the public gardens . . ."

"You were? How?" Jessl exclaimed.

"Moved in with the sightseers. Lothara's full of Eclipsers, so . . ."

"Eclipse will be tomorrow night," Harlan said, startled.

"That's the answer!" Jokan exclaimed.

"Don't be absurd," Harlan mocked him. "I couldn't get within ten feet of the palace wing in any disguise. With a discreet alarm out for me that would be the most closely watched place on the entire planet."

"*You* don't need to go," Jokan grinned, looking at the faces of his friends to see if they had guessed his intention.

"You certainly aren't planning to send Jessl in? Or Cire, or old gray-head here?" Harlan jibed and stopped, turning as they all did, to look at me. Surprised, I nearly choked on a much too generous mouthful. Jokan's grin broadened and he laughed with the gathering momentum of relief and delight.

"Me? Don't be ridiculous," I managed to say over my food. "I wouldn't even know . . ."

Gartly stood up abruptly, "Are you mad? This little country girl? We need someone like Maritha . . ."

"Who is so unknown at court," mocked Jokan. "Maritha would never do. Her fondness for Harlan is well known."

"It isn't her fondness, Jo, that would worry me," Harlan remarked wryly. "It's the fact that it was at her table I collapsed under such suspicious circumstances."

This deflated Gartly into a semishock, for he sat down immediately, his face rather pale and tight.

"I gather that was never made public," Harlan continued quietly. "But Sara can't go."

"Sara's perfect," Jokan went on enthusiastically, winking at me. "We can think up some absolutely idiotic quest for her."

"Quest?" I asked.

"With that face, she could pass into Gorlot's very room."

"It is not in Gorlot's room that we want her," Gartly grumbled primly, eyeing me with distaste.

My appetite deserted me.

"Aha," Jokan crowed gleefully at Gartly's expense, "beauty has the key to any room."

"Now, wait a minute," I demanded, rising. Harlan put a big hand on my shoulder and gently, but firmly, reseated me.

"Sara can't go. She has risked enough already," he said with quiet authority.

"What's the matter with you, Harlan," Jokan demanded, leaping to his feet, his eyes flashing his irritation. "It's got to be her. It's so simple a ruse it can't possibly fail. All Eclipsers have the right into the palace on that night."

"There has to be someone else," I insisted, now that Harlan was backing me.

"There is no one else we can reach in the short time we have. And it may be shorter than we know," Jokan insisted, turning to glare at his brother. "Ferrill may be almost completely broken down now, Maxil was worried sick. And we know it's not his constitution that's weak, it's drugs he's been fed. You know what drugs can do, Harlan. We've got to reach him and save his life. Or is that no longer of primary importance in your life, Harlan?"

Harlan was on his feet, the chair crashing to the floor behind him, as he faced his brother, stung, angry, silent.

"Stop it," I cried, pushing them apart. "I'll go, Harlan. I've hazarded this much already. Why not all?" I turned to Jokan once I saw the bunched muscles relax in Harlan's neck and he ceased to crouch as though about to spring. "Jokan, it's as Gartly says. I'm a little country girl. I've never even been to Lothara. But if you'll tell me exactly what I have to do, I'll do my best to do it."

Jokan's eyes gleamed down at me and he bowed ceremoniously to me.

"I like the country you're from, Lady Sara, if it breeds
courage like yours," he said.

Involuntarily I turned for reassurance to Harlan. Did
Jokan know of my origin? Harlan had said I might tell
him if anything went wrong. Had Harlan already done so?
Harlan's imperceptible nod indicated it was merely Jokan's
curious choice of words. He gripped my arm at the elbow.

"There *is* more at stake, Sara, than just Ferrill's life,"
Harlan said persuasively as he pushed me gently back
into my chair. "Which, any indication to the contrary,
means a great deal to me," he added acidly to Jokan who
shrugged. "Something very peculiar is happening on Tane
if Jessl's report is as accurate as they always are."

Jokan's eyebrows went up in mockery. "What's peculiar
about a war?"

Harlan ignored him. "It's absurd to maintain that the
Tanes would have initiative enough to revolt. Those people are no more capable of taking a life or planning a
cohesive rebellion like this than a restoree." Harlan's eyes
flickered briefly as if he regretted making such a comparison. His hesitation allowed Jokan to get in another dig.

"You're prejudiced on behalf of your little protégées,
Harlan. You haven't seen the damage these 'uninitiative'
people of yours have been doing. Ferrill's the real urgency."

Harlan turned angrily on Jokan. "It's not prejudice,
Jokan, and you should know me better. So drop that
attitude. This supposed uprising masks another purpose.
Just as my all too timely collapse and Ferrill's suddenly
failing health are indications of a Millishly well-laid plan
of far-reaching proportions. What I cannot understand is
Stannall's lack of suspicion. Surely he of all people must
realize something's drastically wrong. I cannot conceive
him selling out to Gorlot or whoever is behind this treachery. But one thing I'm sure of, Lothar stands in great
peril . . . of Gorlot getting complete authority, if he hasn't
already; the truth behind the Tane farce and the loss of a
brilliant ruler if Ferrill should have to be replaced."

"He'll be replaced, even if he gets off with his life," Jokan said dully. "He's a ruin already."

Harlan snapped an angry denial, but there was no support from the others. He turned back to me with a hint of the desperation I knew so well.

"Sara, I don't think you'd be in any danger. The idea is so simple, the time so accommodating. It has to be you."

In his eyes were his concern and his fear and a desperate plea. His hand, warm on mine, gripped me reassuringly.

"I hope you know what I'm doing," I said anxiously.

"You know Ferrill, don't you?" Jokan put in, impatiently. "All you have to do is tell him that Harlan is sane and have him convene an emergency session of Council. I assume," he began acidly, "Gorlot has started no antivirility campaigns on Ferrill."

Harlan shot him a surprised questioning look which Jokan waved aside, but Jessl and Gartly snorted derisively so his reference was known to them.

"Stannall," Jokan continued, "will then be able to do what else is necessary . . . if *he's* still with us. He ought to have far less love for Gorlot than we."

"There's no other way to get to Ferrill?" I asked plaintively.

"Our faces are known. Yours is not. In the guise of say, the Searcher," Jokan improvised and I remembered that Harlan had called me his Searcher, "you can gain entrance into the public garden. Slip into the palace wing and up to Ferrill's room."

"No," Harlan disagreed on the last detail hastily. "You said Trenor was sleeping with him to prevent another one of these so-called attacks?"

"Yes."

"Well, Ferrill will have to attend the Starhall festivities, won't he?"

"If he can walk."

"Then Sara will have a far better cover in that crowd than trying to find her way to Ferrill's rooms."

"It's all very well to make her a Searcher, provided you

can find a costume at this late date," Gartly grumbled, "but how are we to get into Lothara at all? Had that entered your glib plans?"

Harlan and Jokan exchanged glances.

"I do have the planecar," Cire suggested. "And I'm not too well known."

"She can fly in herself," Jokan said easily.

I grabbed at Harlan's arm. Sail I could, fly no.

"I don't fly," I blurted out.

"What?" Jokan looked at me startled.

"Never needed to. Lived in Jurasse," I mumbled and then looked frantically at Harlan for support.

"The one girl out of how many thousands who never learned to fly when she reached legal age," Jokan said exasperated.

And Harlan wanted *me* to go right into the middle of the palace. I'd last three steps inside the gardens and make another inadvertent mistake.

"I'd be glad to escort her," Cire repeated and then blushed, "if Harlan permits?"

"I permit all right, but I just wish there were some way we could all get into Lothara."

"As well wish you had a map to the Mil's system," Jessl snapped gloomily.

"If she's to get into the palace wing at all," Gartly put in, "she can go in no shoddy affair. It must be a rich gown or she'd be turned away."

"That can be obtained in town," Harlan remarked easily, dismissing this objection. Gartly stalked out of the room, his face reflecting pain and anger.

Harlan watched him leave, shrugged and turned to rummage on a table for a slate of waxy substance and a pointed stylus. Sitting next to me, he rapidly sketched in a small plan of the giant structure that was the capitol building, war office and palace of Lothar. Except that it resembled an unrimmed, unevenly spoked wheel, its function put me in mind of the Pentagon and the unreality of this adventure bore down on me again. I had no chance for speculation because Harlan demanded my complete attention as he described my route.

One wing of the enormous building was devoted exclusively to the quarters of the Warlord's family, intimates and servants. Between the spokes were extensive gardens. Only the ones adjacent to the palace wing were fenced in and guarded. Into one of these gardens I must gain entrance. While Jokan and Jessl listened absently to what was common knowledge, Harlan explained in detail what I would have to know.

"Get to the point, get to the point," Jokan urged impatiently once.

"Sara has never been to Lothara before and it's easy to become confused in the dark of the double Eclipse. We can't afford any mistakes," Harlan replied calmly and proceeded with my orientation. Jokan contented himself by noisily foraging in the kitchen.

Once I was in the garden, I was to make my way to any one of the ground-floor balconies, enter the room it adjoined and let myself into the corridor. The personnel of the lowest floor changed so constantly I was unlikely to be questioned. Minor courtiers would undoubtedly all be dancing attendance on their sponsors in the Starhall. I would follow the corridor to the Hub which was the Starhall on the fourth level. I would endeavor to get close enough to Ferrill to give him my message. Once that was accomplished, I would merely retrace my steps and join Jokan at the "Place of Birds." Any passenger cab would speed me there over the confusion of the celebrating. If, however, I did not see Ferrill and my presence was being noticed, I was to come back to the apartment and they would try something else.

I had to agree to the plan's simplicity, but I could not help worry that any plan undergoes revision in performance.

"If you find yourself in any trouble, Sara," Harlan remarked reading my mind, "give them one of your beautiful smiles and I doubt their minds will remain on the question."

"Oh, nonsense," I snapped.

Jokan and Jessl grinned knowingly to my further embarrassment.

"What will her quest be?" asked Jessl.

"Well, to get her into the gardens in case there is extra guard on duty, she can ask for a leaf of the Burning Shame plant. That's near the palace wing," Jokan suggested. "Once in the palace, she can say she needs a token from Ferrill to prove she has been claimed. She needs immunity against a priest she doesn't like. I've seen that one used often enough to know it's accepted." Jokan's grin to Harlan and Jessl made me suspect that ruse had a double meaning I couldn't understand.

There were too many cryptic remarks passed and references that puzzled me. Had I known then what Ferrill told me much later I doubt I would ever have consented to be a Searcher. My ignorance of the true story served me well, I admit, and I'm sure Harlan's neglect in telling me was intentional. The Searcher was an historically documented lady of good clan who had become separated from her lover during a Mil raid. She refused to believe he had been taken, and wandered over the planet, looking for him, constantly in danger of being captured either by a priest who coveted her or by the Mil. She would reward those who sheltered her with jewels. Eventually the priest caught up with her. In the joyous festival interpretation, the girl who played the Searcher very often suggested to a male friend that he be the priest to whom she surrendered herself after a token chase. Morals were totally different on Lothar. Female continence over a prolonged period was unfavorably viewed since women were expected to bear as many children as possible to replace a population constantly lost to the Mil or the exigencies of Patrol. Family continuity stemmed from the distaff side with the notable exception of the Warlordship.

"Let's hope," Jokan leered humorously, clearing his face when he caught Harlan's expression, "there aren't other priests along the way who want to claim her."

"That is why her costume is important," Gartly growled as he reentered the room, carrying a wooden box with stiff tenderness. He laid it on the table and with slow hands uncovered it, looking at the contents for a long moment before he stepped back for us to see. Jokan and Harlan exchanged glances and Harlan gripped the old man's shoulder in unspoken gratitude. He later told me the costume had belonged to Gartly's beloved wife.

I saw only the tissue-fragile fabric, deep greens and golds, the heavy ornate jewels, the intricately strapped sandals and the voluminous folds of the glossy emerald-green cloak.

"Why, it's the most beautiful thing I've ever seen," I gasped, touching the dress lightly as if it might fall to pieces.

Gartly grumbled something under his breath and then left the room with quick steps.

I suppose our concentration on the plans to enter the palace and Gartly's unexpected, touching offer had engrossed us. The sound of a knock on the door, at any rate, came like the knell of terror. We all whirled to the door as if it had become dangerous. Cire looked expectantly at Harlan who motioned him to answer even as Harlan edged quickly back to the kitchen.

"Who knocks?" asked Cire with scarcely a quiver in his young voice.

"Sinnall, Cire," and before Cire could answer, the door swung open.

If Sinnall had waited but an instant more before entering, Harlan would have reached the safety of the kitchen. As it was, he was directly in Sinnall's vision and his hand dropped from the door to his knife belt.

"Is it really Harlan?" Sinnall gasped. He didn't wait for confirmation but snapped to attention, saluting smartly. "Second Leader Sinnall, sir, reporting."

I could feel the tension leave the room as if swept out by a brisk wind. Cire, laughing nervously, threw an arm around the young officer.

"I appreciate the gesture, Second," Harlan said with a grin, returning the salute, "even though I am no longer acting as Regent." He beckoned to Sinnall to join the group around the table.

"My father served with you in Quadrant Five, sir," he remarked gravely, coming forward. "He was Nallis, First Prime."

Harlan grinned. "I recall it as being the other way round," he remarked and was rewarded by Sinnall's tentative smile.

"I can see now why there is an emergency at Lothar," Sinnall said, and held out to Harlan a tiny slate.

Harlan glanced at it, his eyebrows raising in surprise. With a burst of relieved laughter, he passed it to Jokan.

"My luck is holding," he practically crowed. "Sinnall, as a loyal officer in this sleepy uneventful little community, has been ordered to bring a loyal picked section to Lothara on special duty."

"Why should that change plans?" Jessl asked, reaching for the slate from Jokan.

"Because our orders are to report not later than noon tomorrow at Central Barracks for assignment. I can think of no better place for Harlan at the moment than right in the midst of the men trying to keep him out of Lothara."

"That'll get us all in," Jokan said, grinning broadly.

"Anyone know of your orders?" asked Harlan.

"I only got them an hour ago," Sinnall replied, "and I wanted to press Cire into section duty. I know *he's* loyal."

"To you and Ferrill, that's what Sinnall means," Cire interjected, his face intense with pride in his friend.

"Yes, sir," Sinnall replied earnestly. "I know what happens to officers who complain about the new Regent and the odd things that are happening. That's why I'm here," and he grimaced in such a way that I realized his present post was a form of military exile.

"Well, your orders do specify a 'loyal' section," Harlan said with a mirthless laugh, "but they do not state to whom, do they?"

Sinnall, relaxing even more in Harlan's presence, began to grin broadly.

"No, sir. And if I can find uniforms to fit, I'm going to volunteer all of you here as 'loyal.'"

"Room to stow my lady on the trip?" asked Harlan.

My relief that he had undoubtedly abandoned the original idea now that Sinnall's presence indicated Harlan would, after all, be able to get into Lothara, was short-lived.

Sinnall considered me with surprise. "Why, I think so."

"I hope so. I don't wish to leave her behind," Harlan remarked. "And Jokan, not you. You take yourself and your planecar and plan an accident in the Jurassan Hills. You've got to have a reason for returning to Lothara, completely unconnected with me. Gartly, Cire, Jessl and I will be the section. You wait for Sara at your place. Even if you are watched, Sara is unknown and your philandering is legend."

Jokan objected strenuously to being excluded but was finally convinced he could not be in the section.

"Why don't I just take Sara with me now? I'd better use tonight to cover my return and give me time for an accident. I could then take her on to Lothara."

Harlan shook his head. "No, Sara stays with me."

"Brother, I'm not about to . . ."

"She stays. I have my reasons," he reasserted so firmly that Jokan shrugged and pressed no further.

What remained of the day was spent in getting uniforms and making what alterations we could to get a reasonable fit. Not even the largest issue jacket accommodated Harlan's breadth of shoulder. The cuffs were halfway up his arm and, even when I had let down the sleeve all I could, it hung unmilitarily high above his big hand. Sinnall decided that regulation issue would be too skimpy for Harlan's frame in any event and the discrepancies would pass as back-country inefficiencies. The assorted ages and sizes of the four men identified them as provincials. Gartly, with darkened hair and a day's growth of beard, would not resemble the correct old soldier.

Cire sprinkled a white powder in Harlan's dark hair and with the lack of eyebrows (his, too, had been singed in the barrier crossing), an unmilitary shamble and slouched shoulders, he looked amazingly unlike himself. He even demonstrated the witless expression he could assume whenever necessary.

Hunger and fatigue vied for first place in my attention

by late evening and, when someone remembered to get some dinner, I could barely eat for weariness.

"Sara, you're barely rested," Harlan said with concern. "It's just as well she doesn't have to be Searcher tomorrow. She'd fall asleep," he laughed gently.

"I still think it's a good plan," Jessl grumbled.

"Sinnall's orders give us a better opportunity. I prefer to take my own risks," Harlan said to silence him. He helped me rise and escorted me up the stairs. "I'll be right back," he assured Gartly and Jessl who looked after us knowingly.

My face must have been burning when I got into the privacy of the room. I heard Harlan closing the door, but all I could see was the big double bed. All I really wanted was to sleep. And certainly if the boat was neither time nor place, neither was this with those men downstairs. My expression must have shown my thoughts, for Harlan took one look at my face and chuckled.

He took off my robe and led me to the bed, tucking me in.

"Sleep, dear my lady, is what you need right now," he said softly. "And I am relieved you do not need to go to the palace. That was too dangerous. Too dangerous, though Jokan's reasoning was good. He does not know, Sara. Sleep."

I did.

CHAPTER SIX

HARLAN WOKE ME, GENTLY SHAKING my shoulder. At first, the sight of a stranger in uniform bending over me was frightening until I recognized Harlan through the powdered hair.

"Fool you?" he grinned.

"Scared me witless," I grinned back, casting a glance at the dented pillow beside me.

"Well?" he dared me, "there are only three bedrooms here and I want it plain how matters stand between us. Remember, dear my lady, on this planet it is considered an honor to share the Regent's bed."

"I don't want to be in Gorlot's bed," I smirked at him wickedly.

"Neatly said," he said respectfully, but still grinning. "Now rise and dress or I'll make something more of that," and he indicated the bed. "After all, Sara, we slept together like innocent babes for who knows how long?"

Realizing myself topped, I gestured him out of the room. It took me a little while to figure out the closures on the green gown. I heartily wished for the simplicity of the zipper. Strange how easily I assumed in a mental leap that Earth would be able to supply Lothar with zippers when I could hardly understand the spatial distances between the two planets. Paper would be a boon, too, I continued in my mental perambulations, instead of the cumbersome Babylonique slates. I was just picking up the cloak when Harlan knocked again. I opened the door to him, the heavy jewelry clinking, tinkling with my movement. Harlan looked at me with a wondering expression on his face. He stepped quickly in the room, closing the door behind him.

"Didn't I put it on right?" I asked with a pang of doubt. "I know it took the longest time. I had to figure things out. Oh, for the lowly zipper."

Harlan began to smile, slowly.

"You are very different as the Searcher, dear my lady," he said slowly.

Pleased with the sincerity of his admiration, I pivoted on my toes, only to find myself locked in his arms, his face and eyes unbelievably stern.

"Are you still the girl who starved herself for me? The girl who sailed me to safety? Or are you . . ."

"Harlan, we've a long trip," Jessl yelled from below.

Harlan's tone had become almost savage, his arms around me tight and cruel.

"I'm still Sara, no matter what I wear," I whispered, startled.

"Sara . . . who?"

"Sara of the Estril, Odern Cave, Jurasse," I whispered, scared.

"We're coming," Harlan roared, turning his head briefly toward the door.

I thought he would release me but, holding me more tightly still, he bent his head and kissed me with rough and demanding lips. I seemed to sink inside him, held up only by his arms, knowing only the reality of his bruising mouth.

"HARLAN," Jessl bellowed and we both heard his steps on the wooden staircase.

"A map of how to get to Jokan's, from the Barracks' airfield," Harlan said hurriedly in a low voice, thrusting a tiny slate in my hand. "Anyone else would know. It's not far."

He opened the door just as Jessl reached it. It was now Jessl's turn to stare at me.

"Well, well." He looked nervously at Harlan. "That's what kept you."

With as much dignity as I could muster because I was still trembling, I gave both men a haughty look and swept out of the room.

Gartly was sitting facing the stair as we descended and he sprang to his feet, knocking the stool over. His face was completely expressionless. At first, I thought he must be equally struck speechless by my transformation. He turned without a word and left the house. I stared after him, hurt.

"The costume was his wife's," Harlan remarked gently. "She, too, was lovely."

Young Sinnall appeared in the door and bowed low. As we left the house, Cire came round the side of the house, and he too bowed.

"A lot better than stolen fishermen's clothes, hmm?" I said.

"That is the truth," Cire said, his eyes wide.

"Hey, where's my breakfast?" I demanded, stopping dead on the path outside the front door.

"Here," laughed Harlan, holding up a metal bottle and a small package, cloth wrapped. "I'll never let you starve again," he remarked, cocking an eyebrow at me.

"Will you two stop that and let's get off the ground?" Jessl snapped, irritably. "It's a three-hour trip from this cave-forsaken stretch of soil."

Laughing, I followed them down to the landing circle where the waiting official planecar idled its rotors. Sinnall had rigged a seat of sorts for me in the luggage area, apologizing profusely for the cramped accommodations. Cire announced that he would take the uncomfortable seat until such time as we encountered official traffic. Consequently I saw a great deal of such landmarks as the immense pit quarries of South Motlina, for Cire had been alone in Gartly's house near Astolla and had taken us south, away from prying inquiries about the wrecked boat. I saw the oil fields of Wingar and finally the city of Astolla itself and the delta we had nearly landed on. Northward into the mountains of Lothar the ship climbed.

I realized that Lothar had been lucky in several respects: a common enemy to unite it early in its history and the geographical accident which linked its two largest land masses from the north pole to the sixty-sixth parallel. At this point the continents split and rapidly separated east and west, leaving a green ocean between their land legs, dotted with several large islands and driblets of isles in the southern hemisphere. The eastern continent, over which we flew, was more mountainous and larger, the western one, a vast rolling plain ringed with bluffs and precipices, periodically penetrated by navigable rivers and deep lagoons. The western sea was shallow, spiked with tiny islands, deepening finally into a great crevasse of several thousand square miles before the sprawling arm and exaggerated peninsular fist of the eastern continent pouted seaward.

Used as I was to the ribbons of roads seen from the air on Earth, it struck me that Lothar had leapt from primitive wheels to a form of jet plane, thanks to the accommodating Mil. The only roads were foot trails, since most transportation, even by the poorer farmers, was done by air. Land was too valuable to be used up in wasteful roads when the whole sky was open for travel. During the trip I was constantly amazed by the gigantic craft that carried freight and the almost fragile vehicles that transported a single passenger: hummingbirds and vultures.

I missed, however, what I had hoped most to see: an airborne view of Lothara. The excessive number of aircars above Lothara, official and civil, flying at distressing proximity, necessitated my retreat behind the curtain. Sinnall answered and satisfied several official summonses before he made the turn into a pattern at the Central Barracks landing field. Here again, we unexpectedly encountered another touch of the fabulous streak of luck Harlan enjoyed.

The one unsettled detail was how I was to make my way from the Barracks airstrip to the city proper without detection. Sinnall had suggested that I remain hidden until nighttime, which meant a long stretch of hours, waiting behind the hot cloth.

I had my directions tucked in the top of my dress and was startled when our planecar was waved off an obviously overcrowded field and directed to an auxiliary civil field.

"As soon as there is no one around, you can just jump out," Jessl remarked to me through the curtain.

"Get an aircab to Place of Birds, Sara," Harlan suggested and passed in a small bag of coins.

I held it gingerly in my hand, acidly commenting to myself that it did me a great deal of good. I had absolutely no idea which coin of this realm meant how much. Just another little oversight. I would be so glad to get to Jokan's. I presumed there would be food in his larder, and I was hungry again. Once on the field, it seemed we took forever parking and three times Sinnall gave someone his orders to read and I heard each member of the unofficial section grumble out his name and a batch of numbers. Harlan, I remember, gave the name of Landar, in a stupidly high-pitched voice that almost got me giggling.

Finally, I heard Sinnall give the order to debark.

Harlan thrust his head back of the curtains.

"Gold coins are worth more, the larger the better. Silver, the larger, are alloy-mixed and worth less. Take care, dear my lady," he whispered and cupping my head with one large hand, kissed me on the lips with sweet speed. I heard him deliberately bumbling out of the planecar and then the retreating cadence calls.

I slipped into the front of the ship and looked cautiously over the windowsills. There was much coming and going on the field and many women among the men. Reassured I climbed out of the planecar. It was easy to guess which way was the entrance by following the direction of the crowd of brightly costumed Eclipsers. I strode forward confidently.

"Are you claimed, lady?" a male voice asked in my ear and whirling, startled, I saw a medium-tall man smiling hopefully at me.

"Yes, I most certainly am," I said and turning, left him standing there.

Two more offers by not as promising companions made me hover close to a large party of mixed revelers until I reached the gates. The women were allowed to pass quickly, but each man was forced to show identification and every tall man was drawn aside. The hunt was on for someone answering Harlan's description.

The novelty of being accosted by admiring males wore off before I got to the next busy street. There were plenty of planecars, but they were all aloft and I had no idea how one signaled them. I suppose I should have asked someone, but I had been so long away from people, all sorts and sizes of people, that faces and forms were entertaining to me. Not so entertaining were shadowy figures at the edge of the masses of revelers: blowsy drunken creatures, beggars with hideous purple scars, whining their pleas. The section bordering the airfield was obviously poor and I followed the flow of the crowd toward the center of the city. Gradually the poor buildings gave way to pleasanter areas of spiraling walks, connecting fluted colonnaded buildings in muted colors. Guards were stationed at crossroads and they constantly stopped the taller male figures in any group. I smiled to myself at the secret joke that Harlan had entered in an official car and been welcomed royally.

I came, finally, into the Great Bazaar, an enormous square with a central park, comprised of successively larger squares of shops, one outside the other, like the top view of a child's nest of blocks. Only the stores were staggered so that, through the separating alleys, one caught enticing glimpses of other treasures. I wandered through the crowds, wide-eyed at the fascinating stores, trying to imagine the purpose of this or that; trying on in my mind the gorgeous dresses. I decided that the jewels I wore were better than many on display and my dress more becoming.

Thirsty, I stopped at a beverage stand of which there were many, some with the air of permanence, some obviously holiday-rigged.

When the counterman looked expectantly for my order, I realized I couldn't ask for lemonade or Coke. For a moment I could only stare at him idiotically.

Suddenly, hands covered my eyes. Frantic, I grabbed at them.

"Guess who?" an eager young voice whispered in my ear.

Thinking it was only an Eclipse game, I relaxed.

"I'm not good at guessing-games," I replied finally.

The hands dropped as if my skin had burned them.

"I beg, I beg your pardon, lady," a stammering voice apologized.

I turned and looked up a long expanse of white over-shirt before I came to the boyish face. There was a shocked surprise in his eyes and an appeal for understanding the boy did not expect to find. He was about sixteen, I guessed, and his frame had shot up before he could accumulate the flesh to cover it. It gave him an angular awkwardness; a bag-of-bones appearance to his clothes and an obvious inferiority. His gray eyes regarded me with an unspoken plea not to scorn him. He reminded me so of my brother, Seth ... and someone else I couldn't place ... but he did remind me of Seth at his gawky stage. It was this quality, this puppyish wistfulness that caught my sympathy.

"I mistook you, Lady Searcher. Really I did and I was so pleased the Lady Fara ... I mean ..." and he trailed off aimlessly.

Quickly I put my hand on his arm to reassure him, for he seemed about to take off into the crowd.

"No harm done. This is Eclipse, isn't it? And, truly, I am flattered to be mistaken for the Lady Fara."

A brief eagerness flared in his eyes and he looked as if he were about to smile, but his face turned unnaturally mature.

"Please, buy me a drink and think no more of it," I said quickly. "Something . . . light," I added, indicating two drunken carousers with distaste.

The smile flickered again and was replaced with a guarded expression.

"Two cornades," he said to the counterman, tossing a coin to the fellow.

"Thank you, lord, have a safe Eclipse."

The young boy handed me my drink with the polished grace of a courtier, totally out of character for his age.

It was a fruit concoction, tart and cold, and just what I had my mouth set for. We stood at one side of the crowded stand, saying nothing because I could think of nothing to say.

At the opposite end of this bazaar mall, there was a

sudden commotion, indistinguishable shouts, a startled milling of people and then a trio pushed into view. They were not very sober but not drunk enough to extenuate their obstreperous actions. The first man, a rough enormous fellow, charged with the ferocity of an angry gorilla, his long arms pushing way past those who did not move aside quickly enough. He looked from right to left, head thrust forward, bellowing at the top of his voice.

"Maxil, where is that little runt? Maxil, come here or I'll break you. Maxil? Maxil!" His two companions followed, likewise yelling for the missing Maxil, stopping people and demanding to know where this Maxil was.

I turned to my young man and found him missing from my side, just as the gorilla charged up to the stand, beckoning violently to the counterman.

"He was with this lady a moment ago," the man volunteered, not looking at me, but obviously frightened.

The lout turned on me, his liquor-heavy breath offensive, his sweating body odorous. He put his hands on my shoulders and started to shake me.

"Get your filthy hands off me, you stupid bully," I said, seething with anger at this insult. "I said, get your filthy hands off me," I repeated distinctly in the quiet that had fallen on the mall. There is some quality to righteous anger that has great strength in compelling obedience. He did remove his hands, swaying in front of me, while his thick drunken senses took in the import of what I had said.

"Who do you think you are?" the drunk asked.

"Maxil thought she was the Lady Fara," the counterman said timidly. I shot him a look I hoped would silence him completely.

"Fara? Fara here," the sot said, blinking at me, trying to see me clearly. "C'mere, Lort," he beckoned his two cronies. "Is this Fara?"

The other two peered at me, hemming me in against the counter.

"Never seen her," the one not named said. His breath was vile.

"Can't see anything here," Lort complained.

"He," and the drunk's finger jerked at the counterman, "said she was with Maxil. Everyone knows Maxil's sweet on Fara. Not that it'll do her any good." He cackled at his own wit.

Before I realized what would happen, the gorilla had thrown his cloak over my head and I was hoisted to his shoulders. I kicked, I scratched, I screamed, and then someone hit me on the head.

When I came to my senses, it took me a few minutes to recall what had last happened. My head ached and my jaw and my arms felt sticky. I think it was a concern for the beautiful dress Gartly had lent me that stung me into full consciousness.

I was sprawled on a large bed in an elegantly furnished but barren-looking room. Somewhere beyond the windows a great deal of shouting, screaming, laughing and singing was going on. I rose, carefully because of my headache, and walked to the window. Below me lay beautiful gardens, fairylands of casually riotous blooms, spilling onto the winding paths, nudging against a variety of unusual trees, enhancing stonework and sculpture. Beyond the delicate metal filigree I could see the throngs of revelers and another wing of the building.

It took very little intelligence for me to assume I was in the palace itself.

"In Gorlot's room?" I asked myself feeling very droll and wondering what I did now.

Yesterday everything had seemed very simple. This morning the plan had been foolproof. I sighed and felt like crying, but that would hurt my head more.

I did seek out the bathroom and washed my face and arms. I also dabbed at the stains I found on my lovely robes. When I heard a commotion outside, I hesitated briefly, wondering if a locked bathroom might not be preferable to what I would find in the room. I recognized one raucous laugh as belonging to the drunken gorilla and that decided me not to play the coward.

He was there, all right, propelling my young friend of the beverage stand into the room, roaring with vulgar laughter. I picked up a hairbrush I saw on the dressing table, hefting the handle, glad it was metal.

"You drunken Milrouser, how dare you," I cried, and both turned toward me.

The ghastly sick look on the boy's face enraged me as did his incredulous expression when he saw me tearing into the gorilla.

"How dare you kidnap me? This may be Eclipse, but there are limits to what is done. Get out of here, get out of here and leave us alone."

I am absolutely positive I was never so mad before in my life. Not even the time the Travis boys tried their dirty tricks on an innocent twelve-year-old Sara in their father's old barn. He had taken care of them with a razor strop and I took care of this oaf with a metal hairbrush.

If he had been sober, I should never have succeeded, but he and his two cohorts were definitely drink-fuddled and their reactions, for they did swing out to hit me, too slow for me. They howled when the metal brush contacted their arms and faces, and they backed out of the bedroom. I didn't have to chase them across the living room. I stood in the bedroom doorway and threw whatever came to hand. As soon as they had exited into the hall beyond, I raced over to the outside door and slammed it shut, swinging a heavy bolt in place.

The boy, Maxil, for I was sure it was he, stood, open-mouthed with admiration, looking at me.

I mastered the trembling in my body, got back my breath and grabbed an applelike fruit from a bowl on the table by the door.

"Who was that?" I asked the boy who had started to come over to me, his eyes still shining with his respect.

He stopped at my question and pointed inanely at the door. "You didn't know that was Samoth?"

"Samoth? No, why should I? I've never had the misfortune to meet him before." I took a huge bite out of the applefruit. It occurred to me that I would probably never not be hungry again. Most of my waking time for the last few days had been consumed by eating something.

"Wait'll I get that counterman," I continued wrathfully. "Just wait. D'you realize he tattled on you to that oaf?"

"I guessed he'd have to," Maxil said softly, sadly, looking down at his feet.

"Why?" I asked angrily. "Is everyone in this city scared of a trio of drunken bullies?"

Maxil found his ornate sandal very interesting.

"They have reason to be. You must come from out of the city," he added, looking up at me quickly and then away.

"Jurasse," I replied. "They thought I was the Lady Fara."

He looked up guiltily, flushing. "The counterman overheard us, I guess. I'm awfully sorry. It was my mistaking you for the Lady Fara that got you into all this trouble and now you'll . . ." his chin quivered and he turned away abruptly, striding to the window, his whole figure sunk with dejection.

"Now I'll what?" I urged, trying to keep my impatience out of my voice.

"I can't say it. But it is just horrible you've been dragged here like this. Samoth and the others'll be back and they'll . . . they'll . . ." he turned toward me again, his face blotched with an effort to keep back tears.

"They'll what, Maxil?" I said, going to him in my distress at his conflict.

"They'll say . . . I'm . . . impotent," and with that final dragged-out word he turned back to the windows, a pathetic young man.

"Well, of all the despicable, nasty-minded, indecent, incredible things," I said, beginning softly and ending with full vent to my indignation.

The echo of another scene came faintly to my ears and I recalled how I had helplessly overheard my four older brothers taunting Seth because he had been unable to "make it" with one of the town tarts. Even at fourteen I had known how cruel and inhibiting such taunting was. I had been completely unable to help Seth, but in his name I could try to help this boy.

I took Maxil by the hand and pulled him over the low couch.

"Well, are you?" I asked him point-blank.

He flushed. "Well, I have," he said tentatively. "But not when they're around."

"I should hope not. There *are* some things in this world that should be done at the proper time and place, in privacy." And then I, too, was blushing furiously. All I could think of was my unfortunate borrowing of one of Harlan's phrases and the circumstances under which he had said it.

"Aw, now don't say you haven't heard what they're saying about me?" Maxil said, his face still not quite resigned to tears. "Gorlot's got it all planned. As soon as he kills Ferrill off, he'll have me denounced as unmanly and put that fat-assed gut-stuffer Fernan in as Warlord-elect."

"Kills Ferrill?" I gasped.

"He's so sick and it's *not* his constitution. The Harlan clan is *not* weakening," Maxil exclaimed with pathetic emphasis.

"No, it's not Ferrill's constitution. He's been drugged."

"That's what I've been trying to . . ." Maxil gasped and turned to look at me with startled eyes, "how did you know?"

"I know. And further, they drugged Harlan, too."

Maxil stared at me. He looked at the bolted door. Nervously, he got up and went to the living-room balcony, opening the door and looking out suspiciously, before coming back to sit beside me again.

"I told myself that must have been what happened," he said in a hoarse whisper. "Are you sure it's true?"

"I'm positive. And furthermore," I continued, "he's no longer drugged. He's free and he's in this city."

Maxil stared at me as if he thought I had gone mad or he wasn't hearing properly. He blinked rapidly at me, swallowed his Adam's apple bobbing just like Seth's did when he was nervous.

"If you're just saying this," he growled in a tight, angry

voice, "if you're just saying this ... to ... to ... I can still use my authority to ..."

I put my hand on his arm, catching his eyes and holding his attention.

"Maxil, I'm telling you the truth."

Gradually his face changed as he realized I meant what I said. Hope, concern and then despair crossed his face. Groaning, he turned from me, again lost in apathy.

"It's too late," he said sadly. "It's just too late. And besides," he turned back to me again, his eyes sparkling with anger and a sternness incongruous with his youth, "you shouldn't go around *saying* that where just *any*one could hear you." He gestured wildly, at the balcony, and the bedroom and the hall door, as if overgrown ears would come leaping out of the stonework to us.

"I'm saying it to you."

"How do you know Gorlot doesn't have me under control?" he argued violently.

I found myself speaking softer and softer in an unconscious effort to tone him down.

"Well, I doubt he does if he makes such degrading assertions about you. Besides, Jokan said you were terribly worried about Ferrill. You said you hated Samoth. Well, if Harlan gets the Regency back, you get rid of Samoth. All I've got to do is to get to Ferrill and tell him what's happened and have him convene the Council."

Maxil regarded me as if I had lost my senses.

"That's all you have to do. Get to Ferrill and tell him to convene the Council," he repeated as if reasoning with an idiot. "That's all!" Again the broad dramatic gestures.

"I'm in the palace, aren't I? Ferrill lives here, doesn't he?"

It had occurred to me, suddenly, and I felt rather dense it took me so long to wake up to the opportunity, that I *was* in the palace and I might just as well put into effect Plan A.

"And Ferrill will have to appear in the Starhall tonight if he can walk," I rattled on. "And I presume you can get into the Starhall?"

"Yes," Maxil agreed, paying strict attention to me now.

"Yes, I can, and he *has* to appear." He stopped, dazed, and then his face lit up, his shoulders straightened and his chin jerked forward. The frightened, humiliated boy disappeared and the young man stood in his place.

"Do you realize what you've said?" Maxil asked me. "Do you *realize?*"

"I gather you're relieved," I said drolly.

"Relieved, *relieved,* RELIEVED!" he chorused dramatically. "I feel alive for the first time in twelve months. Nearly a whole year!" he assured me, hooking his fingers in his belt and striding up and down the floor.

"In that case, is there any way you can get me some dinner?" I asked as my stomach impolitely made noises.

"Dinner? Certainly. *Certainly,*" he said expansively. He went to the door, shot the bolt free, and swung the door open. "Guard," he said with a swagger in his voice. "I want dinner for two in my rooms."

I got a glimpse of the startled face of the guard who saluted sloppily just as Maxil swung the door closed again.

"I'd bolt the door again, if I were you. I'm not sure I want to tangle with Samoth when he's cold sober," I remarked.

Maxil was not so overconfident as to forget his conditioned response to Samoth in a half-hour's time. Indecision showed in his face.

"Look, my friend," I said seriously, "I'm glad the news of Harlan relieves you, but let's not overdo it until we can get word to Ferrill and start things rolling to get Gorlot and Samoth out of power."

"Oh," Maxil said breezily, "Samoth was dead drunk. He'll go annoy some of the ladies before he comes back here. And then he'll come in with a whole bunch of his clan and tease me. But he won't be back till he's sober. And by *that* time, we'll be gone!" Maxil's eyes flashed with determination. Then he pivoted toward me again.

"Just where *is* Harlan?"

"To tell the honest truth, I don't know. And maybe I'd better not tell you anymore than I already have."

"But . . ." Maxil urged, not to be denied reassurance,

". . . how did you know he was drugged? I mean, how did you get him . . . out . . ."

The timid knock at the door interrupted him. He looked at me, eyes scared.

"Dinner," I whispered to him and then, with sudden inspiration, nestled against his side, twining one of his long arms around my shoulders.

"Come," Maxil said, his voice not quite breaking, his arm crushing my shoulders as he awkwardly returned my embrace.

I must say he made a convincing show of someone inconveniently interrupted. A single man entered, a mousy fellow, clad in a green apron. He bowed nervously.

"What did you wish for dinner, Lord Maxil?"

"Storner, I want a *nice* dinner. What had you in mind, Lady . . ." and he stopped, realizing he didn't know my name.

"My name is Sara, darling," I said, pouting plaintively. "Had you forgotten, after . . ." and I trailed off. I thought Maxil would explode with laughter. Fortunately his face was turned from the waiter. "And I'm just famished. All I want is food."

"Two of the best . . . whatever you're serving Gorlot," and Maxil spat the name out. From the expression on Stoner's face, he had missed nothing I intended to imply. Nor Maxil's contempt of the Regent pro-tem. Whatever the waiter's opinion, he kept his face blank as he bowed out, promising dinner in a very few minutes.

"Say," Maxil breathed, his eyes wide with admiration. "Did you know what you were doing?"

I grinned at him, bouncing up off the sofa.

"I hope it's all over the palace, real soon," I grinned.

"Gee, you're wonderful," Maxil said sincerely. "I wish I . . . I mean, you've . . . just . . ." he was trying to get something out.

"The Lady Fara?" I asked delicately and was answered by his blush. "Oh, she's your girl."

"She's *my* dear lady," Maxil stated firmly. "At least," he added, "she would be. Stannall wouldn't object, I know. But Gorlot's not convened Council on the flimsy excuse that the Tane crisis takes all his time and it is a time for the Warlord, not the Peace Councils."

The subject agitated Maxil and he began his restless pacing up and down. The resemblance struck me and I realized he was much like a bad copy, a smaller-scale Harlan, unfinished, unmolded, untempered. But the resemblance to his uncle was there.

"The Lady Fara is Stannall's daughter?"

"Everyone knows that," he countered, looking at me.

"I don't. But then, I'm a little country girl," I added hastily.

"Well, you certainly don't look like it," Maxil said with unexpected sophistication. "As a matter of fact, you *do* look like *my* Lady Fara." He had his uncle's disconcerting way with the possessive pronoun. "Same height. Same coloring. And we'd planned to be priest," he fingered his white robes, "and Searcher this Eclipse. That is, before Harlan had his so-called collapse. Oh, she'd've had to wait, but we had an understanding," he ended with stubborn insistence.

"Won't Stannall be here tonight? I mean, as Councilman."

Maxil shrugged. "I don't know. He might be. When I saw you in the bazaar, and thought for just one split second you might really by *my* Lady Fara ..." and he left the sentence hanging. "But I'm glad it was you after all," he said with a very engaging grin.

In spite of all the cruelty he had been subjected to, in spite of worrying, Maxil was a thoroughly nice youngster.

"There's not a damn thing wrong with the Harlan clan," I remarked succinctly and then smiled for fear Maxil might take me wrong.

Another knock at the door ushered in our dinner, a welcome diversion for several reasons.

"Storner," Maxil said imperiously after our table had been placed before us and the waiter made ready to withdraw, "when is the Warlord, my brother, due at the Starhall?"

"The rumor is he will not come," Storner said with a blank face.

"I'm not interested in the rumor," Maxil snapped. "What has his physician said?" Maxil's tone showed his opinion of that gentleman.

"By the tenth hour, my Lord Maxil," Storner replied in so colorless a voice it was insolent.

"Oh, marvelous. I promised to get a token from Ferrill," I giggled. "To protect me from a priest I know," I said, coyly walking my fingers up Maxil's arm.

Maxil waved Storner out of the room and we continued to make stupid faces at each other until we heard the door close. Maxil covered his mouth to smother his laughter, doubling up with boyish glee.

I waited a moment, then the smell of the dinner, steaming in its metal dishes, overcame my manners.

"Laugh all you want. I'm hungry," I announced and started to heap my plate with food.

"I've never seen a woman eat so much in my life. You pregnant?" he asked suspiciously.

"What a thing to ask!" I exclaimed, nearly choking.

"Aren't you claimed?"

There was that word again. "Not exactly," I said loftily. "I've an understanding, though."

"Oh," he grunted, mollified.

My sanitarium diet had not prepared me for such gourmandizing as this and I ate steadily while Maxil talked. He talked as if it were going out of style. I realized what terrible tension he must have been under. As well as the dramatic enthusiasms and passionate opinions of adolescence that not even Samoth's tender attentions had completely subdued, Maxil had a keen insight. His humor, often with a bitter edge to it, was wry and delightful. As long as I could keep eating, I would be able to let him carry the burden of conversation. I was distressingly aware of my all too limited acquaintance with the general framework of life on Lothar. Its everyday banalities, like Joe Dimaggio, hot dogs, Fourth of July and hammer murders, were beyond my comprehension.

I gathered that the "bandsmen" were not orchestra

players but groups of hijackers, burglars or highwaymen, terrorizing unpatrolled regions, resorting to senseless outrages of destruction in property and human life. I had to deduce that such crimes, common enough on earth, had been completely unheard of on Lothar. A step more brings the conclusion that the lawless element usually stayed in the Patrol where it had an outlet for its energies. The decreased need for active patrollers had left too many potential criminals idle. But I was surprised that Maxil had the same conclusion to make.

I learned that insanity, also a rarity on Lothar, was plotting a dreadful, steep upward curve of incidence in medical science. There was no Freud, no Jung, not even a good common-sense minister to instruct and analyze. There was no organized religion of any kind on Lothar. There was only the centuries' old dedication to the absolute and complete destruction of the Mil. This was not enough for the younger generations of Lotharians who had had little direct contact with this ageless menace. They wanted considerably more out of life than freedom from fear and the stringent safeguards evolved by ancestors buried hundreds of years ago.

Perhaps, I thought, Harlan was wrong about not seeking out the Mil now. Certainly that would absorb the restless elements. Once Lothar had laid the scourge to rest, she could progress more normally. Normally? Was my Earth any more normal with its constant, useless international bickerings? At least Lothar had a mighty purpose and pursued it relentlessly, valorously.

As we finished the sweet fruit of our final course, I made a particularly noticeable blunder.

"Sometimes you act as if you didn't know what I was talking about," Maxil commented, frowning. "And you've got the oddest way of talking. Where do you come from?"

"Jurasse. My mother was from South Cant. I guess that's why I have an odd way of speaking. Mother always said Jurassans murder . . . [I was about to say the King's English] . . . human speech."

"They certainly do," Maxil agreed, pushing back the

table. He belched without apologizing and I wondered if this were customary or adolescent. I cleared my throat instead.

We had grown accustomed to the noisy crowds outside the gardens. Now suddenly a roar of angry voices drew our attention to the windows. Maxil strode over, beckoning me.

"Another protest on the Tane wars," he remarked, pointing out banners being dipped and glided above the heads of the crowd.

"Damn the Tane wars," Maxil growled. "That's all anyone talks of."

"It masks some other purpose," I said remembering Harlan's fears.

"I'll just bet it does. And you know why that war's a farce?" Maxil demanded. "Because Gorlot's men command the patrol now. Men," he sneered, "like Samoth. *All,* even the emergency session of Council Gorlot calls, they're all *his* men. He hasn't missed a trick. Not one."

"Yes," I contradicted him, "one. Harlan's escape."

"That doesn't do any good unless Harlan can appear *sane* before the Council and *prove* it. And I'll bet Gorlot can think of a way to prove Harlan is as mad as ever."

"I doubt it. Because Harlan never was mad."

"I know it. You know it," he said gloomily.

"Sitting here won't do any good. Seeing Ferrill will. Let's go. It must be near time now," I said, standing up. Maxil's depression was contagious.

CHAPTER SEVEN

THE STARHALL WAS THE FINAL beauty in the flawlessness of the palace wheel. The vast dome-ceilinged room accommodated the throngs of people without seeming in the least crowded, without being noisy. The constellations that shone from the darkened ceiling changed perceptibly as the planet itself turned round its primary. The mocking lights glittered on hundreds of maskers who danced, drank and sported in the gigantic room. I had never seen such a magnificent crowd, nor felt so dwarfed by a walled structure. Maxil and I paused, by mutual consent, in one of the five soaring archways that gave on to the Hall proper, watching the fantastic revelry.

"Where's Ferrill?" I asked.

Maxil shrugged. "It's not yet tenth hour. He may not come in until the Eclipse." He pointed to the ceiling where facsimiles of the two satellites closed the gap that separated them and their rendezvous with their sun. "It's a frightfully noisy night for him. Not like other times. Oh, we had lots of guests but ..." His inference was directed at quality not quantity. "See that blond girl over there by the second archway. The one in the purple overdress? That's my sister, Kalina." He grimaced with distaste. "She's drunk and she's got enough face paint on for a Clan Mother. And the other blonde, the one on the couch under Ifeaus (a constellation, I later learned), that's Cherez. She's only thirteen. It's bad enough for Kalina to be here acting that way. She's already claimed. But for Cherez!"

A servant approached with a tray and paused in front of us. Maxil peered into the ornate metal goblets, snorted and waved the man away.

"Gorlot's serving delinade," he gritted out.

"What's that?" I asked without thinking.

"An aphrodisiac. Don't you know *anything*?"

93

I was spared the necessity of replying by the change of expression that came over Maxil. It was a combination of fear, hatred, disgust and expectation.

"Where's Samoth?" a cold voice said behind my back and I didn't need to wait until I was roughly turned toward the speaker to know it was Gorlot.

"You aren't the Lady Fara," Gorlot said, staring at me.

"Samoth got drunk," Maxil said quickly, taking my arm and trying to move away.

"You are not to leave your tutor. Especially not to pick up prostitutes. As if they would do you any good," Gorlot snapped. "Go find him."

"He's supposed to nursemaid me, not me him," Maxil replied with a show of more spirit than Gorlot evidently expected from him.

"I see," he drawled enigmatically and flicked a hand at the guard behind us. "Take this trollop out."

"Immediately," a feminine voice seconded beyond Gorlot. A woman, elegantly dressed in a yellow Searcher's costume joined the temporary Regent. "I gave explicit orders that I was to be the only Searcher here," she said vindictively. Her eyes narrowed suddenly as she noticed the flash of my jewels in the starlight. She peered more closely at the fabric and cut of my gown. Its rich green made her costume too glaring a yellow by contrast. "Who is she?"

"Lady Sara, the Lady Maritha and, of course, the Lord Regent Gorlot," Maxil said with cold politeness.

"Lady Sara, indeed," Maritha sneered and snapping her fingers at a passing traybearer, took an unladylike gulp of a fresh goblet.

"Lady Sara, indeed," I replied calmly, bowing as graciously as I could, to make her rudeness more apparent. My palms were sweating.

A gleam flickered in Gorlot's eyes as he noticed the exchange. He looked from Maritha's studied blond beauty to me.

"The blond Searcher and the brunet. An interesting contrast. The Searcher has always been my favorite mask, particularly so when I complement it," Gorlot drawled, indicating his white priest's robes.

"You make a truly authentic priest," I murmured, not meaning flattery but smiling up at him from under demurely downcast eyes.

"Get her out of here," Maritha snapped to the guard, her eyes flashing angrily. "Impertinent wretch," and she tossed off the rest of her drink.

Gorlot, to my surprise, canceled that order with a flick of his hand.

"We cannot be so ungracious to Maxil's Searcher," he said as Maritha glared first at me, then at him. She had sense enough to be quiet. "However, every Searcher knows the priest who will claim her, doesn't she?" and his cold eyes flicked once more up and down my body.

Gartly's apparently prophetic words rang in my ears: "It isn't in Gorlot's room we want her."

I took Maxil's arm, more for support against my nervousness, and pulled him forward, away from Gorlot. The backward glance I shot him he could interpret any way he chose. I merely wanted to be sure he wasn't following me.

I was not the only one shaken by the encounter. Maxil's arm trembled beneath my hand. He kept his back straight and his step measured as we walked into the dancers. And there was more pride and confidence in his bearing than there had been since I met him.

The dancers and revelers parted around us to catch us up in their whirling numbers. A fear, deeper, more intense than the momentary shock of the episode with Gorlot, engulfed me in choking terror. The pressing bodies suddenly seemed to compress me in on myself. The various limbs that brushed against mine felt wet or cold and I grabbed at Maxil with both hands. He took one look at my face and brushed rudely past the maskers to get me on the safe, uncrowded sidelines.

I stammered my thanks, unable to explain my ghastly claustrophobia, clutching at Maxil as the only reality in the whole huge room.

He urged me to a brightly decorated buffet table where

tall crystal columns sparkled with liquids. Culinary masterpieces were desecrated to slide down palates dulled by drink. Maxil indicated an almost full dispenser of cornade. We were served by a haughty man who gave the impression of losing dignity by presenting so mild a brew. I gulped down the tart beverage and its cold sweetness reassured me out of my sudden nightmare. I was recovering enough of my senses to see the surprise on the servant's face as he was required to serve another goblet of cornade.

"Greetings, Maxil," said a voice whose cheeriness was another touch with reality.

Maxil's face lit up first, then flushed. I turned, hopeful of seeing Ferrill but barely able to cover my dismay when Maxil grabbed the arm of a well-groomed, wise-faced older man.

"Stannall," he cried eagerly.

"The Lady Sara, is it not? I noticed you passing inspection at the door," and the First Councilman bowed deeply, his shrewd eyes not leaving my face. "Do I congratulate, Maxil?" he asked.

"No, no," Maxil said hastily. "Isn't *my* Lady Fara here?"

"*Your* Lady Fara?" Stannall repeated, lightly questioning the possessive pronoun. "No, Fara is not here," Stannall continued before Maxil had a chance to say anything. Stannall turned a disapproving face toward the shrieking revelry beyond us.

"I mean, is she in Lothara at all?" Maxil persisted hopefully.

"Yes," Stannall said, unbending enough to reassure the boy.

"I'm just filling in for the evening," I felt constrained to say when I caught Stannall's austere expression.

"Rather to the discomfiture of the Lady Maritha," Stannall observed.

"Gorlot called Sara a trollop," Maxil exploded.

Stannall held up a quieting hand. "Evidently the . . . ah . . . Lady Maritha did, too. She chooses to forget she no longer wheedles Harlan but placates Gorlot."

Maxil and I exchanged glances. I couldn't decide whether to say any more to Stannall or not.

"Have you seen my brother ... Ferrill, Sir Stannall?" Maxil asked anxiously.

Stannall dropped his pose of urbanity and became deeply troubled.

"I have, indeed, and ..."

"Where is he?" Maxil interrupted breathlessly.

Stannall ignored the discourtesy and nodded toward a far doorway where two figures stood watching the revelry. I could not see distinctly, but I thought I recognized the taller figure as Ferrill by his stance. Maxil was about to make a straight-line plunge through the dancers for his brother, but I twitched his robe and held him back. Actually, my thought was not caution but a return of the tongue-drying fear that had struck me when we had first gone into that weaving mob. We watched as Ferrill, slowly, almost as if movement were effort, stepped down into the crowd and was swallowed up.

"I can wait for my token," I said with forced gaiety, turning to Stannall. "I need one from the Warlord against a priest I don't like."

"There is no known token for one priest I can name," Stannall remarked calmly, adding in a lower voice that Maxil didn't hear, "unless, of course, that is your purpose in being here."

I smiled at him. "Sir, it was at this priest's instigation I came and believe me, I have no intention of leaving his side this evening."

Stannall bowed and excused himself. I watched him disappear among the dancers and wondered, fleetingly, if I should have mentioned Harlan to him. Still, wasn't he powerless until Council was convened? Surely, any attempt of Harlan's to communicate with the First Councilman would be intercepted. Yet—I had been in the position to speak.

And how was Harlan even to get into the palace at all? Where was he now? Did he know I wasn't at Jokan's?

Maxil touched my arm and led me with a secure grip around the fringe of the revelers, making toward the archway where Ferrill had been. We had circled halfway round the room without a sight of him when he stepped out of the crowd right in front of me.

I was appalled at the change the last few weeks had made in him. The effort I had noticed across the enormous room was tragically obvious close up. His face was very pale, the skin almost transparent. His breath came unevenly, his eyes had sunk into his head, the sockets darkened with pain and sleeplessness. His voice, no longer vibrant, as it had been at the asylum, shook nearly as much as his hands. Maxil put out a quick arm to support Ferrill as the aging young Warlord mounted two steps and joined us.

"I have been wracking my poor brains, dear Searcher," Ferrill remarked in a wheezy, rasping voice that somehow managed to retain a certain forcefulness, "to remember where I have seen you before. Not here, certainly."

"Your memory is better than Gorlot's," I replied as casually as I could, for tension again clutched at me. "But I have bettered my condition in the past few weeks."

Ferrill held up his hand as he searched his memory, Maxil anxiously watching us and the crowd simultaneously.

"It was in the company of Harlan," and I saw the frail shoulders straighten as if the very name of his uncle was a tonic. He said nothing. "I left his company this noontime at the auxiliary airfield," I continued, beginning to share Maxil's anxiety over Ferrill. "He wants you to convene the Council. He is sane. He never was mad. He was drugged just as I imagine they have been drugging you. Give me a token, anything, to explain my speaking to you. And have courage."

Ferrill's breathing became more shallow. He swallowed several times, all the while maintaining a politely attentive smile on his face. With a controlled gesture, he took a dangling medallion from his belt. I accepted it with a little curtsey.

"He may be too late," Ferrill wheezed, "even for Lothar." He descended three steps, touched Maxil's hand affectionately and moved off into the crowd.

"Gorlot saw us," Maxil said, swiftly, the hangdog expression returning to his face.

To cover my own fear, I smiled inanely and laughed as if Maxil had amused me. I searched the crowd frantically for sight of Stannall, for a doorway with the fewest guards, for some reprieve from the man implacably bearing down on us. Maxil whirled me away among a sudden knot of drunken prancers, back toward the beverage table where we had last seen Stannall. The fear of Gorlot met my claustrophobia in a brief struggle for supremacy and the fear of Gorlot won.

But Gorlot never reached us because a shriek of horror pierced the noise and music. Shouts of "The Warlord. . . . He fell" followed. The entire vast hall was silent for a horrified minute. Then Gorlot's voice called cold orders for Trenor, for a stretcher.

We watched, clutching at each other for comfort at this catastrophe as the limp body of Ferrill was carried away.

"I've got to get out of here now, Maxil," I cried. But as we turned to look, all the doorways were blocked by guards with weapons held at the ready.

"Stannall then," I hissed. Maxil craned over the heads around us and then pulled me roughly after him.

The First Councilman had been about to leave the hall when Maxil urgently tugged at his arm, insisting on a private word. Stannall frowned as Maxil indicated me.

"I've no time to undo your coquetry, miss," he said severely, drawing away.

"Would you class news of Harlan as coquetry?" I stated.

Stannall turned slowly back. "What's this? Explain!"

"Harlan was never mad. He's back in Lothara tonight to prove it. At Central Barracks in the section of Sinnall, son of Nallis, who is *loyal* to his Regent," and I stressed the title, not daring to continue for the press of people around us and the sudden approach of two guards.

"The Regent requests the presence of the First Councilman immediately," one guard said, saluting.

"He's *my* brother. I must come, too," Maxil pleaded.

"Only the First Councilman is required," the guard said dispassionately.

Maxil's eyes clouded and his lip trembled a moment. "But he may . . ."

"Lad," Stannall reassured him kindly, "I'll send for you," and he followed the guard.

Maxil's face wore the old, bitter mask. I tried to comfort him, but it was the appearance of his younger brother, Fernan, drunken, strutting in premature triumph, that stiffened Maxil's resolve. Looking at the youngster, his face greasy and swollen with overindulgence, I could scarcely see why anyone would choose *him* over Maxil.

Deliberately Maxil turned his back on Fernan and ignored the whispers we both heard very plainly. Gorlot had spread his fiction about Maxil with an efficient hand.

We didn't have long to wait to know why Stannall had been summoned. He, Gorlot and another man Maxil said was Trenor appeared in the archway and the maskers quieted expectantly.

"The Warlord Ferrill has been seriously taken with a heart attack. He is resting comfortably at the moment. It is the opinion of his physician that with care and rest he will recover," Gorlot's harsh news rang out into the Hall. "We have been concerned with his health for some time. It is our deep regret that his frailty will prevent him from fulfilling his promise as one of Lothar's great Warlords."

"He regrets," Maxil growled.

Someone was moving through the crowd which parted to make way. As he stepped up to Gorlot, we saw it was Fernan. Maxil winced. I saw Stannall beckoning to Maxil and gave him a prod in the ribs. Because the boy refused to let my hand go, we both made our way through the reluctantly parting throng. I gave Maxil one final push and jerked my hand free as we reached the steps. Gorlot, however, saw me and his eyes narrowed. I returned his stare with a defiance I hoped was convincing.

People began to whisper together and then someone tittered and Maxil, standing by Stannall, turned to face the Hall.

"What makes the eunuch think he can be Warlord?" some self-acknowledged wit quipped from the safety of the mass. Laughter rippled from all parts of the Hall.

"Eunuch?" I echoed angrily, rising to the first step and turning to face the direction of the voice. "Eunuch?" I repeated as the laughter died and attention was centered on me. I snorted with disgust and disbelief. "Can you know," for the wit had been a man, "better than I?"

The mutter from the assembled had an entirely different tone now, one of surprise, and Maxil added the final touch.

"Sara, not here," he pleaded, an agonized expression on his furiously blushing face.

It couldn't have been more perfect. The canary-satiated look vanished from Fernan's fat face. Gorlot's eyes narrowed to angry slits and his right hand clenched and unclenched the knife at his belt.

"In deference to the illness of Ferrill, it is my suggestion that you carry your revels to another place of enjoyment," Stannall announced quietly, motioning to the guards to step aside from the archways. "Lord Maxil," and Stannall stressed the title, "the Lady Sara, may I ask that you attend me?"

Gorlot stepped in between Stannall and us.

"As Regent, I would like to ask the Lady Sara a few questions," he almost snarled.

There was a hint of a smile on Stannall's calm face as he answered Gorlot.

"Gorlot, you were Regent to Ferrill. Your Regency, a temporary appointment in any case, has ended with your acknowledgment of Ferrill's incapacity. The Council will convene tomorrow to install the new Warlord-elect and consider the appointment of *his* Regent."

Calmly Stannall motioned us to precede him out of the Hall. I couldn't resist one backward glance and saw Fernan pulling at Gorlot's sleeve impatiently, his putty face screwed up with childish petulance.

CHAPTER EIGHT

STANNALL BRUSHED ASIDE MAXIL'S impatient questions about Ferrill. As First Councilman, Stannall had apartments on the fourth level of the palace wing. We made a silent progress down the blue, softly lit corridor, punctuated with doors and guards, past Maxil's quarters. At the door of his suite, Stannall paused, motioning the guard aside. He produced a curiously shaped rod and pressed it into the small panel in the center of the door. A low whine was audible and then the door opened inward. Lights came up immediately, exposing the graceful main room of the apartment and a filigree-framed balcony.

When the door was closed, Stannall turned to me sternly and demanded an explanation of my cryptic remarks in the Starhall. I gave him an expurgated edition of Harlan's recovery from the drug, intimating that "suspicions had existed in certain minds" over the cause of Harlan's unexpected collapse. I told him of our escape, my meeting with Maxil and my subsequent abduction. As far as I knew, Harlan was in Central Barracks in a detachment from Motlina, under the Second Leader Sinnall.

"I realize now why I was suddenly invited here for the Eclipse," Stannall mused, rubbing the side of his nose thoughtfully. "My presence has not been required much lately. Obviously Harlan could be kept from seeing me here," and he nodded toward the guarded door. "But there are other problems now to be surmounted."

He turned toward Maxil thoughtfully.

"Although . . . ah . . . *the* Lady Sara has already neatly undone much of Gorlot's plans to undermine your election," Stannall began, inclining his head graciously toward me.

"But we . . . she . . ." Maxil stammered.

Stannall frowned and looked at me for explanation.

"We met for the *first* time this afternoon," I said meaningfully.

"Then the boy could be . . ."

"Nonsense," I snapped, regardless of Stannall's position and age. "He doesn't think he is and he should know."

"My daughter, Fara . . ."

"You *know,* sir, Fara and I have had an understanding for just *years,*" Maxil blurted out.

Stannall regarded him with a kindly expression. "I had hoped that would develop into a constant feeling."

Maxil swallowed hurriedly. "It has. I mean, it would if you'd ever let her come back to the palace."

Stannall raised his eyebrows. "More of Gorlot's machinations clarify suddenly. Yes, of course, it wouldn't be to his advantage to have Fara at the palace. Placing you under a tutor the like of Samoth . . ." Stannall shook his head. "Believe me, I was not in favor of that appointment. But I felt at the time it was only for a little while."

"Little while!" Maxil snorted, revealing the abuse he had endured all too long.

"However," Stannall said more briskly, "we shall take care of that little detail right now. Before anything else."

He touched an ornate switch on a bare wall which slid back, revealing a complicated set of panels, desk area and closets. Flipping a series of switches, Stannall activated a vision circuit on which a picture clarified of an old man, clad in a dressing robe.

Stannall greeted the man as Cordan, explaining the Warlord's collapse and asking Cordan to contact Luccill and Mallant and bring them immediately to the palace wing to confer with Trenor.

"With Trenor?" Cordan shouted indignantly.

"Yes, Trenor," Stannall reiterated clearly. "We shall need a full report in the morning for Council. You will then insist, I repeat, insist on seeing me, no matter what the hour, to give me, as First Councilman, your opinion. I cannot overstress the urgency of this. Do you understand?"

Cordan nodded gravely and Stannall broke the connection. Maxil sighed with relief and flopped down into an armchair.

"Why didn't you tell me of Harlan's escape before you rushed off to Ferrill?" the Councilman asked me sternly. "You realize, of course, that the news was too great a strain and brought about his attack? I could have effected a convention myself, given your information."

Maxil turned a horror-stricken face to me.

"I didn't know that," I said, tears springing to my eyes.

"But, my dear girl, I *am* the First Councilman. Surely you know the prerogatives of that office."

"The Council was not in session," I argued in defense. "Harlan didn't dare get in touch with you at your holdings."

"Harlan made a poor choice as messenger, then," Stannall retorted, anger in his voice.

"I wasn't even supposed to *be* a messenger," I cried. "I just had the misfortune to tangle with Samoth and the next thing I knew I was in the palace and in Maxil's room. I thought it would *help* Ferrill to know Harlan was all right."

"Please, Sir Stannall," Maxil interposed, alarmed at my tears. "I'm the one to blame. *I* knew how *sick* Ferrill was. And I knew all about Harlan. It's my fault, not Sara's."

"Oh, my situation is absurd," I cried in my frustration. "Accusing me doesn't heal Ferrill now and it doesn't get Harlan into the palace and make him Regent again."

"He couldn't be made Regent anyway," Stannall reminded us dryly.

"Why not?" Maxil's voice cracked in dismay.

"First, he has to be proved sane. Second, the same condition I cited to Gorlot applies to Harlan. He was Regent for *Ferrill*."

"But what if I want Harlan as *my* Regent?" declared Maxil with dawning comprehension. "I'm over fifteen, so I can choose."

"That's perfectly true," Stannall replied as if he, too, had only realized this fact. He brought his hand down hard on the communicator switch, dialing quickly. He turned to me again, his eyes blinking rapidly, his lips pursing in thought. "There is no doubt of his sanity?"

"Of course not. He never was insane. He was drugged into a semblance of mental imbalance. If you are having those physicians here for Maxil, get Harlan here, too. They must be as qualified to judge Harlan's sanity as Maxil's . . . virility."

A voice declared it issued from "Central Barracks," but no picture evolved.

"This is First Councilman Stannall," and the picture came on abruptly. "I need additional sections for special duty at once. Are all assigned?"

"No, Sir Stannall, but the ones available are all provincial reinforcements called in on special assignment," the officer apologized.

"That doesn't matter. Have you any men from my province?"

"No, sir. I could recall those from duty . . ."

"That would consume too much time. What have you got?"

"Units from Motlina, South Cheer, Banta . . ."

"Motlina. Leader's name?"

"Sinnall."

"That would be Nallis' son, wouldn't it?"

"I believe so."

"Fine. Have him report by planecar to my balcony and give him clearance through all that mess out front."

It was too simple. I sat with my eyes closed in relief that Harlan would soon be here. Stannall, pursing his lips in thought, brooded over the length of his right foot. Maxil walked over to the fruit bowl on the table and chose a piece to munch.

"I wonder," Stannall mused aloud, "what else Gorlot has been busy doing."

"Harlan seemed to think the Tane uprising was covering something up," I remarked into the silence.

Stannall shook his head in disagreement. "I've checked and double-checked the reports on that from the first attack. I've interviewed some of the survivors of the first raids. Those that were paralyzed with cerol. Wicked stuff that. I suspect some connivance with Glan or Ertoi. They have always been so complacent about their role in the Alliance. It isn't natural. And then there's that treaty concerning the Tanes that Gorlot has been trying to ram through Council."

I shrugged, not having heard anything about that. The sound of Maxil's munching was infectious. I rarely needed an excuse to eat lately, so I wandered over to have another bite.

We were all expecting it, but when the whir of the planecar's approach suddenly drowned out the muted revelry beyond the gardens, we jumped to our feet, startled.

The car hovered, connected with the trelliswork of the balcony and disgorged its passengers. Stannall held up a warning hand and allowed the group to file in. The planecar was closing its slot door when the door to the hall burst open and the guards rushed in, weapons drawn. The masqueraders, acting on reflex, pulled out their own arms. The two forces glared at each other suspiciously even as Stannall's easy chuckle dissipated the sudden menace in the room.

"I'm pleased to see such alertness," he remarked to his guards with that measured calm of his.

Weapons were sheepishly replaced.

"Mark these men well, guards," Stannall continued, indicating Sinnall's section. "They'll be coming and going all night. Oh, and when the physicians Luccill, Mallant and Cordan arrive, they are to be admitted immediately. They are expected."

The guards backed out with one final suspicious glare at the newcomers.

As the door closed behind them, Harlan spotted me where I had been half hidden by Maxil.

"Sara, how did you get here?" he exclaimed, striding to me.

Stannall snorted. *"That* reaction proves he's sane," he commented almost sourly. "You've heard the news?"

Harlan, one arm around me, turned back to the First Councilman.

"Bad news needs no announcement," Harlan said heavily.

"Your emissary," and Stannall gave me a curt nod of his head, "was too literal in the discharge of her duty. In consequence she also robbed you of yours."

"Stannall, that isn't fair," Maxil interposed before I could explain anything.

"Sara, you were supposed to get to Jokan's," Harlan muttered, gripping me tightly in his concern.

"Best laid plans," I sighed. "I ended up here, talking to Ferrill after all."

Stannall frowned and went into bitter detail of the events leading up to Ferrill's heart attack.

"Sara wouldn't have known you could help us, Stannall," Harlan said firmly. "Had I even the slightest hope you would be here at Eclipse, I would have . . ."

Stannall waved off the rest of his sentence. "You realize, of course, Harlan, that your Regency also is terminated by Ferrill's incapacity?"

Harlan nodded, settling himself beside me. I sat there inanely holding the core of my fruit because I didn't see anywhere to dispose of it. Behind Stannall's back, Harlan took the core and tossed it at a seemingly bare spot in the wall. A slot opened as the core neared and closed silently behind it. Harlan's grin and the squeeze he gave my hand mitigated Stannall's scathing disapproval.

"However," Stannall continued, pacing, "young Maxil here is next in line. He claims he's ready to stand up and cry for you in front of Council."

Harlan turned to Maxil, a mixture of emotions on his face and a flurry of unspoken thoughts muddying the color of his eyes.

"With thanks for the honor, young Maxil, I'm not at all anxious to be saddled with the Regency again."

Everyone in the room turned to stare at Harlan.

"But you were . . . driving us like cavehunters to get here," Jessl stammered out.

"To save Ferrill's life, yes. It's in good hands now. And neither Gorlot nor I is Regent."

"But Harlan, you're the only one who *can* be Regent,"

Maxil cried out, his voice cracking perilously in his distress.

Harlan regarded him a moment with tolerance.

"You could certify me for good if I agreed with you, young Maxil," he said lightly. "You'll find dozens of men eager for the job. I'll give my personal recommendation that you'll be easy on the new Regent."

"This levity is uncalled for," Gartly growled disapprovingly. "There aren't dozens of men qualified for the Regent of the Warlord in these troubled times. And you know it."

"You're one, friend Gartly," Harlan pointed out. He rose. "I had been Regent for seven years," he said, directly to Stannall. "That's a slice out of a man's life. I've got other plans for the next six years while Maxil grows up," and his eyes slid enigmatically in my direction.

"For instance?" asked Stannall with an edge to his voice.

"You know my preferences well enough, Stannall," Harlan replied sharply. "You've vetoed my requests for more exploratory ships. You've overridden my insistence that we must find more allies for the final attack on the Mil homeworlds."

This seemed to be the prologue for the renewal of an old battle of more than unusual importance to both men. Stannall opened his mouth to reply and then dismissed the subject with a sharp wave of his hand.

"It does you no good to find new planets for Lothar if she is in the grip of men like Gorlot and the petty bullies of his clan. You were, as I recall it," and Stannall's voice was heavily sarcastic, "the one who initiated the colonization policy that would give the run-from-the-Mil his first chance for independent holdings . . ."

"If there were not two but eight, nine, ten planets to divide, there would be no such struggle," Harlan interposed.

Stannall snorted his contempt. "Of course, it doesn't signify that such men as Lamar, Newrit, Tellman—and I could name a dozen others—are no longer available as prospective Regents."

This was news to the others as well as Harlan.

"Yes, that surprises you, doesn't it," Stannall said with calculated scorn. "Newrit and Tellmann were killed in the Tane revolutions; Lamar and Sosit are in survivor asylums in pitiful condition. In their places we have such notable personalities as Samoth, Portale, Losin . . ."

"Bumbling incompetents," Harlan exploded. "I've kept them on the Moonbases since they aged into section leaders because they blasted well can't do much harm to raw rock."

Stannall smiled mockingly. "Yet they are now *quadrant* leaders and the only choice besides Gorlot that Maxil here would have."

Harlan glared fixedly, almost sullenly, at Stannall. "I have already done more than my duty for Lothar," he muttered.

Stannall's eyes narrowed angrily, but he controlled his face into an appearance of good humor.

"Yes, you have," he agreed. "So has Ferrill."

"I have the right to lead a private life, now," snapped Harlan, jerking himself away from Stannall and stamping over to the balcony.

"How would you lead it under the Regency of a man like Gorlot . . . or Losin?"

"Gartly qualifies. So does Jokan."

"Aye, and Gartly's willing," the old soldier spoke up sternly.

"Jokan's reputation as a philandering dabbler disqualifies him, however," Stannall pursued, "in the eyes of the conservatives as much as it enhances him in the halls of the liberals. You know where that would end: stalemate."

Harlan stopped pacing and stood, his back to all of us, staring out at the revelry beyond the palace and absorbing the quiet of the still gardens. There was resignation and tired defeat in the set of his shoulders.

I wondered in the tense silence that fell if his reference to exploration made me indirectly responsible for the outburst that had stunned the others. This change of face was unlike the dedicated man I knew. He had thought of nothing for the last weeks but to get back to Lothara, be reinstated as Regent and save both Ferrill and Lothar from Gorlot's plans. It was incredible that he would suddenly separate duty to Ferrill and duty to Lothar when he himself had given me the strongest impression that the two were indivisible in his eyes. Hadn't Stannall's revelations impressed on him that Lothar needed him more than ever before? Why did he hesitate?

"My friend," Stannall began in a subtly persuasive tone, "your return and the fact that you were really drugged into insensibility are the final pieces in a puzzle I have been meditating ten months. Does it not appear all too propitious that Gorlot should have been in Lothara at the time of your collapse when you had ordered him on Rim maneuvers? That three days after your ... illness, the Tane wars break out? That Socto, Effra and Cheret are replaced within the month, leaving Hospitals, War Supplies and Records in the control of Gorlot adherents? That petty officers with records as martinets and incompetents are suddenly promoted to quadrant leaders? That Ferrill, whose health has never been as robust as we could wish, is suddenly afflicted with a strange debilitating malady and is successfully treated only by Trenor, a relatively unknown physician from a back province in Gorlot's holding? That Maxil is shepherded, disgraced, shamed, humiliated by a bullying byblow, while Fernan is feted and cozened? That Council is left unconvened except for the emergency quota all during a long summer and that that quota is composed of those barons who have opposed your reforms? They fit in, these pieces, don't they?

"And don't think I haven't left a cave unsearched to find out what is really going on. I've seen every report from the quadrants, talked with the wounded; seen the shivering wrecks that were our most promising patrol leaders and tried to convince myself that nothing was wrong. Because there has been no discernible evidence of illicit activity.

"And then, miraculously, you return as sane and hearty

as when I saw you in the Starhall two hours before your collapse."

Stannall paused. He looked at Harlan to see what effect his disclosures were having.

"Tell me," the Councilman's facile voice changed flavor again, "have you no personal quarrel to pick with Gorlot for taking ten months out of your life? Can he shame you with the stigma of insanity and not expect to answer to you? Or are you still insane? The man who tells me his duty was done with Ferrill's deposition does not sound like the Harlan I knew ten months ago. It sounds like a drug-weakened dreamer, filled with delinade, not guts and blood."

Instead of being stung by the insults, Harlan turned wearily from the window. He looked toward me first, but his face was expressionless.

"You touch a point none of us have brought up, Stannall," he said slowly, heavily. "It is necessary *first* to prove I *am* sane, to the Council, to the planet, and to myself."

Jessl and Gartly exhaled tightly drawn breaths. Stannall allowed no expression of triumph whatever to cross his features.

"Harlan," Maxil burst out, his voice cracking again, "if you don't want to be Regent for me . . ."

Harlan crossed quickly to the boy and threw an affectionate arm across the rigidly held shoulders. "My . . . hesitation . . . has no reflection on my fondness for you, lad. Or, I should say, my lord."

"That, too, has not yet been decided," Stannall said briskly. He sat down at the desk by the communicator and pulled out slates as he continued talking. "The physicians will report here after they make their examinations of Ferrill . . ."

"There's no chance that the initial verdict can . . ." asked Harlan.

"None," was Stannall's emphatic answer. "I presume Gorlot has been merely biding his time before he brought up the matter of the lad's health officially. Perhaps he didn't expect Ferrill to collapse so completely."

"But you said he'd be all right," Maxil said anxiously.

Stannall frowned slightly at this interruption. He turned and looked at Maxil as if the boy had changed completely.

"I said he'd live. The extent of his invalidism we'll know when we receive the full medical report. At the same time they are here to see you, my lord, they can make a preliminary examination of Harlan. Undoubtedly a more extensive one will have to be made at the War Hospital Clinic at a later date." Stannall added a final mark to the slate he had been writing on and handed it to Sinnall.

"Section Leader, this must be delivered at once to Lesatin. I believe he planned to be in Lothara for the festivities, but I doubt he was invited to the palace." Stannall smiled wryly. "His sympathies have never paralleled Gorlot's interests. Once the message is delivered, consider yourself under Lesatin's orders. Try first at his town residence, Place of the Triangle Red. Someone there may be sober enough to remember where the man went.

"Gartly, I want you to contact every old patroller you know, in town or not. Jessl, get your younger friends together. I want word spread that Harlan is back, that he is sane. That he never was mad. Your group can spread the news quicker than the Mil can evacuate the city. By the way, where's that ladies' man, Jokan? I'd've thought he'd be along tonight."

"He's waiting at his place for Sara. And I think she'd better go there," Harlan said.

"On the contrary," Stannall countermanded, turning to look at me. "The young lady must spend the night in Maxil's suite."

It was Harlan's turn to frown.

"I don't see the necessity of . . ."

"You don't see, Harlan," Stannall interrupted testily, "that she is essential to counteract Gorlot's campaign to have Maxil set aside as impotent. In front of the entire Starhall, she admitted his claim on her."

Harlan turned white and stared at me.

"I did not," I cried, although I didn't understand the undercurrent between Harlan and Stannall that was directed at me. "I said nothing of the kind. And I only met the boy this afternoon at a cornade stand in the square. Then . . ."

Stannall waved me silent. "That *must* not be known," and he pinioned with his glance everyone in the room separately, exhorting unspoken compliance with this essential lie. "The *impression*," and as his voice underlined the word, he looked squarely at Harlan and then Maxil, "must stand."

"A moment," Harlan said in a too-quiet voice. "I had a prior claim."

Stannall turned to Harlan coldly. "I cannot help your private plans for the Lady Sara. The fact remains unalterable that Lothar must remain under the impression that this girl is Maxil's lady. That voids Gorlot's scheme to have Maxil set aside in favor of Fernan. Gorlot neglected to include an element of chance in his calculations. We cannot permit his neglect to go unutilized because of private feelings or dealings. I'm certain that both Lord Maxil and the Lady Sara are aware of the circumstances in which they now find themselves and will conduct themselves accordingly."

"Sara, I'm sorry," Maxil pleaded with such adolescent embarrassment that I swallowed the words that rushed to my lips.

"There is so much at stake," I began, directing my plea to Harlan whose jaw muscles were clenched with his unspoken anger. "After all, it is an honor to be the Warlord's lady. If I ever dreamed a simple glass of cornade would lead to all this . . ." and I made an attempt at a carefree laugh. Maxil gave me a rather sickly grin of gratitude, but Harlan refused to unbend.

"With *your* permission," he grated out between his teeth at Stannall and then drew me out to the balcony. Stannall watched us leave and then beckoned to Gartly and Jessl to leave and for Sinnall and Cire to join him at the desk.

Harlan was gripping my hand painfully tight. He shut the glass balcony door and drew me into the balcony shadow.

"Sara, that gesture may cost you your life," he began.

"Don't be silly. I've braved the worst that Gorlot could do and . . ."

"Gorlot is nowhere near as deadly for you as Stannall," Harlan said in such earnest my levity failed me.

"You never come right out and explain," I wailed softly.

He shook his head irritably. "It is not a simple thing to explain. I don't understand how you came to let Maxil claim you. Surely you must realize how little you know of this planet."

"I couldn't agree more."

"Then how can you expect to play a part which calls for constant public appearances where everything you do and say will be remarked. The tiniest slip will be noticed. Sara, Sara."

He took me in his arms, pressing my head against his chest, folding me carefully but tightly against him, his lips on my forehead.

"What else could I have done? I've been as backed into a short cave as you have."

At my choice of words, he gave a little chuckle, and released me. I could see his face in the shadow, his eyes on me were tender.

"There was one chance in several thousand you'd manage to carry off what you've already done. But I'd far rather see you safely on my holdings until we find out more about how you got here. And preferably, find your world."

"Is that what you meant when you said you had other things to do with your life?"

"Yes," he said sadly. "Yes. There's more than just finding your world and helping them defend themselves against the Mil. But that's scarcely an issue to throw into the confusion of this mess."

"But *why* is my origin so dangerous?"

"It's all wrapped with the horror of restoration," he said

in a tight voice, "which I have no time to explain. But you say you've come from another planet. The only *way* you can have got from another planet that I know of is by way of a Mil ship. And traveling on a Mil ship ... well, it follows that you must be a restoree. And to almost everyone, a restoree is a horror to be exterminated at the first opportunity."

I stared at him, my throat dry.

"But I'm not horrible, am I?" I whispered, scared deep inside me by the intensity in his voice.

"Dear my lady," he said softly, framing my face with both hands, "has not half of Lothar acknowledged your loveliness?"

"But your restoree talk scares me," I said, biting back my tears. Fatigue, hand in hand with fright, seeped past the barriers excitement and novelty had created. I was desperately tired.

"I know, Sara, but I must scare you enough to make you doubly cautious. I feel so powerless to protect you."

"I'm too tired to think," I groaned, putting my hand to the place on my jaw that ached.

He opened the door and handed me back into the room.

"*My* Lady Sara is exhausted," Harlan said, issuing his challenge at Stannall.

The First Councilman looked up at Harlan for a long moment.

"Maxil, you have heard Harlan's claim."

"Yes, sir, I have," Maxil agreed somberly, rising to his feet.

"All right, both of you escort her to Maxil's apartment. Then I want *both* of you back here," Stannall said with exasperation.

Harlan, bowing slightly to me and then Maxil, gave Maxil my hand and opened the door to the hall for us.

There was no doubting the shock of surprise on the faces of the guards as they recognized Harlan on the way to Maxil's quarters. Neither Maxil nor Harlan looked right or left. Maxil palmed open his door and stood aside to let me and then Harlan pass while the startled hall guard snapped to attention, his eyes wide and rolling around to get the closest look at the Regent.

Maxil closed the door and let Harlan lead me to a bedroom, opposite the one in which Samoth had dumped me that afternoon. The lights came up immediately in the lovely room.

"How do you turn them off?" I whispered urgently to Harlan.

He pulled the door to and waved one hand over a panel of darker wood by the doorway. The lights went out. I saw the whiteness of his hand move again and the lights came up.

He stared at me fiercely.

"By all the mothers of all the clans, I should have claimed you on that boat after all. Remember, you are *my* lady."

The incredible possessiveness of his look stayed before my eyes long after he left. I realized suddenly what the formality of "claiming" and using the personal possessive pronoun must mean. I had got myself married to Harlan without even knowing it. I fell asleep trying to see all the ramifications of my paradoxical situation.

CHAPTER NINE

THE NEXT MORNING WHEN I woke, I felt rested completely and, of course, hungry. I was torn between a bath and something to eat. On the bed was a heavy green robe. I glanced at the other side of the large bed and assured myself I had been its lone occupant. I rose and belted the robe and tiptoed to the door. I peeked out into the living room, saw a clear path to the fruit on the table and started for it.

"Lady Sara, I hope I didn't wake you," and I whirled to see a young blond girl in a blue overdress, her eyes wide and anxious.

"No," I muttered.

"I am Linnana and at your service. May I draw your bath? There are gowns for your choosing and, if I may suggest it, the others will soon arrive for breakfast." She glanced at the hall door nervously, expecting an invasion momentarily.

Beyond her, I saw on the raised level at the balcony door the table set and awaiting diners. I nodded but nevertheless grabbed up an applefruit before I returned to my room. I didn't care what she thought. I was hungry.

I bathed and then allowed Linnana to show me the clothes she had mentioned. It was a mistake because there were far too many of all colors, lengths and fabrics, and a small chest of jewels as well.

"I'm just a simple country girl," I began finally as even Linnana showed impatience at my indecision. "I don't know what to choose to wear in the palace for breakfast."

She giggled. "That's easy. With your permission?"

She held up a knee-length tunic and overdress in contrasting shades of a soft rust, and took from the jewels a simple chain of gold with jadelike buttons in the links. When I had dressed, no longer worried about unfamiliar

117

closures because she took care of that, she set me down again and opened a small metal box. With a brush, she recreated eyebrows for those I lost in the force screen. She added a touch of color to my lids and a blush of paint on my lips and studied the effect. When I glimpsed myself in the mirror, my hand inadvertently went to my nose. I snatched it back into my lap for fear she would interpret the gesture.

"My pardon, Lady Sara," and she brought out powder for me.

It was a little reassuring to know that women still used such guiles on Lothar.

Evidently she felt no more was needed and followed me to the door.

When I stepped out into the room, I stopped abruptly on the threshold. Linnana had neglected to tell who had been expected for breakfast and I had not bothered to count the place settings. It would not have been so overwhelming if I had known what to expect. Over twenty men were gathered in that room, of whom I knew only Stannall, Harlan, Maxil and Jessl. Following Maxil and Harlan's example, those seated at the crowded table rose instantly. I believe I was the only one who saw Harlan prod Maxil forward to greet me.

Maxil struggled with his embarrassment as he took my hand to lead me to my place. Our flushing faces only compounded the desired impression.

A servant came quickly with the steaming chocolaty beverage which was the Lotharian equivalent of coffee. It helped clear my head, certainly; hot, tart and stimulating.

"You'll be pleased to know, Lady Sara," Harlan began formally but with a wicked twinkle in his eye, "that the Lord Maxil and I have been cleared of the various physical and mental deficiencies attributed to us. And, by the foremost physician of the world, Monsorlit."

I grabbed frantically to balance the cup in my hand before my trembling spilled the hot stuff all over me. Maxil hastily proferred a napkin and a servant materialized to mop up and produce a fresh cup. I muttered inanely about hot cups and tried to catch Harlan's eye. His remarks were addressed to the table in general and he did not look at me.

"Gorlot was ... obviously ... mistaken about Maxil," he continued blithely. A polite ripple of laughter forced a bright smile from me. There were no lascivious sidewise looks at me from the men at the table. Actually fathers were quick to urge a likely girl to become the unofficial lady of a Warlord. A child of such an alliance might well be Warlord-elect if the father died without other, more legal issue.

"The most exhaustive tests brought by Physician Monsorlit failed to show me mentally defective but he's to try his worst this afternoon in that precious Clinic of his. I am, evidently," and here Harlan's laughter was echoed by the others, "to be congratulated on my astounding return to sanity."

"Physician Monsorlit," the name rang in my brain and I couldn't believe it. Could there be two with the same name?

"Remarkable luck, that," said a man standing by the balcony, "getting one of Gorlot's own to validate your sanity."

Harlan frowned at the comment.

"I say I find it difficult to believe a man of Monsorlit's caliber is connected with Gorlot. He's too fine a scientist and physician ..."

"Not too fine a man to have dabbled in the vile practice of restoration," snapped Stannall with such massive hate and condemnation in his voice that it filled the room with tension.

I stared, amazed at the First Councilman for the passion of his denunciation.

"He was severely disciplined for that youthful attempt," a gray-headed, senatorial man remarked, "and has turned his remarkable energies toward our truly pressing problem of insanity. Look what he has achieved with that Mental Clinic of his. He's been able to train useless idiots to perform simple duties perfectly."

Stannall was not impressed.

"He has sought the proper cave in company with Gorlot."

Then why, I asked myself, did Monsorlit say Harlan was sane. Don't they realize that Monsorlit was responsible for Harlan's collapse?

"Gorlot will have difficulty now keeping Maxil from the Warlordship and Harlan from being appointed Regent," someone stated.

"I wouldn't be too sure," Stannall said sourly. "Remember, there was little Monsorlit could do when three other noted physicians were sincerely convinced of Harlan's recovery."

"Then you expect trouble tomorrow when the Council convenes?" Grayhead asked worriedly.

"Of course I do," Stannall said. "Do you think Gorlot will simply step aside because Harlan has returned unexpectedly? No, the man is incredibly cunning, else we should have suspected him long ago. How many of you doubted his report of Maxil's impotency until last night? How many of us have questioned any one of his other unusual acts? The appointment of a back-province physician for Ferrill instead of Loccan or Cordan?"

"But Trenor effected some relief for the War——the boy," another voice interposed. "There *was* a definite improvement."

"Yes, a cessation of whatever drug they used to debilitate the boy," Stannall retorted.

"Did the physicians find the residue of any such drug in Ferrill's body?" Grayhead asked.

Stannall snorted. "There are many drugs with peculiar properties, my dear Lesatin, whose traces are completely absorbed in the system within a few hours. Cordan suggests that perhaps cerol was used since Ferrill's motor system has suffered most. But that is confidential information."

"Cerol?" Lesatin exclaimed in horror, "but that's a Tane-grown drug."

And, I amended to myself, the same thing they used on Harlan.

"Then the Tanes are behind this," someone blurted out.

"No," Stannall replied with such calm assurance that the rising hysteria in that quarter was calmed. "But I have good reason to believe that the Tane Revolution masks some intention other than meets the eye."

Stannall smiled slyly at the anxious requests for explanation.

"We have already sent a . . . ah . . . qualified observer," and Stannall glanced quickly at Harlan with an accusatory expression, "to Tane to bring us back a firsthand report of the situation. I have not been satisfied with the all too reassuring official reports."

"Neither have I," Lesatin asserted loudly. "They've been . . . ah . . . em . . . too vague."

Maxil muttered in my ear, "Jokan took off on his own last night. Harlan was fit to tie him to a Mil Rock. So was Stannall but not for the same reason."

"But Jokan was supposed to wait for me," I said inanely.

"That's why Harlan was mad. That Jokan!" Maxil chuckled with delight.

Stannall was continuing smoothly. "He will return as soon as he has properly assessed the problem. In the meantime, it is essential that we delve into every corner of Gorlot's administration and bring up from the depths of each cave those inconsistencies which can bring the majority of council to its senses with regard to this tyrant."

"I should think poisoning Ferrill would be sufficient," remarked a wiry, black-headed man later named to me as Estoder.

Stannall pointed a finger at him, punctuating his words, "*If* we had proof of it, which not even Cordan can find . . . except by the process of eliminating other factors. Indeed, without Harlan's miraculous escape and return, we would not even be possessed of the suspicion. The action of that new drug is comparatively unknown, you realize."

"Just how did Harlan escape, if he'd been so heavily

drugged? No one's clarified that point," Lesatin remarked, pointedly staring at me.

Harlan shot me a quick encouraging smile but allowed Stannall to speak first.

"The ... ah ... Lady Sara," Stannall had difficulty for some reason in deciding on my title, "managed to penetrate the sanitarium and became assigned as Harlan's attendant."

"We are doubly indebted to the Lady Sara," Lesatin remarked, bowing in my direction.

Lesatin seemed to me to be the sort of person who dotes on being possessed of the fullest information on any given subject that attracts his attention. He reminded me unpleasantly of an officious junior executive at the agency library who had plagued me unnecessarily for infinite details about this or that. I steeled myself for the questions Lesatin, if he bore out the resemblance, might throw at me.

"Can it be possible to assume," Estoder spoke before Lesatin could, "that Socto, Effra and Cheret were removed from Hospitals, War Records and Supplies more by Gorlot's intervention than the normal course of events?"

"Possible, probable and entirely feasible," Stannall agreed, "and I suggest we begin our checking immediately with these offices with the thoroughness of the ancient priesthood in examining a novice."

Everyone now had a question or an opinion or a suggestion. The breakfast broke up into little groups of debaters, calling to Harlan or Stannall for approval. Men departed in pairs or singly. Finally there were only four of us left. Harlan reached for a heavy surcoat. I tried to catch his eye so I could tell him about Monsorlit's visit to the asylum. I was also afraid of being left alone with Stannall after his remark about restoration.

Harlan spared time only to grip my arm and mumble about seeing me later. As the door swung shut behind him, I felt awfully alone and vulnerable.

"Maxil," Stannall said, "I think you had better present yourself to your brother's quarters."

"Fernan?" Maxil countered, distastefully.

"No," Stannall frowned, "Ferrill. The morning's report is reassuring. The paralysis of his right side continues. But last night's examination contradicts the theory of a heart seizure. It will look well that you have been to see him. And take the Lady Sara with you. I have assigned four men as your bodyguard. Absolutely trustworthy," and the First Councilman's face relaxed into a reassuring smile for Maxil. "You two," and he flicked his eyes to me, "are not to be left unguarded for a moment. Oh, and when you've seen Ferrill, your new quarters should be ready. I'll see you at dinner. Lady Sara," and he bowed punctiliously in my direction.

"He doesn't like me, Maxil," I said when the First Councilman had left.

"Aw," Maxil shrugged it off. "He will. Harlan'll see to that and when Fara gets here," and Maxil blushed furiously, "I mean, aw," and Maxil rolled his eyes to the ceiling in adolescent embarrassment.

"I know what you mean, Maxil," I laughed, patting his arm consolingly. "It will be a great pleasure to step aside for my competition."

Maxil's face screwed up even more. "Oh, Sara."

"Oh, Maxil," I teased back, trying to reassure him.

A knock at the door disclosed Sinnall, in resplendent Palace Guard uniform, at rigid attention. Behind him I could see an equally rigid Cire and two huge guardsmen. Sober-faced and taking his new position very seriously, Sinnall saluted.

"My orders, Warlord, are to guard, guide and defend you and the Lady Sara. May I present Second-Leader Cire, and Patrolmen Farn and Regel!"

"Second-Leader Cire," Maxil said, grinning broadly at Cire's good fortune. Then he hastily cleared his throat and recalled his new position in life. "My compliments, *Group Leader*," and his voice underlined Sinnall's double promotion, "and my thanks for your loyalty. I wish to see my brother, Ferrill."

Saluting smartly, Sinnall backed out into the hall with

his men, waiting at attention until Maxil and I started before he signaled his men to fall in behind us.

There was a vastly different atmosphere in the hallways this morning. Perhaps it was the green sunlight that flooded the hall from the skylights and balconied alcoves. Perhaps it was the crisp snapping to of the guards who saluted as we passed where last night they had insolently glanced our way. Perhaps it was the obsequious salutations of the men and women who paused to greet Maxil, openly eyeing me. Several would have engaged Maxil in conversation, but he was too nervous to give them any encouragement and, to my relief, they tactfully withdrew.

There was a marked difference in Maxil's bearing as we continued. Last night he had come close to cringing away from passers-by. Today, his shoulders were erect. He held his head high and his eyes lost their apologetic furtiveness. He was beginning to accept the fact that he was Warlord-elect; that this good fortune was his and that he could no longer expect ridicule. No longer was he Samoth's whipping boy; nor the "younger brother" of a promising Warlord, but the heir himself. And I was proud, too, to see him conducting himself in what he considered the proper manner.

Leaving our escort outside, we were immediately passed through to the inner rooms of Ferrill's suite. At the door of the bedroom, a double guard was posted to whom Maxil issued his request with new-found imperiousness. One guard excused himself and entered the darkened room. He returned immediately, holding the door respectfully for the man who entered.

Maxil's confidence disappeared instantly and he muttered a halting request. I was in no position to bolster Maxil because I was staring straight at Monsorlit. I trembled with fear and apprehension. Round and round in my mind whirled Stannall's words, and the volume of his revulsion and contempt seemed to grow with each cycle. I looked frantically around for some exit or something I could do that would remove me from Monsorlit's notice.

"Certainly you may see Ferrill, Lord Maxil," Monsorlit assented smoothly. He stood courteously aside to let the boy pass. "I must, however, caution you to keep your visit short so as not to tire him."

"He'll be all right, I mean ... that is, he's not going to die or anything, is he?" Maxil asked anxiously.

Monsorlit shook his head, smiling enigmatically. I turned toward the outer rooms.

"No, Sara, stay with me," said Maxil pleadingly.

Monsorlit turned, curious, to me.

He started to incline his head in an acknowledgment, stopped, stared puzzled for a split second and then straightened. There was nothing in his expressionless face to indicate whether he recognized me as Harlan's whilom attendant or not. I was certain it would be only a matter of time before he pulled my identity from storage in his orderly mind. Maxil saw all this, but his interpretation of Monsorlit's stare made him flush. I wrenched myself around and escaped into the darkened bedroom.

A greenish glow, pleasant, restful, fell on the book-piled desk, the panel of communications screens, shelves of souvenirs and slates that covered the inward walls of the room. Against a side wall was Ferrill's wide bed, flanked by chairs and an austere hospital table with its neat array of medicines.

"Greetings, Maxil," said a low voice from the shadowy heaps of pillows. "Come to view the departed?"

"Aw, Ferrill," Maxil groaned, dropping on to the bed.

"My lord," I heard the low hoarse chuckle, "I couldn't be more pleased at this turn of events. In all truth, it's been hard to play Warlord. No idealist, no dreamer like myself should have to come to grips with the realities of ruling a world. His heart is not sufficiently armored against sentiment and suffering for the strict impartiality essential for the domination of millions. I would soon have failed Harlan, my father's memory ... and Lothar."

The voice trailed off into a cough. Maxil, a gangling awkward shape, shook his head in denial.

"Ferrill, if I'd only known how awfully sick you were, I'd never have let Sara tell you about Harlan. Stannall says that's what made you collapse," Maxil confessed brokenly.

"Good thing she did," the sick man stoutly reassured his brother. "The only thing that saved my life, believe me, was fainting last night. Otherwise you would really be gazing on the departed."

"What do you mean?" cried Maxil aghast.

"Simply that I'm positive Trenor would have administered a lethal dose of his palliative last night. The moment Sara told me Harlan was free I could feel the prick of that final fatal needle in my arm. As it is, I'm extraordinarily lucky to come out of this with just a mild paralysis. Cerol is dangerous stuff. I'd've died a lot sooner did I not come of stout-hearted stock. That heart attack rumor is false."

"You mean, you *knew* you were being poisoned and never told anyone?" Maxil cried out.

Ferrill snorted. "Who would have believed me? 'The boy's delirious,' " he quipped in an elderly voice.

Cerol, he had said and that was what they had used on Harlan but the results were so different. On Ferrill they caused debilitation ... on Harlan only a senseless stupor.

"Stannall believes you were poisoned."

"Certainly he believes ... *now*. Who is that lurking in the shadows? Come here," Ferrill commanded. "Ah, the Lady Sara. My harbinger of good news. Again thanks."

"I'm relieved to know that last night's message was good news to someone," I said gratefully. "Even if Stannall objects."

"My dear girl, you ruffled his feelings. Stannall has been thwarted of late, both personally and politically. He dislikes most of all being uninformed on curious happenings. A failing of his, but it makes him an extraordinarily capable First Councilman. Almost too capable. Gorlot must have had a paragraph in his plans for him, too."

"Have you any idea what Gorlot was building up to?" I asked curiously.

"Apart from complete domination of Lothar," Ferrill said with a nasty laugh, "I have only vague suspicions."

As I looked down on the gaunt-faced man who had still been a boy a few weeks ago, it was difficult to realize that there were only four years between Maxil and Ferrill. It looked more like forty. "I suspect he gave the Tane planets away to those who have backed him. After Harlan's convenient sick-leave had been arranged, Gorlot descended on us like a Mil ship that didn't bother to orbit. Everyone had a good word for him. Took me a while to come to my senses, I want to tell you. Then it was already too late. His men were in strategic positions. The Tane war was under way and I was kept almost too sick to care. After that, patient optimism and intestinal fortitude seemed my only alternatives."

"Is Monsorlit really helping you now?" I asked, speaking my fears. "He isn't just another Trenor for you?"

Ferrill's smile was very knowing and wise. He waggled a weak finger at me.

"Don't doubt our leading authority on nervous diseases, sweet lady."

"But he's the one who was drugging Harlan in the asylum. And I know there were others in there just as unwilling as Harlan. And Trenor was their physician."

"I don't doubt it."

"And you still let Monsorlit treat you?" Maxil quavered.

"Yes. For the simple reason that *I* trust the man."

I stared at him.

"Why he is allied with Gorlot, I don't know," Ferrill continued. "He is an oblique fellow but it will be a sorry day for Lotharian medicine when he is gone."

"But . . . but . . ." I stammered.

"Monsorlit is not a proper cave-mate with Gorlot, no matter what the appearances show," Ferrill said with more vigor than you would expect from so frail a person. Then he frowned at me. "You are certain that he drugged Harlan? Monsorlit was *not* at Maritha's the night Harlan was taken ill."

"But I *saw* Monsorlit give Harlan an injection and he called it cerol. They thought I was a moronic attendant. And I know that there are nine other men in that sanitarium, drugged by Trenor, with the same stuff Monsorlit used on Harlan."

Ferrill raised a thoughtful eyebrow and pursed his lips, a gesture imitating Stannall.

"That's when you decided to help Harlan?"

I nodded. Ferrill shook his head, frowning as he tried to correlate this information with his picture of Monsorlit.

"You must retire now, my lord and lady," said the soft, respectful voice of Monsorlit.

I jumped and Maxil got to his feet, for none of us had heard the door open. I waited breathlessly for Monsorlit to denounce me. "You will tire the young patient," was all he said.

But as we passed him on the way out, his eyes glittered at me and I wished passionately I knew how much he had overheard.

Maxil turned frantically to me once the door was shut.

"We've got to tell Stannall, Sara," he said breathlessly.

I shook my head violently. At the moment I didn't know which of the two men I feared more, the physician or the statesman.

"Stannall will find out all he needs to know by himself, I'm sure. You know his opinion of Monsorlit. And if Ferrill is to recover from this poisoning, Monsorlit is undoubtedly the only man who can do it. We *can't* take away Ferrill's chance of recovery. Let's forget, right now, what we said in there. Completely."

Before he could object, I pulled him into the filled entrance room. We were greeted by queries after Ferrill's health. Twice Maxil was importuned with unveiled hints for patronage. At first I thought Maxil didn't catch them. Once we had reached the quiet of the corridor, he snorted out a bitter remark.

"You should have seen them all laughing yesterday when Samoth dragged me back with you over Varnan's shoulder."

Our guards filed behind us as Maxil led me down the corridor beyond Ferrill's suite.

"We have the rooms my father and mother had, I think. They're the only ones vacant I could use."

There were guards at that doorway, too. Sinnall received the salutes and replaced them with his own men. He then opened the door wide, stepped inside and quickly checked each of the doors leading into the reception hall. Evidently reassured no assassins or Mils lurked anywhere, Sinnall threw open both of the big doors leading into the main room of the suite.

Stannall's charming rooms seemed barren, cramped and cold in comparison with the spacious splendor of this four-balconied living room with its various levels. A wide window overlooked the riotously blooming gardens, backed by the towers of the city, magically iridescent in the green sunlight, sparkling in an incredible panorama to my alien eyes.

Linnana and a white-tuniced young man approached and both bowed.

"My Lord Maxil, I've checked Ittlo's credentials and Stannall has already approved Linnana," Sinnall said with stiff formality. "Subject, of course, to your approval."

Whatever comment Maxil may have had was drowned by an uproar outside. I had heard that bull bellow only once before, but it had been indelibly engrooved on my eardrum.

My reaction was annoyance. Maxil turned white, his shoulders resumed their slump and he crouched as if to hide. I caught him by the arm and gave him a shake. He didn't see or hear me. Sinnall expressed his annoyance actively by opening the door with an angry jerk.

"What is the meaning of this disturbance outside the Warlord's suite? Get rid of that man."

I doubt that Samoth would ever have passed the guards for all his burly strength. He was at the moment impotently raging against their crossed weapons. He quieted a moment as he saw Maxil and then began bellowing.

"I'm the Warlord's appointed guardian," he yowled.

"The Warlord's appointed guardian is the Council, not an individual," Sinnall answered with a snort at such ignorance. "Remove this nuisance," and he beckoned to two guards farther down the hallway. "Hold him in custody. The only reason he was permitted to remain free was the generosity of Lord Maxil. This has been exhausted. Off with him."

The guards promptly took over and there was a certain overzealousness to the restraints they applied. Sinnall cut off the indignant mouthings of Samoth by slamming the door. He apologized to the stupefied Maxil for the unwarranted interruption.

"Maxil," I said in a wicked way, for the boy still looked scared stiff, "think up something juicy for Samoth to do. Like decontaminating Mil ships."

Maxil's eyes began to gleam. Sinnall had difficulty retaining his official face as the boy's unguarded expressions showed his reflections on suitable vengeance.

"Maxil," I began, having wandered around the room, peering into a study, a small anonymous room, a room set aside for communication panels, three bedrooms. There wasn't a bowl of fruit in sight, but there were plenty of flowers. "Maxil, I hate to mention this but I'm hungry."

Maxil looked at me with disgust.

"I've never seen you when you weren't. Are you sure . . ."

"Maxil, order me some fruit at least," I pleaded cutting him off in midsentence because I knew perfectly well what he might be going to say.

"My apologies, my lady," Linnana said, coming forward swiftly. "A terrible oversight. I'll remedy it immediately. Ittlo!" and Linnana gestured the other attendant toward the communications room with a fluttery hand.

A knock on the door and a gentleman entered, bowing, followed by boys carrying a variety of uniforms and other masculine apparel.

"Ahem," Sinnall said discreetly behind his hand, "there will be a formal dinner, Lord Maxil. If you please . . ."

Maxil looked up at the ceiling in dramatic exasperation at such matters but went obediently into his bedroom.

We were eating a marvelous lunch when Maxil was called to the communications room for a call from Stannall.

"Council will convene tomorrow morning, Lord Maxil," Stannall said formally. "Your presence is required. The Lady Sara will hold herself in readiness to attend the convention."

"Yes, sir," Maxil agreed readily.

"I trust your quarters are satisfactory?"

"Yes, sir," Maxil agreed enthusiastically.

"You are satisfied with the personnel?"

"Indeed I am," Maxil replied, grinning broadly at Sinnall and Cire.

"Then until the dinner hour this evening, Lord Maxil," and Stannall courteously signed off.

"Formal dinner," said Maxil gloomily. "I knew Stannall would put them back in."

There was another tap at the door and one of the guards motioned to Sinnall. There was a brief conference and then Sinnall went out into the hallway, looking over his shoulder at Maxil. I moved so I could see into the hall and caught a glimpse of an anxious young face. It took me a minute to get the significance and then I turned to Maxil.

"I'll bet I got a glimpse of Fara in the hall just now."

"Fara," and Maxil's face lit up with joy. He ran to the door and yanked it open. Sinnall and the girl were deep in earnest conversation. She caught sight of Maxil, her mouth made a round O and she looked like she would burst into tears.

"Get her *in* here," I hissed at Sinnall.

Poor Fara had no opportunity to run as I was sure she wanted to. Maxil had her by one arm and Sinnall by the other. I motioned to Sinnall to close the doors to the inner hall so that just the five of us were in the main room.

"Maxil, father will be furious if he knows I'm here," she wept and then she gulped back her sobs as she came face to face with me.

Her emotions were painfully obvious. She had heard all the gossip and had been hurt by it. She had been betrayed in her love and denied sight of him by her father whose political common sense dominated his personal preferences. She did look like me, even with her eyes red with her tears and with her hair disheveled. A younger, prettier, gentler, totally different girl.

What impressed me more than her delicate loveliness was Maxil's tenderness toward her. He drew her against him, one hand holding one of hers to his lips, the other arm drawing her possessively to him. There was no hint of the gawky adolescent who had clumsily tried to embrace me the previous night as we deceived the waiter. He was Romeo to his Juliet, strong and loving, tender and sure.

"Fara, I'm so glad to see you. What do you mean, your father will be furious with you? I've asked for no one else but you," Maxil was saying.

"But ... but ... we were sent from the palace and no one would let us come back and Father wouldn't let me come to the Starhall last night and then ..." and she glared at me. She drew herself up to her full height, suddenly regal for all her youth.

"You heard those *rumors* about Lady Sara," I finished for her.

She swallowed hard, too proud or too hurt to answer.

"Well, Lady Fara, they are only rumors," I said. "Lord Harlan has claimed me as his lady."

Her eyes widened and she gasped, looking trustingly to Maxil for confirmation. I don't know how, but Maxil kept from blushing as he nodded solemnly to Fara.

"Now, will you stop glaring at me and sit down while we tell you the whole thing?" I suggested. "I think I can see why your father was not anxious for you and Maxil to meet right away," I added as her emotions of uncertainty, curiosity and distrust crossed her transparent little face.

By the time she left in Cire's company to dash back to her suite, we had the whole thing pretty well thrashed out. She didn't much like it, but she understood. Maxil was so relieved I thought he'd explode.

"She'll accept my claim. She'll accept," he cried, sliding down into his chair with delight. Stretched out full length, his long legs stuck out at angles, he sighed deeply and closed his eyes. Then, slamming both hands down on the chair arms, he propelled himself up with astonishing force, careening around the room. It was obvious from

Sinnall's expression he did not consider this proper behavior for a Warlord-elect.

"Leave him alone," I laughed at Sinnall. "You're only this young and in love once and I've presented a terrible complication. You must admit that."

Sinnall shook his head. "What if they give themselves away?"

"They only have to play along for a few days."

Sinnall still wasn't convinced, but at that point Linnana and Ittlo suggested it was time we dressed for dinner.

CHAPTER TEN

FORMAL DINNER MEANT JUST THAT, but it was a formality that very few of the main participants enjoyed. Harlan and Stannall, alone, at the head table, behaved as if they were enjoying themselves.

A portion of the Starhall had become a dining room, with a head table on the raised circular section between two of the five archways, while four long tables splayed out from it on the level below.

I don't know who was more nervous, Maxil or me. His behavior vacillated between an almost unbearable imperiousness when addressing his younger brother and sisters to adolescent sullenness when he gazed at the table where Fara sat with adult members of Council. Stannall, of course, was at the head table between Maxil's sisters. I was seated at Maxil's left, and Lesatin, the curious councilman, sat on my left. Harlan sat at the end, too far away from me for the conversation I wanted to have with him.

It was not a cheerful meal although the food was excellent. Kalina and Cherez, Maxil's two sisters, were dressed as befitted their age and station, their pretty faces much sweeter devoid of last night's excessive makeup. But they were sullen. Maxil told me that Kalina had been told she was to deny the claim of the man Gorlot had mated to her. Fernan, completely cowed by Stannall's presence and under Harlan's scrutiny, ate the sparse meal set before him. His glowering fat face with its pasty pimpled complexion was not a pleasant sight at dinner. I avoided his direction as much to keep from seeing him as to keep myself from Stannall's notice.

I must correct myself. Lesatin thoroughly enjoyed himself. He made conversation for us to agree with, commented on one course after the other. I felt terribly conspicuous and surreptitiously waited until I saw what Harlan used as silverware. Perhaps I felt a constraint because in Harlan's presence I was so conscious of inadvertently tripping over my own ignorance. With Maxil or Sinnall I could laugh off a slip or divert attention. But Harlan was so preternaturally concerned with concealing my origin, I was unnerved. The menace of Stannall and Monsorlit completed the top-heavy pyramid of my anxiety.

By the time the entertainers whirled out into the center of the huge hall, I was weary. My back ached, my stomach felt overfull and churned with odd tastes and textures. My neck felt stiff with tension and I wondered if I could ever relax again.

When we finally filed out of the great hall, I tried to stay by Harlan. He gave me a warning look as he handed me over to Maxil. I was furious and frustrated. I desperately needed a few private words with Harlan on what to do tomorrow if the Council should actually call me. I was forced to go to bed without that reassurance and I was filled with worry, worry, worry.

In the alarm-clock way I had acquired since coming to Lothar, I awoke suddenly and completely. My head still ached, the room was unreal in its luxurious appointments and my body felt logy and disjointed. Linnana was evidently a skilled keyhole listener because I no sooner stretched than she appeared to announce my bath was ready.

I chose the simplest of the rich gowns and a single strand of contrasting beads as much to forget the extravagance of last night as to present Council with the "simple country girl" I had styled myself in jest.

The breakfast table held a surprise for me. Jessl was at it, chatting companionably to Sinnall, Cire and Maxil. The boy had recovered his equilibrium this morning, it seemed, for he rose with a spring as I entered. Jessl seated me with a flourish and a flirt. Linnana and Ittlo bustled about with dishes.

The mood in which I awakened could not linger with such gay breakfast talk. Jessl insisted on a ribald recounting of town gossip about Maxil and me and he was so deft with his recital I couldn't be offended. Even Maxil, now that he had set himself straight with Fara, laughed. The morning beverage stimulated me and unbound the knots of tension at the back of my neck.

"Sara, Harlan said not to worry about Council calling you. Today at least. We can all watch in the board room," Jessl indicated the chamber devoted to communication panels. "It's a closed circuit into this room from the Chamber. It will be a real pleasure to follow Gorlot's downfall."

"You're sure of it?" I queried hopefully.

Jessl scoffed at my unspoken doubts and leaned forward across the table in a mock conspiratorial fashion.

"The things we've uncovered about that man would make your skin curl off. Remarkable, isn't it, how the slightest breath of scandal on any public figure brings forth previously forgotten slights and errors."

"But will these things discredit him as a candidate for Regent?" I wanted to know.

"Sure, surely," Jessl agreed expansively. I wondered then if Jessl had been purposefully sent to allay Maxil's doubts or whether Jessl was an incurable optimist.

"What's the gossip about Harlan's return from insanity?"

Here Jessl did hedge. "There's a great deal of controversy about that. I only wish we had some conclusive proof that he never had been insane."

"But he never was," I insisted forcefully. "He was drugged. Gorlot and Gleto drugged him." Why I inserted Gleto's name instead of Monsorlit's, I don't know. "I heard that from Gleto's lips myself."

"Does Harlan know that?" asked Maxil anxiously.

"Of course he does," I assured him.

"Then why doesn't he have you appear before Council today?" the young Warlord fretted.

"Perhaps you are the main issue today, not Harlan's sanity," I suggested.

Jessl shook his head.

"No, Maxil's as good as confirmed right now. Stannall had an inspiration and had the physicians check Fernan over, too. The kid's heart has suffered from his overeating and he could never stand even normal acceleration. Maxil's therefore practically the only choice. But it's the Regency that's to be the heavy contest. Don't worry, lad. I mean, my lord," Jessl said with sincerity. "Harlan and Stannall know what they're doing."

I fell to mulling over exactly what I had told Harlan concerning himself in the asylum. I had mentioned Gleto and his being drugged but not Monsorlit's visit, nor one other, possibly very important fact. Yesterday I had told Ferrill that there were others held under drugs at the sanitarium. If those men all recovered as Harlan had, and told their stories, it would be definite proof, by association, that Harlan never had been insane. I tugged Jessl's arm.

"Has anyone checked into the medical histories of Gleto's other recent patients? I mean, say other squadron commanders or men of position who have also suddenly and unexpectedly gone mad."

Jessl swiveled around to look at me with dawning comprehension.

"Trenor had nine other patients at that asylum," I continued. "At least that's what Gleto said. If they could be restored to sanity the way Harlan was, wouldn't that prove that Harlan, too, had been drugged, had never been insane? And I *know* those men were drugged."

Jessl was at the communicator panel before I finished my hypothesis. The screen lit to show Stannall's crowded living room. Jessl asked Stannall to close his circuit. The background of the room blurred and only the first Councilman's face was distinct. Jessl repeated what I had told him. Stannall's face quickened with obvious interest.

"How long does it take to recover from the effects of the drug?" he asked, excited.

"About five days' abstention from the drugged food," I reluctantly advised him, knowing how important the time factor was. "But maybe there's an antidote or a stimulant."

"We can try. It would be very interesting to check this. It would implicate Trenor still further. Can you identify the patients concerned?"

I couldn't. Stannall pursed his lips over this disappointment. Then he thanked me with absentminded courtesy and the screen dimmed. Jessl came thoughtfully back to the table.

"Sinnall," he asked, "do you recall anyone going off his orbit recently?"

Maxil came up immediately with one name, a communications man at the spaceport who had run berserk all over the flying strip. Then there had been the case of a police official in the city. Jessl himself thought of two group leaders. Sinnall suggested a veteran trader on the Tane routes who had come home babbling some strange tale before he had been drugged quiet by physicians.

"What kind of a tale?" Jessl asked.

Sinnall frowned. "Oh, he made a rhyme of it, the way I heard the story." Sinnall shuddered at the memory. "Went like this:

> For a change the Mil can eat
> The gentle, juicy Tane meat.

Of course, there hasn't been a Mil raid for the last two Eclipses. And only a few Perimeter skirmishes reported."

A few skirmishes in two Eclipses: that would mean more than a year. Was I in one of those ships? Could I have been on Lothar that long? But Harlan had only been in the sanitarium ten months. And the Tane war started a week afterward. When had I been taken? Before or after? And how? Harlan could only guess that I must have been transported from Earth to Lothar in a Mil ship. How then did I get off the ship; where did I go from there for Monsorlit to change my skin and my nose? I was certain now that Monsorlit had been responsible. How did I get into the sanitarium where I should have been a patient, not an attendant?

"Sara's thinking. Maybe she knows another official for our missing four men," Jessl jibed, startling me out of my frightening contemplations.

"Me? No, I haven't followed that sort of thing. I was too busy with Harlan."

"Which reminds me to ask you," Jessl began forcefully, "where did you meet up with our Regent? Jokan doesn't remember ever meeting you, but he's been on and off Ertoi gazing into crystals. I've been underfoot and I don't remember meeting you in our closed circle," he ended with a complimentary leer.

"Which should prove to you that Harlan is pretty good at minding his own business all by himself," I hedged archly.

This would not put Jessl off. "Where do you come from, lady of mystery? Your accent is slightly southern, if anything, but your appearance is northern."

"A girl can't keep anything secret around here," I laughed.

"The lady minds her business pretty well, too," laughed Jessl in good part. "I'll bet I'll figure you out yet. That's my specialty."

Sinnall and Maxil laughed with him. But I could see he was a little piqued at my continued evasion. I hoped he wouldn't pursue the subject before I had the chance to talk with Harlan. Clan, cave and mining engineering notwithstanding, I had very little knowledge to fortify me against the determined curiosity of a friend. Or had he felt that his own would not question the girl who had restored him from the living dead?

"If you guess correctly, I'll tell you true," I promised easily.

Jessl merely smiled at me queerly and I noticed he was looking at my hands. It was all I could do to keep from jerking them into my lap. Harlan had been singularly interested in my wrists, too. Examine them as I might, I could find nothing to warrant such scrutiny.

The guard entered to say that Council was assembling.

Maxil rose with an excess of nervous energy, while Jessl, putting a reassuring hand on the boy's arm, got more casually to his feet. He guided Maxil to the door and watched him down the Hall, Sinnall and Cire flanking him.

In his unguarded face as he returned to the table, I saw the weight of Jessl's own doubts. He had been careful to hide them before the boy. The dread that had bothered me on waking returned in double measure.

Jessl and I went silently into the board room. I signaled Linnana to bring more to drink as Jessl flipped on the screen to the seething Council Hall. He yelled at Ittlo to leave off clearing the breakfast table. Then he settled himself beside me on the couch, to stare moodily at the screen.

CHAPTER ELEVEN

HAD HARLAN AND STANNALL been aware of how many people Gorlot had touched in establishing his massive plans, they would have approached the Council Hall with even more trepidation that morning. Gorlot had chosen his victims well.

I know my own sense of foreboding was lulled in the first hour of that crucial meeting. The very familiarity of a roll call for the Councilmen as they named their provinces and districts (The Council consisted of scientists, military men and landed gentry instead of the proportional representation practiced on Earth) was reassuring to me.

Stannall as First Councilman called the session to order with a few words about the gravity of the situation and a reassuring report on Ferrill's condition. If it deprived Ferrill of his birthright, at least it did not mean his death.

An ancient-looking, heavy collection of tablets was rolled to the front of the chamber right up to the raised dais where Stannall and the seven senior Councilmen were seated. (The significance of the number "seven" harked back to ancient history and the first Harlan's Seven Brothers.) An old man mumblingly read from the tablets the names of Fathor's children. At a motion from the floor, Ferrill's name was ceremoniously canceled as ineligible for the Warlordship. Maxil was named as next in line and he was asked to step forward and present his claim. All this was couched in the floweriest language, with great gestures and ceremonial pauses.

Maxil came forward, holding his tall gangling figure erect. He bowed gracefully to the eight in front of him, to the Council behind him, and presented a much bemedaled slate to the secretary. A great show was made of reading it. The legality of his birth was then formally recorded.

Stannall took over and the simplicity of the procedure of investiture was refreshing. It amused me, for it sounded

so like an Earth marriage ceremony. Stannall asked if
anyone present knew of any just reason why Maxil, second son of Fathor, son of Hillel, son of Clemmen, true
blood and seed of Harlan the First, Defender of the
People, should not be Warlord-elect in this, his sixteenth
year of life.

A massive silence prevailed. I gathered that this would
have been the opportunity for Gorlot to bring up Maxil's
supposed impotency.

Stannall's words of formal acceptance of Maxil in the
name of the Council were drowned by the roar from this
august body. The entire room was on its feet, shouting the
boy's name, and saluting continuously. Maxil smiling nervously accepted the acclaim with poise.

When the furor had subsided, a tense, uneasy restless-
ness took hold of the assemblage. Stannall motioned to
Maxil to be seated on the single raised chair to the right of
the eight elders.

"Since our young lord, Maxil, is under the legal age, it
will be necessary for the Council to consider those men
who are qualified to instruct him in the military duties of
the Warlord and, with the aid and guidance of this Council, in governing and guiding this world toward its great
and recognized goal, the extermination of the Mil from the
skies."

Stannall consulted a slate in his hand.

"We note that Lord Maxil is over fifteen years of age
and therefore considered to have reached the age of reasonable discretion. Following the custom of our laws, he
has the right to agree with or disagree to our choice of
Regent, and to propose, if he should have a qualified
candidate, a man sympathetic to his personality and his
welfare."

Jessl chortled to himself at that speech and I noticed a
definite stirring among the Council members. I could not
see either Harlan or Gorlot.

Stannall turned slightly toward Maxil and the boy rose
as if forcibly ejected from the chair.

"I do have a choice, one acceptable to this Council
since he has been Regent to my brother, Ferrill," and

Maxil's voice stumbled a little over his brother's name. "By my legal and accustomed right, I will choose Harlan, son of Hillel, son of Clemmen as my Regent, with the Council's permission."

"But the man's been mad for months," a voice from the back of the room protested quite clearly in the stunned quiet. Others chimed in with similar sentiments and a general arguing shout rose in volume. Stannall folded his arms to ride the noise a while before he called for order.

"We call Harlan, son of Hillel, son of Clemmen, before this Council."

The great doors at the opposite end of the Hall opened and Harlan marched in, looking neither left nor right. He held himself so proudly, so regally, tears of pride came to my eyes. Harlan bowed to Maxil, to the Council, to Stannall. Not all of the seven elders had had a chance to see Harlan before this appearance and he was scrutinized carefully. Stannall indicated the empty chairs drawn up on the left of the main platform and Harlan, bowing briefly, seated himself there.

"We see that the name of Harlan, son of Hillel, is on the list of those men eligible by their age, conduct and military experience to be Regent. We also call before this board the following men, their merits to be weighed before Council this day."

Stannall began to call off his list. The first three names were unfamiliar to me and at each one a Councilman arose to ceremonially remind Stannall that so-and-so had died, or was over the maximum age. The fourth name was Gorlot, son of someone—I didn't hear because the name of the implacable man echoed in my mind harshly. Gorlot strode in, his square face as still as ever, his square frame devoid of the grace and litheness that characterized Harlan. He bowed to the young lord, to the elders, to the Council and was gestured toward the waiting chairs.

Gorlot hesitated at the chair next to Harlan and then, with deliberation, left two seats empty between them. His action had the appearance of being cautionary rather than insulting. But it was a well-calculated piece of business. Jessl groaned and cursed with vehement originality.

I started again as Gartly's name was called and this gray warrior stepped forward. He was but a year under the maximum age. He took the seat next to Harlan, flicking his cape contemptuously in Gorlot's direction. I could have kissed the old grump. Jokan's name, too, was called and a mutter arose from the Council. Stannall turned to the seven with the comment that Jokan was absent on a special mission for the Council. As he was well known, his record would have to speak for him.

There were other names called, men I remembered Harlan using as examples for candidates for the Regency: men who were reported dead or in survivor asylums. I wondered if any of them were among the nine unwilling guests at Gleto's. Jessl seemed to have the same thought, for he glanced at me significantly.

At any rate, by the end of Stannall's little list, only three were seated at the left of the seven. No one doubted that the contest was between Harlan and Gorlot.

"We are fortunate indeed," Stannall began with a slight smile, "to have as candidates two men who have already had experience in the arduous position of Regent to the Warlord-elect." His bow was impartial.

"At the young lord's request, we first consider the eligibility of Harlan, son of Hillel, son of Clemmen."

A sigh ran through the Council and was echoed by me. Stannall made a sign to the secretary who nervously cleared his throat and read off in a rattling way the personal history of Harlan. I couldn't always catch his mumbling or the stilted phrases and ceremonial longhand he spoke. But it was evident that Harlan's early career as a fighting man had been brilliant, crowned with the discovery of the Tane planets as well as some daring innovations in perimeter patrol techniques.

The secretary came to the last slate of the pile before him, and his voice noticeably slowed.

"On the twenty-third day of the thirteenth moonset, Regent Harlan was stricken ill and relieved of his duties toward the Warlord until such time as his recovery was effected."

Stannall smiled slightly and there was a loud spate of excited whispering among the Councilmen. I wondered who had slipped that helpful phraseology in the document or whether it had been there all the time. Stannall raised a hand and the whispering died.

"As is customary, Council asked all candidates to present themselves to the War Hospital to be examined as to their physical . . . and mental fitness. Physician Monsorlit, as head of that establishment, may we have your report on Harlan, son of Hillel."

Stannall stepped aside as Monsorlit, whom I had not previously noticed, rose from his side seat in the front row of the Council and took the center of the room. He bowed to Maxil, to the eight men, to the Council, to the three candidates. I caught myself holding my breath. Perhaps now would come the bombshell to our hopes. Monsorlit's duplicity with Gorlot was certain in my mind. He may have lulled the suspicions of others, but would he show his true self now? If restoration were such a heinous crime as I gathered it was, Monsorlit would not care to risk Gorlot's exposing him. For Gorlot certainly must have known Monsorlit was restoring people.

Monsorlit spoke well and without a plethora of confusing technical terms. He summarized being called by Stannall with the other three physicians to determine the state of Harlan's mental health.

"Even a cursory examination without benefit of special equipment proved that Harlan had recovered from the grip of mental disease that prostrated him ten months ago. You can imagine, gentlemen, how delighted and surprised my colleagues and I are. No other patient suffering from similar symptoms has recovered to such a marked degree."

I glanced at Gorlot to see what his reaction was and, in spite of the man's studied carelessness, I thought I detected a smug satisfaction to his patience.

"Naturally, such a superficial examination was not conclusive proof. Harlan himself suggested a more thorough one at the Mental Clinic." Monsorlit paused to thumb through tissue-thin metal sheets in his hand. He finally sorted one to the top. "I have here the results of our most exhaustive tests which we compared with the last physical examination of Harlan, taken shortly before his illness." Again he paused and I took another deep breath. Harlan was looking with obvious but not anxious intent at Monsorlit. Gorlot sat, showing that trace of smugness. Maxil fidgeted continually.

"There was a noticeable discrepancy between the two reports," Monsorlit continued. Gorlot's smile broadened slightly. "It was apparent that the reaction time in certain coordination tests and in the general response to spoken and written questions was shorter."

Gorlot's semi-smile disappeared and there was an agitated rustle in the Council Hall. Monsorlit had thrown his bombshell all right but not in the expected direction.

"In short, Harlan is in better general physical health today than he was eleven months ago, the time of the last full physical examination."

"What about mental health?" a voice demanded from the floor, heedless of protocol.

Monsorlit glanced unperturbed at his notes.

"My colleagues and I are in agreement. On the basis of the most exhaustive tests in our means, Harlan is both mentally and physically capable of any duties or offices required of him by Lothar."

Maxil clapped a hand to his mouth to suppress his glad shout. Others in the Council had no inhibitions about expressing their approval, but the jubilation was not as widespread as I had hoped it would be.

Gorlot was glowering now and he watched angrily as Monsorlit resumed his place, in the front row, oblivious to any censure from that direction.

Stannall stepped forward again, bowed to Harlan and held up his hand for silence.

"This is indeed good news for the entire world. I trust that you and your colleagues are already working to effect similar recoveries on others of our leaders who have fallen victim to this new scourge."

Monsorlit contented himself with bowing his head briefly in assent.

"A question, Sir Stannall," a loud voice interrupted. Our attention was directed to a portly individual in the right rear of the hall.

"You have the floor, Calariz of South Cant," said Stannall after a very brief pause.

"I recall the physician for further questions. I, and I am certain there are others of my mind, am not sufficiently reassured by this ... this glib certification to trust the tender mind of an untried youth to a man so recently mad beyond speech."

Monsorlit came forward again.

"Physician, have there been other recoveries from this form of illness?"

"Yes," replied Monsorlit blandly, to the consternation of his questioner.

"As complete as Harlan's?"

"No. As I remarked earlier, Harlan is in better condition than before his collapse. Due, no doubt, to the rest and quiet with which we find it best to surround our mentally disturbed."

"Why then, and particularly since you have been the physician in charge of Harlan's case, was not the improvement noted and reported? I believe I am correct in stating that this Council expressed a deep interest in being kept abreast of any improvement in our ... ah ... former Regent's health."

Monsorlit did not hesitate with his reply. "In such cases as we have been able to observe where an improvement has been noted, it has been either so gradual as to escape the untrained eye, or a matter of instantaneous return to normal."

"And Harlan's recovery was in which category?" prompted Calariz.

"Instantaneous," was the bland reply.

"The liar," I exclaimed.

"What else can he say?" muttered Jessl.

"Ah, very good, I'm sure," Calariz was saying. "Were you there?"

"Unfortunately, no. My time has been heavily scheduled by the weight of our rising mental disease and the supervision of casualties from the Tane war."

"Quite so." A neighbor beckoned to Calariz and had his ear for a moment. The smile on the face of the man from South Cant was not pleasant as he straightened.

"Tell me, Physician, is there any guarantee that Harlan will remain sane? I mean," and Calariz had to raise his voice to top the sudden whispered agitation, "can we be sure that say, six or seven months from now, Harlan will not collapse under the stress of the Tane war and the task of training our new Warlord?"

Jessl and I groaned together over this loaded question. Monsorlit considered carefully.

"There is no such guarantee."

Gorlot's face lost its angry blackness. Harlan appeared unmoved, but Maxil's distress was obvious. Poor boy, he saw himself with Gorlot as his Regent whether he wanted him or not. He probably pictured himself dying slowly of some poison as Ferrill nearly had.

Calariz looked around him triumphantly and sat down. Before Stannall could take the floor again, another man rose to be acknowledged.

"You know me, gentlemen, as one who has supported Sir Harlan in many of his policies and moves," this fellow began with the oily ease of one accustomed to long perorations before arriving at his point. "I have stood squarely behind him, as I did behind his brother, our late and much loved Fathor. I was the first to deplore the illness which deprived us of Harlan's brilliant leadership and I want to be one of the first to welcome him back officially to our midst. But ... I have a serious duty. For ten long months, this fine commander and statesman has been out of touch with the struggles and trials of our daily living. He has been unaware of our internal battles with mental illness, unemployment, crime and general unrest. Can we put upon him the added burden of reassessing past months when we can't hesitate so much as a millisecond in forging strongly ahead? Can we ask him to take up again a part of our world's life that nearly deprived him of his health and personal happiness forever? That he has allowed himself to be drafted to resume the onerous duties of state is indeed a credit to his patriotism and honor. But . . . my friends and worldsmen, is it fair to the man, to Harlan?"

"That old . . ." and Jessl finished the epithet under his breath. "He's one we were certain was loyal to us. How did Gorlot reach him?"

I slumped down in my corner of the couch, utterly miserable. I got more depressed as the next hours were filled with debates for and against Harlan, only more were against. The text of their arguments was substantially the same: Harlan had been mad once, he could go mad again. Harlan was not sufficiently attuned to the political and social scene and this was made to seem essential. Others tempered their views with the feeling that Harlan had served his world long and well enough. Other personalities were needed. There were those who did speak out for Harlan, couching in general terms their dissatisfactions with Gorlot's Regency. But it was a negative approach where a positive one was necessary. One man used the thinnest possible veil for hints that Ferrill's health had declined rapidly and concurrently with Gorlot's Regency. He was shouted down by Calariz and the oily representative from Astolla.

Stannall finally called a halt to this verbal massacre of Harlan and turned the discussion to Gorlot's suitability. The old firebrand, Estoder, who had hinted at Ferrill's suspicious illness, rose first to cite inadequacies in Gorlot's administration and conduct of the Tane war. Calariz and the Astollan gave him little time to speak and talked loudly with their neighbors during his remarks.

"Jessl, he'll never win at this rate. What happened?" I wailed.

"It's the insanity angle. A lot of those who would follow Harlan through a Mil raid are afraid of that. Frankly, if I didn't know Harlan had been drugged, I'd be worried, too."

"Then why doesn't someone come out and say he was drugged?" I demanded. "I can prove it."

"How?"

"I was there. I saw it done. I heard Gleto talking about it. He said he was afraid Harlan could throw off the drug and he wanted to increase the dosage."

"That *isn't* proof we can substantiate, unfortunately. It's hearsay. And it would be ridiculous to stand you up against the testimony of men like Monsorlit. No, my dear. We'd have to have a physician's report that traces of the drug were actually found in Harlan's blood. We tried it, but his system had absorbed whatever they used."

"They used cerol and you know it," I reminded him sharply.

"And cerol is rapidly absorbed into the system," Jessl retorted angrily. "Besides, all we'd need to prove to them that Harlan was still unstable would be for us to come out with a statement that he'd been drugged all along. We'd be laughed off the planet. If only we had had more time and could revive one of those men at the sanitarium."

"They're setting it to a vote," Linnana cried out.

I had to watch but it was horrible to witness this defeat.

"But Maxil won't have Gorlot," I said helplessly.

"He'll have to take him," Jessl muttered.

"But they can't do that to Maxil," I insisted. "He'll be poisoned like Ferrill and what Gorlot's intended to do all along will get done and then where will Lothar be?"

The roll was being called with droning fatality to Harlan's chances. I wanted to break the connection so I wouldn't have to watch. I was halfway to my feet to shut it off when there was a commotion at the Hall doors. They burst open suddenly to a scene of struggling guards.

"I am Jokan. I have the right to enter. STANNALL!" a voice rang out above the scuffling and shouting.

"Let Jokan advance," Stannall bellowed with more power to his voice than I imagined he'd have.

Jokan ran up the aisle. He spared no time for ceremonial bowing. Catching Stannall by the arm, he spoke softly and urgently. The First Councilman's eyes widened with disbelief. He backed up, his hand reaching behind him for the support of the table. Jokan stopped speaking, his face grim. Stannall stared at him. He managed to ask a question to which Jokan only nodded slowly and gravely. You could see the effort with which Stannall drew himself erect.

"I have grave news. The gravest. I must speak of something I never thought would be said of a Lotharian. I must speak of treachery so abominable that the words gag in my throat." Stannall's voice did choke, before he gathered strength and volume and venom. "There has been no war on Tane," he declared in a tight, measured way. "And furthermore there are now no more Tane on their two silent planets. Why? Because they have been taken by the Mil."

A concerted gasp of horror rang throughout the Hall.

"How, you may well ask, did the Mil get the Tane? How did they, for that matter, penetrate so far in from our Perimeter Patrol? Because the Patrol has been withdrawn from the Tane sector.

"There is only one man who has the power to do that. I accuse Gorlot," and Stannall's finger pinioned the traitor, "of the highest, most gruesome treachery. I accuse him of the foulest . . ." and here Stannall was drowned out by the savage roar that came up from the very floor of the Hall. There was a mass stampede toward the traitor.

Jokan had leaped to Gorlot's side during Stannall's denunciation. His weapon was pointed at the man's throat. Ironically enough, it was Harlan who kept Gorlot from being torn apart alive by the hysterical Councilmen. It was Harlan who brought the mob under control and back in their seats while guards formed a tight ring around Gorlot.

It was Harlan who called squadron outposts along the Perimeter to report their positions. It was he who reassigned them and called up additional units from the spaceport to rush to unprotected areas. It was Harlan who kept his head, the man they considered unsafe to trust with their government.

But it was Stannall who recalled the business of the day long enough to insist on a re-vote which was dispatched with unanimous haste. Harlan was again Regent!

CHAPTER TWELVE

I HAD A SAMPLING OF THE general reaction to this startling news from the three people in the room with me. Linnana started to weep hysterically, throwing herself at Jessl's feet and imploring him to take her to the Vaults where she would be safe from the Mil. She evidently supposed the Mil to be on their way from Tane to Lothar although this had not even been hinted. Ittlo cursed monotonously, alternating his curses with "How did he do it? How could he do it?" This was substantially what Jessl wanted to know.

First he managed to calm Linnana by reminding her that the inner network of alarms gave them a full day's warning before the Mil could possibly land on Lothar. There was no possibility of Gorlot's tampering with those sentinels. She continued to weep quietly, falling into a little lump on a chair, until I thought to have her go with Ittlo and get quantities of the stimulating beverage. I had a feeling we'd need it.

With something to do, both Ittlo and Linnana were in better shape. The door flung open and Fara came racing in, her eyes wide in her white face.

"I had to come, I had to come. Maxil will be so upset," she pleaded with me.

Jessl and I exchanged looks. She was, of course, quite right. True, I didn't realize that tradition would require a sixteen-year-old boy to be on the flagship of the fleet that would undoubtedly meet the Mil the next time they came thundering down on Tane.

Her concern for this crisis and its effect on the boy was instinctive and creditable to the unselfishness of her devotion to him. I felt ashamed. All I had considered was the fact that Gorlot was finally exposed and Harlan vindicated.

"Help me get to him," Fara cried, looking first to me,

then to Jessl, gesturing at the pandemonium in the Council Hall.

"Harlan will bring Maxil back here, I'm sure," I said encouragingly. "And I don't think anyone could get through to him right now. Look."

Fara and Jessl turned to the hectic picture on the panel. Harlan, Stannall and Maxil were easing themselves out of the Hall, all the while directing various agitated groups of Councilmen. The comic relief was supplied by the secretary. He was trying to keep his unwieldy table of tablets from being upset in the push and shove. He kept jumping up and down on one leg, weeping in distress at the ghastly news he must record.

Ittlo's questions, "How did he do it? How could he do it?" were answered in the course of the next few violent days. But there were a lot of other questions that were never adequately answered.

The perfidy toward the gentle Tane who had so recently been reviled as expendable savages shocked Lotharians of all degrees out of their petty squabbles and united them once more in their ancient crusade against the Mil.

"How could he do it?" was answered by the blazing personal ambition of the man Gorlot, who had correctly assessed the greed of barons and patrol dissidents, seizing upon the unrest of the time to implement his scheme. There were many who had wanted the Tane planets as their own playgrounds, or for their business monopolies. They were not especially interested in having the Tane there. They gave Gorlot the support he needed in Council when he needed it, in return for his extravagant promises of large grants when his colonization reforms went through. His choices of squadron leaders were promoted through rigged military boards and the incumbents thrown out, moved up, or liquidated in one manner or another. In return for their explicit, blind obedience, Gorlot substituted in all key Perimeter positions the incompetent men who had formerly been denied promotion. The few who went along only far enough to get suspicious of Gorlot's ultimate goal or who found out inadvertently were silenced. Some ended up as mental cases, others as complete paralytics doomed to a short and useless life in the thrall of cerol, conscious but unable to blurt out the frightful truths held locked in their brains.

Gorlot had withdrawn the Perimeter defenses on the Tane sector, creating a funnel down which the Mil, encouraged by the lack of resistance, headed toward their new prey. The routine engagements Gorlot reported during his period as Regent were actually those few Mil ships he had had to destroy to control. Some of the men supposedly in cerol shock from Tane attacks had been captured by the Mil. Frantic appeals, like the case of the rhyming trader, had been put down to the ever-mounting toll of mental health. I wondered how Gorlot, once the Tanes' planets were stripped, planned to turn back the Mil the next time they approached the funnel. Or would the Mil know they had had all the life those two ill-fated planets bore? Would Gorlot have risked a Mil raid on Lothar? My private opinion was yes, he would have dared, particularly if he could be the hero of the occasion. Perhaps he meant ultimately to discard the "weakened line" of Harlan and start a new dynasty, the vigorous "line of Gorlot."

The real miracle in the affair was Jokan's role. He had started back for the north and staged a realistic crash in the mountains as planned. The men who rescued him were patrollers on leave. They recognized Jokan as the man who had been experimenting on Ertoi with the crystals. These crystals had enabled the Ertoi to keep the Mil off their planets long before the Alliance. The sonic vibrations of the crystals were powerful enough to disrupt the cellular construction of the Mil and reduce them to a battered jelly. The Ertoi were a much older race than the Lotharians. Thanks to the magnetic storms with which their planet abounded they had early found a means of defending themselves against the depredations of the Mil.

Jokan had worked for several years on a project to incorporate similar electromagnetic crystals on every Lotharian ship. Laboratory tests had proved that the crystals were effective if the Mil victim could be encircled. It was this new weapon that had given Harlan the hope that Lothar might seriously consider attacking the Mil home planet. However, there was as yet no adequate way to shield humans against the effect of the crystals. A man, because of his relatively denser cell composition, could stand a much higher frequency than the Mil. But man still suffered from the vibrations emanating from this weapon.

Jokan's patrollers mentioned that all the ships they had seen or served on recently were now equipped with the crystal resonators. There was considerable secrecy attached to these installations. Jokan was deemed the permissible exception. He had, after all, been instrumental in their development. But Jokan had not known that the installation of the crystals was so widespread. He was immediately concerned and questioned the men closely. What he learned was enough to send him back to Lothar to make his desperate and successful attempt to get to the Tane planets. He had left word at his apartment of his intentions, believing me soon to arrive safely there.

The patrollers had also told him they had been in maneuvers off Tane, using the crystals on Mil type transports, driving the ships toward Tane. There had been several of these "war games," combined with expeditions on the Tanes in which the "rebellious" Tanes were herded into cantonments to await punishment for their "offenses" against Lothar.

I don't know where Gorlot was taken immediately after the fiasco at the Council Hall because it had to be a well-kept secret. The palace was mobbed by endless throngs and deputations, screaming for possession of the traitor. Numerous attempts to invade the palace by force to seize Gorlot were repulsed.

Fara's concern for Maxil was just. He returned from the Council Hall in grim silence. He made continual appearances on the balcony overlooking the great Square, reassuring the people that the Mil were not lurking in the clouds above, ready to swoop down and depopulate Lothar. With a sternness astonishing for his relative youth, he assured them of punishment for the traitor. The only reason for a delay in dealing with Gorlot was to discover how far-reaching his plans had been. However, it became necessary late that night to bring Gorlot from his prison and show him to the frenzied mobs before they could be made to disperse.

Someone had started a rumor that he had been rescued or was going to be rescued. What group of zealots might do such a mad thing no one ever said. But Maxil showed them a Gorlot, manacled with ship-anchor chains, bruised and bloodied, quite a different man from that morning.

The enflamed people had to be satisfied with effigies of Gorlot which were burned, tortured, dismembered, tied to Mil Rocks all over the planet, thousands of times throughout the night. Vengeance was easy to accomplish by pointing fingers at those who had enjoyed Gorlot's favor during the past ten months.

Maxil proved himself a true descendant of Warlords, carrying himself with great dignity during his trying personal appearances. I appeared with him, as did Fara, Stannall, Jokan and Jessl. But I think it was Fara's presence that steadied him most. Once Stannall recognized this, at my insistence, there was no longer any problem about Fara remaining in the Warlord's suite.

I think all the arrogance and imperiousness went out of Maxil that day. The glamorous trappings, the little dignities and privileges that went with his position had been brutally torn aside to show him the ugly mechanics underneath. It was a frightening initiation into manhood.

The Regent and the First Councilman seemed to be on strings, in and out, back and forth. Jessl stayed with Maxil but apart from one public appearance with Maxil, Jokan was not in evidence. He joined us very late that night as Jessl and I sat up, listening to the disturbed sleep of the new Warlord, far too keyed up to rest ourselves. The noise from the streets was still audible. I was, as usual, eating. I'll say that for my participation in events that day: it was I who remembered that people had to eat occasionally, particularly people under stress. And I made everyone have dinner, including Stannall and Harlan.

Jessl took one look at his half-brother and did not offer

food. He poured him a full cup of a potent patrol brew. Jokan showed every minute of the forty sleepless hours of his trip to and from Tane. He was no longer the debonair man-of-the-world, playboy and wit. Jokan was too dead-tired to play any role. He had lost the last of his few illusions. Jessl and I waited as he drank, his legs sprawled out from the chair, his chin on his chest, one arm limp over the back of the chair, the other cradling the tumbler against his cheek between gulps.

"You know Jessl," he said finally, "I circled those damned planets and I quartered them. I went to every sacred grove on both Tanes. They were fenced round with forcers. Only the forcers were off and there wasn't anyone around. Used to be, there was always someone in a grove.

"And quiet? You've never been on such a quiet world. Those Tanes were always making some kind of noise, that silly croon of theirs. You always heard it. But there was always some kind of noise. I tell you, it was the weirdest thing I ever felt. And those burned-out acres where the Mil ships had landed. You could smell them. It made me sick. I was sick until I couldn't stand and crawled back to the ship on my hands and knees."

I noticed that he wasn't exaggerating. The knees of his now disheveled flying suit were torn and mud-caked.

"Jessl, if I hadn't been there," he continued, miserably, his eyes filling with tears, "I wouldn't't've believed a man, a Lotharian who knows what the Mil do, who's been brought up to kill the rotting species, could conceive such a scheme." He shook his head and drained the rest of his cup, holding it out for Jessl to refill.

"Didn't you find *any* Tanes?" asked Jessl hopefully.

Jokan shook his head slowly from side to side, from side to side. "A whole race of gentle natural people who never hurt anyone, who didn't suspect treachery in others until it must have been too late. A whole race wiped out. By one man. One man."

Draining his cup again, Jokan flung it viciously against the wall. It clattered and bounced noisily onto the carpeting. Jokan sat there looking at the battered cup with

narrowed eyes. Jessl reached for another tumbler, filled it
and passed it over to his brother. He and I watched until
Jokan drank himself into a complete stupor. Then we put
him to bed.

I went to sleep in the final hours of that night, listening
to the dull rumble of public frenzy which showed few
signs of dying down from sheer inertia. There was no less
noise than there had been the previous night with Eclipse
festival going full blast. But there was a different feel in
the air now . . . a feeling of hate so strong it smelled, so
tense it pressed against you like heavy fog and made
breathing difficult.

CHAPTER THIRTEEN

WHEN I AWOKE AT MY usual hour the next morning, I felt oddly refreshed by the short sleep and curiously alert. I was up well before Linnana this morning, I thought with a grin. She didn't even appear when I drew my own bath. In a way it was a pleasure to be alone, feeling as I did, and I hummed to myself as I bathed. Gorlot had done his worst and it had backfired on him. The yoke of apprehension was lifted from the back of my neck. Somehow, to me at any rate, the Mil did not seem as terrifying as Gorlot had.

I threw on a robe and walked out onto my balcony. The gardens lay below me, trampled and battered by yesterday's surging mobs. Beyond, the city was preternaturally quiet, the way New York could be, early Sunday mornings. A sudden muted drone caught my attention and I located the sound from the trail the ship made as it needled upward into the greenish morning sky. The trail was barely thinning when another roar split the air and a second, a third, a fourth line of smoke spurted upward. I watched this exodus for some time before the knock on the door roused me.

Harlan came in and motioned to me to stay on the balcony where he joined me. There were circles under his eyes and fatigue lines drawing down the corners of his mouth. But his step was quick and his voice firm.

"Good morning to you, Regent Harlan," I said and gave him a full court curtsey.

"Very graceful," he grinned back and gave me a hand to steady my rising. "I didn't hope to find you up. But I took a chance. Jokan is far beyond wakening."

"He was very tired last night," I tendered.

"He was also very drunk," Harlan remarked, teasing me. "Hardly blame him. Wish I had the chance."

I could think of nothing witty or apt to say because Harlan's very masculine presence disturbed me.

He leaned against the wall, facing me, folding his arms across his chest, regarding me with disconcerting directness.

"What is all the activity at the spaceport?" I asked, nervously gesturing at the smoke trails.

Harlan didn't bother to glance over his shoulder. "Sending out replacements and technicians for the Perimeter. Have to replace nearly every man Gorlot appointed with someone competent. He did a thorough job of removing, permanently or temporarily, every able man in Patrol unsympathetic to him."

"You *are* afraid the Mil are coming back in force."

Harlan frowned at me intensely. "There is always that possibility."

"It's what everyone seems to fear."

"Well, they might. Gorlot gave the Mil a wide-open field with Tane. What's to prevent them from assuming that the entire section isn't wide open? Especially since we've always maintained such a vigil."

Harlan moved to the balcony railing, looking out over the battered gardens. Then he turned back to me, leaning against the iron support.

"Have either Jessl or Jokan been after you? About your origin?" he asked anxiously.

"Jessl calls me the lady of mystery," I laughed lightly.

Harlan frowned.

"I can't keep both of them away from you and they're curious. Look, I'll send you some vision tapes about Jurasse. You can't read Lotharian yet, I gather? Hmmm. That's too bad and there's no chance to teach you. Well, you'll have to assimilate as much from the historical and vision tapes as you can."

Harlan stared thoughtfully into space, scrubbing his chin thoughtfully. I noticed he must have just bathed, for his hair gleamed damply in the rising sun. His lean profile stood in bold relief against the green sky, emphasizing the strength in his rough features. I put that picture into a special corner of my memory for easy reference. He turned back toward me suddenly. The wry grin on his face set as he caught my absorbed expression.

"I've never thanked you, have I, Sara?" he said gently. "If you hadn't had the courage of . . ."

I shook my head to stop him.

"You forget, you were the only way I had of getting out of that ghastly place."

He reached for my right hand, raising it to his lips without taking his eyes off mine. Then he pulled me slowly toward him.

"Maxil's Fara has joined him," Harlan said with a meaningful grin. His arms held me tightly against him and his eyes compelled me to look only into his face. "Maxil is as eager to claim *his* lady as I am to claim mine."

Slowly he bent and lifted me into his arms, his eyes never leaving mine. I could feel the warmth of him through the thin fabric of his overtunic and hear the beating of his heart, fast and strong. I felt I must be only one loud, frantic pulse beat. He put me on my feet by the side of the bed, his eyes warm and intense with feeling.

"This is not a smelly fishing boat, dear my lady," he said softly as his hands unfastened my robe. "And it is much too early for anyone to be up and looking for the Regent." He shed his own tunic and I swallowed hard with nervousness. Quick concern crossed his face and he framed my head with gentle hands. "Is this body you cared for so long offensive to you?" he asked softly. "You know it so well."

"I know it well, yes, but not the man within it," I whispered.

He smiled then, a wonderful tender possessive smile.

"When the man I am is within you, you will know all of me well and I, all of you. And you will no longer be afraid of me."

My arms, of themselves, slid up around his neck and our bodies touched. I couldn't control my trembling.

"Dear my lady Sara," he said very softly, his voice rough with passion. "I'm claiming my own. *Now!*"

A long time later, I heard his soft chuckle in my ear.

"You know, you were untouched after all. Those bully boys Gleto used as guards weren't above rape."

"I know," I said in a very small whisper into his chest, "I was terrified they might have when I wasn't in possession of my senses."

He tipped my head up so I had to look him straight in the eye.

"Afraid of *me* now?" he asked gently. He wouldn't let me duck my head and he grinned at my furious blushing. "I can see you aren't and I'm glad." He kissed me quickly and settled me against him. "I'll do better by you next time, sweeting. But I can't give a guess when that'll be. This is stolen time." He sighed deeply and the lines loving had lifted briefly settled back into place.

"You look so tired, Harlan," I murmured, worried, touching the raggedy scar on his cheek.

"I feel a lot better now than I have for some time," he grinned wickedly at me and kissed my breasts. His hands tightened on me roughly. When he looked up at me, his face had changed completely. "If anything should happen to you now ..." He sat up abruptly, his strong back to me. I could hear him slap one fist against the other palm.

One long arm reached out for the overdress he had dropped to the floor. In one fluid movement he had thrown it over him and buckled it into place. He looked down at me.

"That's why I can't stand to have you stay on here. Too many people get to see you. You've too unusual a face to be easily forgotten. Someone who knows where you were before you were made my attendant is going to remember you. But ..." and he sighed deeply, "there's no possible chance of whisking you away to a less public place."

"Nothing will happen, Harlan. Surely someone would have come forward by now. I've been seen so much," I reassured him. "And I've been doing quite well. I've had to."

"You've recalled no memories, not even fragments that would give us a lead?"

"None I want to remember," I said, suppressing a shudder.

He bent to kiss my forehead in apology for stirring up those memories.

"By the way, we got those nine men out of Gleto's tender care," he said, sitting down beside me. He took my left hand in both his, stroking my wrist gently. "They're coming round and furthermore, we found enough cerol in Gleto's medicine room to supply an army. There wasn't much of that stuff available before the Tane wars, too new a drug, so it was obvious someone has been importing it in quantities. We'll find out who soon."

"Then you *can* prove to anyone that you never were insane in the first place. Not that it matters now."

"It still matters," Harlan assured me. "But what is more important, we should be able to learn from those nine when the Mil first got to the Tanes . . . in what force. . . ."

"Can't you get Gorlot to tell you?"

"We're working on him, too," Harlan said grimly. "We've had more success with his cronies in Records and Supplies, but they don't know the total plan."

"What about Monsorlit?" I asked hopefully. It would be nice to be rid of one menace.

Harlan looked at me questioningly.

"He drugged you, after all. And Gorlot appointed him," I argued, not understanding his reluctance to indict the physician.

"No. Monsorlit has always been in charge of the staff at War Hospital," Harlan said quickly. "Gleto has been accused," he added to pacify me. "But other than Gleto's counteraccusation there is no proof Monsorlit was involved. Gleto's such a wretched cave-blocker his word doesn't go for much."

"But mine does," I replied, trying to ignore the fear that sank like lead into the pit of my stomach.

"Look," and Harlan closed strong hard hands around my shoulders. He gave me a little shake to make me look at him. "We'll have to forget about Monsorlit's duplicity. If restoration is once brought into this, you'll be killed just as if you were any other restoree. Monsorlit must have done the restoration. He's the only one who would dare or who could do such a superb job. But how he did it and when, I am not interested in finding out. And neither, dear my lady, should you be. By the mother of us all, Sara," and he threw his hands out in an exasperated gesture as I stared at him, unconvinced, "do you *want* to be discovered?

"Monsorlit has covered all traces in this affair," and Harlan swung off the bed to pace restlessly up and down the room, "just as delicately as he covered all trace of restoration on your body."

He turned and pointed his stumpy finger at me. "If his hospital ship had once been on Tane at any time, we could accuse him of hiding treasonable information or of direct collusion with Gorlot. But he's clever. He kept his ships in orbit one hundred miles above the planet. The wounded were ferried up to him by small rocket. We can't pin a thing on him.

"There's just enough cerol in his hospitals for experimentation. And his staff is so cave-bound loyal to him they wouldn't spit unless he said to. How can we pin anything on him that would remove him as a danger to you?

"He's got Ferrill back on his feet and to top it all, he's come up with an antidote for cerolosis. That makes us grateful to him. And his clinics for mental health all over the planet have touched too many little people for us to try to defame him."

"But he drugged you," I insisted inanely.

Harlan shrugged. "I can do nothing that won't endanger you."

"What if Monsorlit remembers me?" I pleaded, desperately afraid.

Harlan dropped to my side again. "Sara, Sara, please. Go on making yourself into a Lotharian. It's safer." He smiled plaintively and kissed me tenderly. "You're one now anyway. But remember, fear of a restoree is almost as deep as fear of the Mil and to many ... you heard Stannall ... just as hideous."

I was about to say something when a gentle knock startled us.

"Just be careful, dear my lady," he whispered urgently as the door opened to admit Linnana.

CHAPTER FOURTEEN

I OFTEN FELT IN THE next few days as if I lived in the old Grand Central Station. Harlan and Stannall conducted much of their business in Maxil's living room and board room, including Maxil in all discussions. The boy would reel to bed late at night exhausted, rise the next morning and grimly plunge back into the tedious reports from Councilmen and Patrolmen, or broadcast reassuring messages to the planet. The palace seethed with feverish activity and the air was punctuated day and night by the blasts of shuttling rockets and great ships.

A full report of the death of the Tane was partially cushioned by the discovery of a lone group of sixty badly frightened, suspicious survivors.

All Patrol reserves were recalled for reexamination and assignment. The fiction that this was due only to a reshuffling following the collapse of the Gorlot Regency was not fooling many, but it kept hysteria under control. Every available ship, no matter what size, was being refitted with Jokan's electromagnetic resonators. Busy as the spaceport beyond Lothar was, Maxil assured me that the Moonbases were bedlam. Jokan spent most of his time with Ertois and Glans although I didn't get to see any of these extraplanetary allies until later. Jessl was occupied with some radical planetary defense system and appeared only once at the formal dinners that Stannall insisted be continued for public morale.

Maxil announced plans for a speeded-up colonization of one of the Tane planets. Applications from all walks and trades would be acceptable. With a wry afterthought, it was also announced that both Tane planets were being equipped with the Ertoi defense crystals to prevent a return of the Mil. I realized then that that must be what occupied Jessl, the erection of a similar last-gasp defense for Lothar itself. To have admitted this publicly would have crystalized everyone's nightmare.

My public appearances as Maxil's companion continued, but I insisted that Fara also be included. Maxil always felt more at ease with her than with me although I know he liked me. But I was eight years his senior and, as Harlan had made plain he had a prior claim, Maxil was uncomfortable when the three of us were together. With both Harlan and Maxil bringing pressure on him, Stannall finally conceded that people would be too concerned with the Mil crisis to worry about such "minor details."

However, members of the palace circle soon took advantage of the fact that Maxil had made no formal claim on me and pressed their attentions. Stannall would not, however, permit Harlan to make his formal claim public, which infuriated the Regent.

If Linnana ever mentioned finding Harlan in my room that first morning he claimed me, she never passed the information along. I was deeply grateful to her and she became very helpful in dissuading importunate suitors who tried to enter my room.

My private time I spent listening to the tapes Harlan had sent me until I felt I knew Jurrasse intimately and could tour its eighteen hills blindfolded. Fara and I went to the Great Bazaar and I listened to the talk of the crowds, shopping, watching, familiarizing myself as much as I could with Lotharian ways.

Lothar was an odd contrast of technical advances and primitive inventions. There were no land vehicles other than animal-drawn carts of the crudest type. Women baked on wood stoves while the land Patrol and the palace cooked with a form of thermal energy in gigantic ovens. There was radiant lighting, but a crude type of radiant heating. Cloth was all handloomed. There was efficient refrigeration but no canned supplies. No paper but the awkward slates or thinly extruded metal sheets for more permanent records. Widespread television existed and recording tapes but nothing approximating typewriters or printing presses. Epic poems were sung by skilled bards using stringed instruments and drums, but there were no dramas other than mummeries. Glass and high-grade plastics but no china, porcelain or clay.

My days were busy, but I waited impatiently for the few hours Harlan could spare to be with me. He would come late at night, waking me from sleep, or early in the morning as I could not break my habit of early rising. If he came at dawn, he would bring cups of beverage and fruit, teasing me about my ravenous appetite.

"When do you ever sleep?" I asked him, half anxious, half amazed at his inexhaustible vitality.

He rolled onto his side and ran a caressing hand the length of my body.

"Here and there," he answered absently. He stroked my wrist softly. "Remember, I had months of sleep in the asylum and," he added with an engaging leer, "as long as I have access to the greatest of all restoratives, I'm doing fine. When I think of the time I wasted in that asylum, the opportunities I was oblivious to . . ."

"You are absurd," I protested, laughing.

"And you are delightful, dear my lady," and we would be off again.

He never completely forgot my exposed position and my lack of background. But I became more at ease and lost my fear of self-betrayal. I was full of confidence.

The communicator panel, which was always busy, flashed on one morning just as I was rousing from a post-breakfast stupor. Harlan had been with me late that night. Jokan said the call was for me.

I recognized the speaker as Councilman Lesatin. In most courteous terms he asked me to attend a meeting in half an hour at Stannall's office beyond the Great Hall in the administration wing.

My curiosity, not my concern, was aroused. Lesatin had been a dinner partner twice and I dismissed the man as an amiable, exaggerating character. He happened to be the representative of the mining interests in Jurasse and we had chatted about my coming from there. The only question I hadn't been able to answer was what shaft my father had worked in. I had fobbed that off by confessing to a sudden lapse of memory. Very silly, I had said airily, to forget a title I knew as well as my own clan. Lesatin had helpfully named a few shafts and I had picked one eagerly. He had not seemed unduly concerned with my forgetfulness.

When I reached the office, not only Lesatin was there but also Stannall and several other senior Councilmen whom I knew by sight. I still had no apprehensions.

I was greeted most courteously and asked to be seated.

"One purpose of this meeting," Stannall began in his most formal tone of voice, "is to acquaint you with the public approval of this Council and the citizens of Lothar for the considerable part you played in exposing the traitor, Gorlot. Had you not suspected and been able to effect Harlan's release, we might have discovered all too late the perfidy planned against the entire Alliance. Our gratitude takes this material expression," and Stannall handed me a much decorated slate. I glanced at it with what I hoped was intelligent comprehension and thanked them most fervently.

"We feel we can never adequately recompense you for the danger in which you voluntarily placed yourself."

I muttered something to cover my embarrassment.

Stannall's official countenance relaxed into as pleasant a smile as he had ever directed to me. The other five men beamed paternally at me. I wondered if Stannall had now forgiven me my various sins. He had been less curt, certainly, since Fara had joined Maxil's suite. Perhaps she had championed me.

"We would be interested in knowing just when you first suspected Harlan was being drugged. Also anything you can remember that would lead to the apprehension of other traitors."

"There's Gleto, of course, and his armed guards."

Stannall nodded and remarked that they had been in custody for some time. "Gleto makes some odd charges," Stannall added absently, "which we are unable to substantiate."

"Oh?" I remarked hopefully, not at all suspicious of this line of questioning.

"He had involved several men of prominent position whom many would like to see cleared of such basely derived suspicions," the First Councilman continued smoothly.

"I'm not sure I could give you any help. I was shut up constantly in the one cottage. I had no opportunity to overhear or see any visitors of consequence. Except when Ferrill came to see Harlan. I think that was the first inkling I had of irregularity," I said truthfully.

"Oh?"

"Ferrill asked particularly to be informed of any change in Harlan's condition, you see," I continued, goaded by Stannall's noncommittal reception. "Gorlot made a sign to Gleto and he smirked. I mean, Gorlot was plainly indicating that Gleto should not inform Ferrill if Harlan got better."

This was considered and commented on.

"Did Physician Monsorlit ever attend Harlan at the asylum in your presence?"

My throat dried up suddenly and I coughed evasively. The truth, the truth is the one thing you never stumble over. But I couldn't tell the whole truth. Not now when I saw what Stannall was after: an indictment against Monsorlit. But they all knew that Monsorlit had been the attending physician.

"Yes, he came," I admitted slowly.

"What did he do?" Stannall seemed to leap on my confirmation.

"Made a routine examination of Harlan, administered a drug and left."

"Did you have any idea what drug?" Stannall snapped.

I swallowed and claimed ignorance. Stannall stared at me with such a menacing intensity it was very difficult to act unconcerned. My throat was parched.

"Tell me," Stannall began casually, turning his back on me for a moment, fiddling with slates on his desk. "How did you obtain the position as attendant to Harlan?"

"The usual way."

"Which is through Monsorlit's Mental Defectives Clinic,

according to the records," Stannall retorted, wheeling back to me with blazing eyes.

"Well, certainly," I replied with mock amazement that he should consider this remarkable.

My admission confused him and Lesatin muttered something to one of his colleagues.

"You *admit* having gone through the Clinic?"

"Certainly," I was forced to reconfirm. "Mental Defectives Clinic" I heard my mind echoing and an icy finger twisted deep into my stomach. I fought the sudden panic. I must think clearly now. I must. I had just admitted to having been insane ... no, no, I was seriously disturbed, that's all. It meant I would be shielding Monsorlit whom I wanted to expose. It meant, more certainly, I hadn't given the proper thought to my background story at all. No one was asking me how many hills Jurasse had nor the position of the Odern Cave Vaults nor the placement of the inner labyrinths. Nor what shaft my father had worked in.

"Why were you in the Clinic?" Lesatin asked into that chill silence. I looked at him and realized that this affable man with the insatiable curiosity was quite capable of correlating odd pieces of information into logical theory.

"I went there for help," I said slowly. "You see, I'd had several very bad experiences that upset me. Some friends thought I might get help there."

"What kind of experiences?" Lesatin urged gently.

"Remember the apartments near the sign of Horn? The ones that collapsed in the earth fault? Well, I was trapped in my room for hours before they could get me out. Then my father was one of the men who was killed in the fault. I didn't have any relatives and I never could get to see my Clan Officer. I'd have these terrible nightmares," that was true enough, "and finally, I went to the Mental Clinic."

I wondered if neurotics were acceptable in this Clinic. Certainly in terms of earth psychiatry, those two traumatic shocks were sufficient to cause a psychosis ... if you tended to be psychotic. I looked pleadingly in each face to see the reception of my fabrication. I was relieved to see sympathy replace skepticism and suspicion.

"Then you are naturally grateful to Monsorlit for curing your ... ah ... nervousness and nightmares," Stannall suggested.

"Well, not Monsorlit, certainly. I wasn't a very unusual case and you had to be pretty bad to get his attention what with the Tane war."

This was not the answer Stannall hoped for, I knew, but it was plausible.

"Did you ever see anything ... unusual ... while you were in the Clinic undergoing treatment?" asked Stannall conversationally.

"Unusual?"

"Yes. Cases where men were perhaps completely bandaged from head to foot. Patients with scars on their wrists, ankles or necks?"

"Oh, no," I replied hastily. I knew now what he was driving at. He wanted to be able to accuse Monsorlit of restoration. And here was Stannall's proof sitting in front of him. "Oh, no, no. No restorees, only men he had repossessed," I blurted out without thinking.

"Repossessed!" and Stannall snapped the word up hungrily and turned triumphantly to the others.

"What exactly do you mean?" asked Lesatin anxiously.

"I don't exactly know," I stalled. "I mean, the other girls in the sanitarium were called 'repossessed' and some of the technicians too." I recalled the conversation Monsorlit had had with Gleto about restorees and repossessed. "I guess I mean people who have been ill mentally and he has repossessed them of their senses. People he's trained to do certain things. I guess you could almost call Harlan repossessed, except that he was never really insane."

The qualification had an effect on the Councilmen. They talked quietly among themselves.

"Perhaps we have been wrong in our suspicions," Lesatin began without his usual pomposity. "The two terms, repossessed and restored, have similar meanings. This young lady's statement bears out what we already know.

And we have certainly examined every hospital record and each patient carefully. *I* have found no evidence of restoration."

Stannall turned angrily toward Lesatin. I gathered he wished Lesatin had not been so outspoken. Lesatin shrugged off the silent reprimand.

"All we have is the word of a low Milbait like Gleto against the innumerable proofs to the contrary from unimpeachable sources," Lesatin said. "Surely, Sir Stannall, you must realize the splendid contributions Monsorlit has made toward the insidious problem of insanity . . ."

"I realize that Monsorlit, in some way, despite all oral and written proof to the contrary, aided and abetted Gorlot in his treachery. If just one, just one of those casualties had been capable of speech, we would have discovered this obscene plot. Why couldn't *one* of them speak?"

"Monsorlit received all casualties in the orbital hospital ship. There was ample opportunity for someone like Trenor, who has admitted his complicity, to silence them effectively with cerol," Lesatin pointed out.

"Can't you help us?" Stannall said fiercely to me, his eyes blazing with a fanatical hate. "*Won't* you help us?" His intensity startled me so that nothing could have made me speak out. I comprehended too well the logic behind Harlan's advice to forget Monsorlit's part in his incarceration.

Stannall advanced on me, to my growing terror, for the mild-mannered First Councilman was as one possessed, his face gray with emotion, his wiry body trembling with rage.

Harlan burst in the door. At sight of him, I cried out in relief. Harlan's entrance was explosive, not casual. The news he blurted out with no preamble cleared the room of all other interests.

"The Mil are coming," he cried in a tight voice. Striding to the communicator wall, he snapped on the picture to a scene of complete confusion. A gasping older man in uniform was shrieking out his message.

"The Mil! THE MIL ARE COMING!"

"Report position, report position," Harlan said in a

controlled voice, forcing comprehension through the man's hysterical repetition of his ghastly message. I could see the squadron commander, for I realized this was a ship's signal room, gulping for control. The slate he held in his hand shook violently, but his voice lowered.

"I beg to report," he gasped, seizing on the inanities of protocol to reassure himself, "infiltration past the first ring. Twenty-three Mil ships, fifteen Star class, five Planet, with three attendant satellite trailers. Moving directly Taneward at equatorial intersection."

"Twenty-three," Stannall murmured incredulously. "The largest force in three centuries. And moving toward Tane."

"Spur infiltrations?" Harlan demanded, his voice metallic with command.

"No, sir. Just the direct route unless ..." and the squadron commander's hand shook more noticeably, "they break off later."

"What is their pace rate and interception potential for supreme task force?"

"Base is working on it now, sir," a shadow voice put in.

"Proceed with Prime Action, and, Commander, are *all* your ships equipped with the new electromagnetic crystals?"

"Yes, sir, they are, sir. But we've had no test runs."

"No matter. Maintain surveillance but under no circumstances, repeat, under no circumstances, attempt standard delaying tactics. My respects to you and your squadron, Commander. You will receive additional orders shortly."

The picture faded as Harlan punched another dial. Before the picture had been fully established, I heard a piercing wail outside, the eerie panther-cry of a warning siren. Stannall and the others left the room, walking stiffly as people in the midst of a horrible dream. I heard Harlan's voice, calm, unhurried, the unusual metallic burr of command adding its harsh note, as he announced to the planet total, immediate mobilization and complete civilian evacuation.

I listened stunned through this electrifying broadcast.

Then he switched with unhurried sureness to the vast globular room I identified as the Moonbase Headquarters of the Patrol. Here also was the unfumbling dispatch of trained men reacting to an emergency that had been theory for three generations and was now, unexpectedly, grim actuality.

I saw Gartly and Jessl among the men in the Moonbase and, for the first time, representatives of the Alliance planets, Ertoi and Glan. The former were as humanoid as a saurian species can appear, complete with gills and scaled armor. The second, the Glan, were willowy skeletons with three digits and an opposing thumb. Their bodies were covered with a fine down, their faces, long and narrow, were sensitive. Their apparently ineffectual bodies were deceptive for the Glan were structurally twice as strong as Lotharians and equal to their scaly space neighbors, the Ertois.

From them, Harlan received the news that their entire force was speeding toward the penetration point. I thought this was excellent cooperation until I saw the spatial tank and realized that their relative position had a great deal to do with such all-out collaboration. Spatially speaking, they were above and beyond Tane and Lothar but only as the apex of an isosceles triangle is above and beyond its base points. It was to their advantage to deflect any further penetration of the Mil at Tane or Lothar, for the angle of the Mil advance made the triangle two-dimensional and therefore Ertoi and Glan were not galactically far from Lothar.

The Alliance contingent, however, had the farthest to come and there remained the calculation of experts to determine if it were better to wait for their reinforcing navy before joining battle or whether to attempt it with only the Lotharian fleet. That decision ultimately rested with Harlan as Regent and, in this emergency, the de facto Warlord.

The decisive figures were not to be completed for several hours and Harlan signed off with the advice that he would presently board his command ship. All further communications were to be forwarded there. He made one more call and I saw the startled boy-scared face of Maxil. He was being dressed in a shipsuit by a grim Jokan.

"It is my duty to inform my lord," Harlan began formally, "that Lothar is in gravest danger. I must now assume all rights, responsibilities and privileges. Will you accompany me on board the flagship?"

"What do I say?" Maxil asked, his voice steady.

Harlan gave him a reassuring grin.

"You acknowledge the danger, relinquish to me your rights and responsibilities and say you'll join me. You're a little young for this, lad, but I don't think you'd want to miss it. And, if you're feeling scared, you're not alone. I'll see you in half an hour. Now, please let me speak to Jokan."

Maxil nodded and stepped aside.

"Jokan, you'll take Sara along with Ferrill to the Vaults. Stannall and the Council will be assembling there presently. I've got the power so they can't object to any emergency measure I propose. Space help us if Maxil and I go down together. I'm ordering you alternate Regent this time," and he snorted at his behindsight.

"Now wait a minute, Harlan, I'm going with you . . ." Jokan objected, his eyes flashing angrily.

"No, Jokan. You can't," Harlan said with absolute finality. "It could be more important to Lothar's future to have you alive if something goes wrong with our attack plan. I haven't more time to explain now. Jo, you know I wouldn't ask it if I didn't have to."

Jokan glared helplessly, searching for an argument strong enough to sway his brother.

"Jokan, I _count_ on you. I can't trust anyone else," Harlan repeated, his voice tight with the desperate urgency of his appeal.

Jokan set his teeth and bowed his head once in stiff resignation.

"Where's Sara?" Harlan asked.

"Here," I reminded him.

Harlan whirled around and stared at me fiercely for a moment. I didn't know whether to be amused or hurt he had forgotten I was there.

"Jokan, I call you to witness that I claim the Lady Sara to be *my* lady," he said formally, drawing me by the hand into the range of the vision screen.

"I accept the claim of Harlan, son of Hillel," I said proudly and Harlan kissed my hand formally. Even now his thumb paused over my wrist.

"Jokan, I'll give Sara the alternate commission of Regency. And Jo, if something should happen, guard Sara. If I don't come back, she has something very important to tell you. Now get Maxil off to the spaceport. I'll meet the boy there."

He flicked the panel to one more station, ordering his planecar brought to the balcony of the office in twenty minutes. Turning away from the set, he looked at me with such avid hunger in his face I had to turn my eyes away from his naked desire.

When I looked up at the slam of a drawer, I saw he was swiftly styling a slate. I sat down and watched him as he wrote, thinking with a sense of despair that this might be the last time I ever saw him. I memorized his face so that my mind would be able to recall the image faithfully should I never see the original again. It was difficult to reconcile the fierce and gentle lover I knew best with this grim warrior, urgently writing last-minute instructions for the safety of a world he might never walk again. He finished one slate quickly, tossing it aside with a clatter to clear space for the next. This, too, he wrote quickly. The third one, however, did not come as readily and he frowned as he wrote, blended out, and restyled. He punctuated this final message noisily and flipped a protecting film over it which he sealed. He gathered the three together and then stood up.

He came toward me and I rose to meet him. I had lead in my stomach and I needed iron in my thighs which did not seem strong enough to support me as I stood. In a few moments he would go out the balcony windows and . . .

He put his strong fingers on my shoulders and gave me a little shake to make me concentrate on what he had to say. His face had softened its grim expression and his eyes wandered lovingly over my face.

"If I don't come back ... but I will," he reassured me quickly as I gasped at his fatalism, "give the third slate to Ferrill. To no one else. Ferrill is the only one who would be able to help and stand up to Stannall. Jokan can guard you because I have pledged him to it, but only Ferrill can help against Stannall. Stay with those two as long as I'm gone and watch that quick tongue of yours."

"Harlan ..."

He gave me another little shake to hush.

"If I were a soldier on your world and going to battle ... but maybe your world doesn't have wars ... pretend, anyway. How ... Oh Sara," and he pulled me into his arms, holding me tightly. "I have known you such a short, little time."

I threw my arms around his neck, choking back a sob.

"Not with a tear, Sara," he reprimanded me gently. "Surely not with tears?"

"No, not with tears," I denied, crying, lifting my lips to his kiss.

I clung to him desperately, for the passion that his slightest caress evoked in me welled up to meet his. Abruptly he took his mouth from mine and held my head fiercely against his shoulder, burying his lips in my hair.

Slowly he released me, holding my hands gently as I struggled to hold back my tears.

"Honor my claim to you, dear my lady."

A horn blasted outside and I saw the hovering aircar. I felt his hands pressing mine around the slates and, through my tears, saw him stride out to the balcony and into the car. I watched until I could no longer see it over the arc of the palace gardens.

My head ached with the pressure of stifled grief and my body from the stimulus of his caresses. I would always associate the mingled odors of car-fuel, fresh slate wax and mid-morning musty heat with that scene.

CHAPTER FIFTEEN

I CARRIED THE SLATES, holding them stiffly in both hands just as Harlan had placed them there. I walked down corridors that were obstacle courses of hustling men and equipment. There was no panic, just urgent dispatch. No hysterics, only grim determination. But I was oblivious. Their haste, their muttered apologies bounced off the numb shell of my exterior.

I don't think I had quite accepted the fact that Harlan really cared for me. I accepted the fact that he was grateful to me; that he found me useful in sailing a ship; that he liked to be seen with me; that he liked to go to bed with me, but not that his emotions were involved. I knew he was concerned for my safety, but I had irrationally connected that with the fact that only I could recognize my own home planet in space and Harlan keenly wanted more allies to help overthrow the Mil. It was just difficult for me to assimilate the knowledge I was Harlan's lady, me, Sara Fulton, late of Seaford, Delaware and New York City.

It seemed an age before I reached Maxil's suite where a pacing Jokan waited. He looked at me sardonically, the muscles along his jaw working. I handed him the slates and he glared down at them as if they, too, were enemies in the alliance to keep him planet-bound when all his soul wanted to be in space with the fleet. He handed one slate back to me brusquely.

"That one's for Ferrill, not me," he said with no courtesy. He scanned one quickly and placed it in his belt. The other he read, his frown deepening. He glanced at me twice during the reading and then sat down. His anger drained out of him and a hopeless impatience took its place.

"Oh, sit down, Lady Sara. I won't eat you," he said kindly, seeing me still standing in the same spot.

I sat down and promptly burst into tears, gulping out apologies as I sobbed. He leaned over and roughly patted my shoulder, muttering reassurances. When I didn't stop, he fetched a drink and made me get it down.

"Patrol issue," I choked.

"Of course, we're pretty lucky," he said with no prelude. "Harlan's the most brilliant commander we've ever had. We're better prepared for this sort of thing than ever before in our history. Never thought there would be a Prime again, but we've got it and there's no panic. It's not as if the Mil were able to swoop down on us with no forewarning the way they used to. It could be a lot worse, you know. We could have Gorlot as our Regent and I bet we might just as well skin ourselves if he were. But he isn't. It's Harlan and he'll save our skins if anyone can. Because, my dear brother's lady, right now we can annihilate the Mil in the sky."

It was not the words he said but the way he said them that stopped my senseless weeping; I looked up at him in amazement because there was triumph in his voice; a certainty that exceeded the trivial phrases of his verbal assurance.

"I hope so," said a wry voice from the doorway. We both turned to see Ferrill there, supported by two men. "I'm being conducted to the Vaults," he said, indicating the escort with amusement. "Coming?"

Ferrill's smile, oddly mocking, made his old-man's face younger.

"There's really no need for me to be bulwarked by all the ingenuity of the Vaults. The Mil wouldn't bother a wreck like me," Ferrill continued amiably. "I gather," and his face grimaced ruefully at Jokan, "Harlan has made you stay behind to guard the sacred persons of the Warlord's progeny. You've worked as hard for this contingency as he. Pity you can't witness it. But I'm glad it's you that's here!" Ferrill's sincerity reached Jokan through his bitterness.

"It is my honor, sir," he replied in a neutral voice, but the bow he made the ex-Warlord was deep and respectful.

Jokan indicated I was to precede him to the Hall. I hesitated at the doorway so that Ferrill might precede me as I felt his due. He bowed slightly and I continued. We made our way to the down-shaft through hurrying people who stopped and stepped aside respectfully to let Ferrill's party pass.

"Nuisance to be sent scurrying down so early," Ferrill commented as we reached the shaft. "Nothing will happen for a day or so."

"True," Jokan conceded, "but they have activated the spatial tank below and set up the remote connections there rather than in the Council Hall. It's more reassuring to the general public to vault themselves anyway. Too much has happened to unsettle them. They fancy themselves more Tanes, I'm told."

"Hmm. That's reasonable," Ferrill replied thoughtfully.

When we reached the cellars of the palace, we passed a six-foot-thick section of wall that would swing up into place, closing off the entrance to the Vaults beneath the palace. Huge guards saluted as we passed this impenetrable lock.

We walked down a short corridor to an enormous, low-ceilinged room where partitions blocked off working, resting and eating areas. The busy occupants spared Ferrill a grave smile or bow. The next corridor was doubly sealed by more six-foot sections. The precautions were so formidable I wondered what kind of attack armament the Mil mounted which could penetrate such fortifications. Maybe the effect of the doors was more psychological than necessary.

"I haven't been in the Vaults in years," Ferrill remarked. "I often wondered who dusted them and how frequently."

Jokan gave a mirthless snort at such a fancy while I surprised myself with a genuine laugh at such drollery.

We paused before a final heavy door and were admitted by guards into the innermost section, the retreat of the Council and the Warlord's family.

The huge room, which appeared to be as large as

Starhall, was dominated by a spherical tank some ten feet in diameter. I did not have the chance to examine it because Stannall approached us from one of the cubicles beyond. He bowed gravely to Ferrill, glanced at me curiously and clasped Jokan's arm in welcome.

"Sir Ferrill, your quarters are prepared in Room Seven. I regret you must share them with your attendants and your brother Fernan but . . ."

Ferrill shrugged off the inconvenience and excused himself. He rested more heavily on his helpers although he had moved along the public corridors with a semblance of vigor.

"I had not expected the Lady Sara," Stannall said severely.

"Lord Harlan has claimed the Lady Sara in my presence," Jokan said bluntly. "I have, here, an alternate commission of Regency," and Jokan handed over the slates to Stannall, "as well as Harlan's official record of claim and acceptance."

The First Councilman glanced quickly through both, scowling at me again with intense irritation.

"Very well," Stannall acknowledged sourly.

"You mean my appointment as Regent," Jokan said pointedly.

"No, of course not. I approve of that heartily." He looked up, conscious of Jokan's stare. I had not exactly expected Jokan to come to my defense, particularly against Stannall, so his attitude was very reassuring. "My congratulations, Lady Sara. I know the Lady Fara will be glad to see you."

"Did Maxil . . ." Jokan began.

"Fara accepted the honor," Stannall said quickly.

"Congratulations all around then," Jokan said with a wry smile.

"Maxil claimed Fara?" I repeated, hoping that at least one area of irritation might be erased between Stannall and me.

"Thank the mother of us all for that," Jokan muttered. "Room Four?" he asked and when Stannall nodded, he drew me off to the side where I saw numbered doors, closed against the noise of the main room.

"There is much for me to order, Lady Sara," Jokan said, opening the door for me.

"And I am tired."

A droning voice muttering unintelligible syllables in a room beyond penetrated my sleep and woke me, startled, in an unfamiliar darkness. Frightened, I lay still until the mounds of deeper shadow became distinguishable as Fara, Linnana and two empty beds.

The drone continued and I had been so startled on awakening that my ability to sleep was gone. I rose and stumbled across to the bathroom.

The lights of the main hall and the muted conversations that blended under the theme of the droning voice were a shock after the dim quiet of the sleeping room. I stood in the doorway, looking over the bustle for Jokan or Ferrill. Stannall was standing in front of the cubicle that was his office, his slight body slumped with weariness. While he talked to a Councilman, his eyes were fixed on the space tank and the measured tread of the blips within it. There were few in the room who did not glance frequently at the tank, frequently and apprehensively.

I located the drone as issuing from one of the twelve big screens at the top of the room. A communications man was talking, calling off sector units and parsec figures. In turn, clerks noted down these figures at tables that circled the screen and tank area. From the other big hall messengers came and went, officials in patrol uniform or Council robes met and conversed quietly in the linking corridor. Their voices were pitched lower than that continuous drone.

Jokan came striding down the corridor and up to Stannall. Ferrill, walking slowly from Stannall's office, joined them. The Councilman who had been talking to Stannall bowed and moved away. Jokan was arguing and Stannall was objecting, shaking his head dubiously. Ferrill added a sentence and Stannall regarded the ex-Warlord with a long scowl. The three of them moved over to the tank and Jokan pointed, scribing a circle with his hands and indicat-

ing its position in the spatial reference. A messenger came
up and handed Jokan a slate. This had a bearing on his
argument because he pointed out several lines for Stannall
to read. The First Councilman shrugged, shook his head
again. When Ferrill added his comment, Stannall lifted
both arms in a gesture of exasperation. Jokan bowed
formally and went to the main communication screen, one
that looked in on the giant refitted Mil ship that was
Harlan's command vessel.

My attention was abruptly diverted from Jokan by a
touch on my arm. To my concern, I saw Monsorlit standing beside me, regarding me with a cold impersonal interest tinged with some private amusement.

"Lady Sara," he said, making a mockery of the title
with a flick of his eyes, "for a moron, you've made
remarkable conquests. I've reread your dossier and find it
fascinating."

"Moron? I'm no moron," I said with all the disdain I
could muster. I turned from him, but his hand, as cold as
his expression and as strong as his personality, closed
round my wrist.

"As I was saying, I have examined your history and I
find it differs considerably from the public version of your
origin."

"Against Harlan's word, what can you prove?" I demanded.

He smiled blandly, his eyes wandering over my face
and body with clinical dispassion.

"Against Harlan's word, I have the facts and witnesses.
Facts that would prove extremely interesting to the First
Councilman, to young Maxil. And, certainly to Harlan
himself, unless you are more of an innocent than you
appear."

"I don't know what you mean," I gasped, trying to
twist my hand free.

He looked down at my wrist, holding it up and stroking
it with his thumb. Then he glanced suggestively into my
face. I had no strength to hide the shock that gesture gave
me.

The smile which was no smile cut across his thin face.

"You are unique, Lady Sara. Absolutely unique and as a serious scientist, I cannot allow the originality to go unremarked. I intend to have you back in the Clinic and I give you warning. You may come of your own free will, explaining your request to your protector any way you wish. Or, I will force you to come, by edict of the Council. I doubt you like that alternative."

"Physician," said Ferrill's soft voice at my side. Monsorlit looked up and bowed to the invalid.

"Do not overexert yourself in this excitement, Sir Ferrill," Monsorlit advised sternly.

"Exert myself? Oh, not likely. I have accepted the role of passive observer. That requires no exertion at all."

So saying, Ferrill neatly turned me away from Monsorlit and guided me toward an unused table in the dining area. He motioned me to sit and gave an order for hot drinks to the servant who appeared.

"Why does Monsorlit terrify you?" he asked quietly, his eyes slightly narrowed.

"He's . . . he's so cold," I blurted out, still trembling with the shock of the encounter.

Ferrill's eyebrows raised questioningly but, at this moment, the waiter returned. I drank hastily, the comfort of the warm beverage dissipating my inner chill. When I raised my eyes over my cup, Ferrill was regarding me with curious intentness. He reached over and lifted my right hand, turned it over and rubbed one finger across my wrist. I jerked my hand away and sat staring at Ferrill in a sort of helpless horror.

Ferrill smiled to himself and then included me in that smile.

"Lady Sara," he began with a rueful grin, "for the short time you have been in our circle, you have managed to elicit an amazing amount of talk. You succeed in antagonizing one of the most powerful men on the planet for some obscure reason and you stand in petrified terror before our leading scientist. You appear out of nowhere in Maxil's keeping, deliver me from evil, and now I understand that our noble Regent, who has kept remote from all permanent entanglements, has claimed you as his lady." He shook his head in mock consternation. "I can dismiss a good ninety percent of the talk about you as the fabrications of envy. I have a good idea of the basis for the antagonism, but I am at a complete loss to explain the terror."

I did not trust myself to answer him. Instead, I pulled out the slate Harlan had given me for him and thrust it across the table. Ferrill took it with a brief glance at the outer inscription and shoved it into his belt.

"Surely it's not restoration that makes you fear Monsorlit. The punishment is the same for the operator as the victim."

I looked nervously around to reassure myself no one could overhear us.

"As I told Monsorlit," Ferrill continued, "I am merely an interested bystander. I consider myself qualified to make all kinds of deep, penetrating observations which, to project my new image, I like to think are acute and perceptive. I have had much time for passive reflection, you know.

"Monsorlit is a great artist, a genius in his field. He is interested in achieving perfection, to which I say 'well done.' But he must have allowed himself to be carried away with his zeal, if he can be said ever to be carried away by anything." Ferrill's grin was a bit malicious. "For he neglected one axiom of nature . . . which prohibits her from duplicating anything . . . even two sides of the same face." He stopped and, narrowing his eyes, stared keenly at me. Pointing negligently to my wrists, he continued, "He was exceptionally deft in disguising the graft joints. I gather he has done a great deal of work on that crucial spot. But he made your features too symmetrical. If a mirror were handy, I could easily prove that both sides of your face are the same, except for your eyes. The left one droops a trifle at the outside edge. I wonder if that irked him in his search for perfection," and Ferrill chuckled. "However, if he had been able to change that, I do believe he would have ruined the total effect. That slight imperfection gives your face a touch of humanity it would otherwise lack."

I wasn't sure I understood all he was talking about. His tone was so light, so conversational, that his disclosures were robbed of their gravity.

"Still," and he frowned thoughtfully, "I doubt anyone has the time for the close scrutiny my conclusions require. And, since Monsorlit has conveniently done away with the one weak spot, the one detectable, unmistakable weakness in a total restoration, what do you have to fear?

"I should say he has proved his point. And Monsorlit doesn't care for the approbation of the multitude as long as he has satisfied his own curiosity. As you know, he has always maintained that restoration itself did not cause mental vegetation. As he expresses it," and Ferrill evidently did not agree completely with the theory, "it is our ancient fear and superstition that breaks the mind. He says we had so many centuries of passive acceptance of death under the godlike Mil that a man unconsciously wills himself to die when he is captured, whether his body dies or not."

His words began to make some reassuring sense to me and I started to relax. After all, Harlan had said that Ferrill was the only one who would or could understand and help me. Had he guessed that Ferrill knew I had been restored? At least, Ferrill did not regard me with horror and revulsion. I sipped my cup and the warm liquid ran down my throat, spreading its comfort to my fingers.

"That's better," Ferrill said with a grin. I realized he had been talking as much to put me at ease as to tell me of his theories.

"I gather," he continued, smiling, "Monsorlit's new techniques of shock treatments worked on you to bring you out of the mental death. You certainly are a far cry from the ghastly parodies that gave restoration its death sentence. I shall suggest to Harlan that he repeal that law quietly if you're the result of the latest techniques of restoration. Or should I say 'repossession'?" Ferrill's smile mocked the semantic hairsplitting. "So you see, you don't have anything to fear from Monsorlit. Anything."

"But I do," I protested. "He wants me to go back to that horrible Clinic of his. He said he'd *make* me if I didn't come willingly."

"He can do nothing to you," Ferrill said blithely. "For one thing ... well, Harlan knows you've been restored, doesn't he? Well, *he* won't permit it."

"But ... if Harlan doesn't ..." I stammered and couldn't finish the sentence.

Ferrill tapped his chest with a thin finger. "Then *I* won't let you go back. Oh, I may be a frail invalid, my dear, but I am still Ferrill," he announced, his voice ringing.

"I'm so terribly sorry ..." I began but Ferrill waggled an admonishing finger to silence me.

"At the risk of repetition, I owe you my life, Lady Sara, or whatever is left of it. Besides, I wouldn't be very good at that sort of thing," and his gesture indicated the spatial tank. "Now, Maxil, as is the habit of younger brothers, has always been a scrapper. You never saw a boy keener on spaceships. Right now, if he isn't free-fall sick, he's having the time of his life. By the way, there's Harlan on the screen now."

I rose hastily, peering over the obstructing partition for the best view of Harlan. I ignored Ferrill's chuckle.

Harlan was addressing his remarks to Stannall, Jokan and the elder Councilmen, continuing an argument that must have been going on for several minutes.

"Sir," said Harlan, stressing the title as one whose patience is also stressed, "I *know* it hasn't been tried before. But neither have we had the equipment or the emergency. I insist, and so do my commanders, that the gamble is worth the game. We are fortunate that so many of our ships were equipped with the electromagnetic crystals during my disability. We may thank Gorlot for that at least," and Harlan permitted himself a wry smile at the shocked distaste occasioned by his remark.

"That is enough to make me distrust that innovation completely," Stannall said stiffly, looking for agreement among his fellow Councilmen. Several of them sided with him by their nods of disapproval.

"You forget, sir," Jokan put in, defending a system he had developed, "that it was Harlan's innovation, a development of war research under my guidance. And you forget that it was Fathor who thought the Ertoi planetary defense mechanism might be adapted to shipborne armament. Gorlot was at least strategist enough to recognize its value as a weapon when no one else considered it more than a toy."

"Sir Harlan," expostulated Lesatin pompously, "a decision of this magnitude cannot be made in so off-hand a manner."

"By my Clan Mother," Harlan exploded, "your own committee of specialists approved the installation of the magnetos two years ago, Lesatin. Why all this time-consuming chatter? I've not asked for your decision. I've already made it for you. I'm telling you what I'm going to do. The battle plan remains as I have outlined it."

"The responsibility," Stannall said forcefully, "of the people lies on our shoulders, too, not yours alone. Your disregard of time-proved successful action . . ."

"Time-proved in the jetwash," snapped Harlan impatiently, "life-wasting, you mean. The resonant phenomenon produced by the electromagnets can crush the Mil with greater personnel safety, less risk and loss of ships and lives than any improvement in our battle tactics since we refitted the first Star-class ship. By all that lies in the stars, I will use the resonant barrage if we have to form before Lothar itself.

"What you grandly ignore, good sirs, in your preference for these time-proved orthodox methods is the plain and simple fact that we've never had such a concentration of Mil against us. You ignore the recorded facts that it takes the concerted action and an eighty-five percent casualty of twenty ships to disable . . . with luck . . . a Star-class vessel. We have *fifteen* out there in the black speeding toward our puny four Stars. And whether we form before Lothar or at the first circle of defense, the casualties from your 'time-proved tactics' will be the same."

Jokan had been writing furiously on a slate. He passed the results to the most disturbed Councilmen. They grouped around him, their voices rising in the excitement his figures aroused. Harlan glanced down at the confusion, at first with annoyance, until he saw the change of attitude in these skeptics.

"We are approaching communication limit. If I don't come back, you can skin me in effigy. If I do, it will be as a victorious commander and we'll debate the ethics involved. In the meantime, Jokan has as many answers as I since he's been in charge of the project. You have the benefit of his talents and I do not. Jokan, jet it into their thick heads, will you?" Harlan urged. "I'll beam you at zero hour and, unless you like the noise, you'd better cut the sound on all screens," he warned.

"You technicians got the spatial coordinates now?" he asked the clerks in the banks around the tank. They raised right hands in reply. Harlan's eyes left the immediate foreground and scanned the space above the Councilmen's heads. I made myself as tall as I could in the hope he might be looking for me, but the expression on his face, set, cold, tired, did not change. The picture began to waver. Harlan looked off to his right in the control room, then back to the Councilmen.

"We're at the limits, sirs. My respects to you all," and the picture dissolved into blurs.

The droning voice had ended, too. The big room was strangely silent for what seemed a long, long time. As if everyone found the quiet unbearable, everyone began to talk at once. The Councilmen turned on Jokan with intense expressions and garrulous queries. Messengers began to move back and forth around the room. I sat down, confused by all the discussion and disheartened by its tone. Ferrill appeared disinterested and I drew some courage from his attitude.

"What was that all about?" I asked, abandoning any pretense of knowledge.

My request did not surprise Ferrill. He leaned forward, planting his forearms on the table comfortably as he enlightened me.

"The Ertois are workers of crystal and quartzite. They had developed a primitive form of energy, electricity, they called it, long before the Mil descended on them. Our force screens are an adaption of their electricity. They discovered, by what freak chance I don't remember, that the Mil cannot stand electrical currents or sonic vibrations. They ringed their planet with gigantic electromagnetos, activating them in case of Mil attack. The metal of the Mil ships became a conductor and the Mil were electrocuted. Now, we had to figure a way to adapt this principle to use in space. Sound doesn't travel in the vacuum, of course, but regulate the frequency of the electromagnetic radiation and you produce a resonant phenomenon in the ship hulls that literally tears the Mil cell from cell. Ironically, though the Mil are much larger than we, they are easy victims to a weapon that we can endure.

"My father was very interested in this application of resonators. You see, we've never had an offensive weapon. That's why our casualties have always been so high. The only advantage we have had over the Mil in battle has been our ability to take higher accelerations and make sharper maneuvers. It's a pretty slim advantage.

"This project has been going on for several decades. It's been expensive and was discontinued when Fathor died. Council had an attack of conservatism and the Mil were quiet on the Rim. Harlan reinstated the project under Jokan who is one of our few creative geniuses.

"The reason our skeptics have been so upset is that they have never seen what the resonators can do to a simulated Mil protoplasm. I have seen it and, granted it was under ideal laboratory conditions, the results were incredible." His eyes narrowed. "There is a minor theory going around, which I am inclined to support, that Gorlot used the resonators to herd the Mil into Tane. It's the only way he could have managed to control their direction."

"Why didn't Harlan mention that?" I asked. "Didn't he know?"

Ferrill shrugged. "Where the Mil are concerned, logic is sometimes useless. Particularly right now. Look what's happened. The Mil have actually been allowed past the Perimeter. They have been allowed to wipe out an entire race. For seventy-five years, they haven't been able to penetrate the Rim defenses for more than a few parsecs.

"Our ancestors were used to the menace of the Mil in their skies. As accustomed as one is able to get to such a thought. But we aren't. Stannall may be our leading Councilman and a very intelligent fellow, but the mere thought of the possibility of the Mil coming back into Lotharian skies turns him into a quivering mass of ancient fears and superstition. And Harlan has just blithely assured him that he will wait to reform before Lothar itself in order to test this new weapon!"

"Why does he have to wait?" I asked confused.

"Because, Lady Sara," Ferrill explained patiently, "the beam attenuates with distance, losing its strength. The maximum effect is gained at close quarters—spatially speaking—from an encirclement, so that each resonator is equidistant from the target, setting up the resonating phenomenon at maximum efficiency."

"If they can't encircle?" I asked, perceiving some of the dread with which Stannall and the others received Harlan's gamble.

"The usual tactics, only we will have a ringside seat," and Ferrill gestured heavenward.

"What *are* the usual tactics?" I insisted.

Ferrill regarded me seriously for a moment.

"You really don't know, do you?" he remarked with amazement. "We have discovered only two ways to dispose of a Mil ship. Both are dangerous to the attacker because we lack an offensive weapon other than speed and maneuverability. We must either knock out their control room, which means a close-range assault with nucleonic weapons that match theirs, or we must make a direct hit on their fuel source. The first is preferable because it leaves us a new recruit for our fleet . . . after decontamination, of course. The second method blows up the ship."

"You heard Harlan mention eighty-five percent casualties, didn't you?" Ferrill continued and I nodded. "He means just that. There are only four Star-class cruisers in our fleet, eighty-five planet weight and forty satellite variety plus about fifty rider suicide ships. Figure out your eighty-five percent against a force of twenty-three Mil ships, *fifteen* of them Star-class and you can see why Harlan is going to gamble on our new offensive weapon."

My mental arithmetic was not up to estimating the odds, but eight-five percent was obviously a Pyrrhic victory.

"Back in my great-grandfather's day, we once had a force against us of one Star-class, four planet and a satellite. We had, at the time, eighty ships. Nine returned. We disabled two planet-types and the satellite. That was the biggest force we have ever attacked until now. The Mil usually send a group of planets and satellites. With their consistent losses in this area of the Great Starry Wheel, you'd think the Mil would have left us alone long ago."

"You mean some of their ships still get through?"

Ferrill looked startled. "No! We destroy enough so that they retreat. But there is always a terrific loss of life for us.

"To knock out the control room, a suicide rider with nine men must approach to maximum penetration range of the nuclear missiles. That's about one hundred land miles. That's too close to a Mil, believe me. The ships are nothing but speed and one long cannon. Their success depends jointly on the skill and diversionary tactics of the pilot and the accuracy of the gunner. Very often, the suiciders are crushed by the impact of their own blast. All too often, the Mil gunners get the range first. And sometimes," and Ferrill shuddered, "the riders are grappled and pulled inboard. Even if we do disable the Mil ship, those men are lost."

"Why?" I asked without thinking.

Ferrill clicked his tongue at me. "One, if the men haven't as yet been touched, they've gone mad by the time we reach them. Two, if they have been skinned, Council's edict about restoration makes euthanasia imperative."

"Skinned," he had said. I had been "skinned," alive! I fought the rising nausea and the shaking that gripped my diaphragm.

"I'll wager that's why!" Ferrill said with a note of triumph in his voice.

"Why what?" I managed to say, pushing to the back of my mind his last words.

"Why Monsorlit tied in with Gorlot"; and he leaned forward so that our conversation could not be overheard. "Gorlot knew some ships and men would fall into Mil hands. He had to have someone make perfect restorations on the victims so they would seem to be no more than Tane casualties. And Monsorlit went one step better. He pulled those restorees out of shock so there could be no suspicion whatever of the men having been Mil victims. To prove his point, Monsorlit would take a far greater risk."

"I'll tell Harlan you're trying to dishonor his claim," said Jokan's voice behind me.

Ferrill grinned up at his uncle with a deprecating laugh. Jokan pulled up a chair and signaled a server.

"Did you manage to reassure the skeptics?" Ferrill demanded with an affectation of disinterest.

Jokan shrugged expressively and threw the slate he carried toward Ferrill who cocked his head sideways to read the slate without having to pick it up.

"The odds *are* favorable," he said with some surprise. "Even if a trifle close to home. Don't they see that?"

"What they see is the space tank and the proximity of the Mil to Lothar," Jokan scoffed. "I believe the older one gets the more the fears and superstitions we should have abandoned centuries ago cloud the thinking."

"Don't they realize that the older one gets the less valuable he becomes to the Mil?" Ferrill pointed out cold-bloodedly. "No fat. No meat. No smooth hide."

Jokan did not hide his distaste of Ferrill's observation.

"I'm not concerned," he said stiffly. Then grinned as he added, "But then, I'm under the largest pile of reinforced rock and metal on the planet. I also remind myself what the resonators can do to the Mil . . ."

"Under ideal laboratory conditions," Ferrill inserted maliciously.

"Under ideal laboratory conditions," Jokan assented without rancor, "which Harlan, with the reinforcement of the Ertoi and Glan, can reproduce."

"If the Ertoi and Glan arrive in time," Ferrill amended.

Jokan's eyes sparkled angrily. "Are you through qualifying the odds against us?"

Ferrill flashed a look at Jokan but thought better of what he was about to say and hitched one shoulder negligently.

"I'm realistic, my dear uncle. Also I find an element of humor in the situation."

Jokan snorted with disgust at this observation.

"Your humor was never so warped before, my dear nephew."

"Nor was my life," Ferrill added quietly, then added too brightly, "Monsorlit has been frightening Harlan's Sara."

"Ha. He's in no position to frighten anyone. Stannall's after him again. Monsorlit had best look to his own defense. And you have the strongest protection, Lady Sara," Jokan said stoutly.

He had finished his quick meal as we talked and now rose.

"You two can exchange insults, if you wish," he said as he glanced at the large time dial above the space tank, "but there are precisely eight hours and thirty-two seconds before encirclement and I intend to use it in sleeping. I relinquish our mutual ward into your safekeeping, Ferrill." He bowed to the ex-Warlord and then to me, with a touch of his old insouciance, and departed.

"He's sure about Stannall being after Monsorlit?" I asked hopefully.

Ferrill shrugged. "Stannall has been after Monsorlit for years. Never did know why. Some old quarrel. Stannall has a capacity for grudges that is astonishing."

"Didn't I hear Jokan call you nephew?" I asked after a pause.

"He is, after all, my uncle."

"Well, why isn't he a candidate for Warlord, instead of Maxil?"

"He and Harlan are only half-brothers to my father, Fathor. But you should remember that only my father's line can inherit under the old laws. If Fathor had died without issue, and he certainly waited long enough to claim his lady, it would have been different. It's a pity, too, because Jokan shows the real Harlan strain."

"Doesn't Harlan?" I demanded, piqued.

Ferrill chuckled and I realized his omission had been intentional. "Obviously. But Harlan's real mission in life is to find more and more new planets. The Tane success went to his head. He's got jet-itch. Besides he's got nowhere near the deviousness of Jokan."

"Then," I demanded, confused by the intricacies of Lotharian governmental structure, "why wasn't Jokan made Regent instead of Harlan?"

Patiently Ferrill explained that Harlan had been a Perimeter Commander. Jokan had never reached that rank nor intended to. Unfortunately, such military experience was the prime requisite for the Regency.

"Is that how Gorlot got in instead of Jokan when Harlan was drugged?"

"Naturally," Ferrill assented, his eyes glittering angrily. "The system has too many faults and this affair should make it obvious to the Council that a revision of the old laws must be made. We are too hampered by age-old superstition and pre-Perimeter contingencies." He snorted derisively. "It's absurd to assume that only a direct descendant of the original Harlan can lead us to victory over the Mil. It's ridiculous to bind the genius of modern military tactics to planet-bound traditions. Just like that argument over there!" and he indicated the group of Councilmen arguing vehemently around the space tank.

"Would they really censure Harlan for disregarding them?"

"How can they?" Ferrill scoffed. "At the moment, he *is* Warlord. That's why he was picked as Regent, in the event of a military emergency an inexperienced stripling could not handle. His plan is law: it's just typical of Harlan to wish to have Stannall's agreement. It *is* preferable to have the First Councilman agree with you if you are Regent or Warlord."

He rose abruptly.

"Jokan's suggestion is contagious. We've hours yet before the crucial test of Harlan's revolutionary tactics. Sleep passes time admirably. But first, join me for a glance at the tank?"

Ferrill and I stood a little removed from the others. He rightly assumed I needed an explanation. The science behind the tank's projection he did not bother to expatiate. Its physical presence, however, was awesome enough. It was composed of an amber, transparent liquid or gas with no apparent material enclosing its circumference. It stood ten feet high and wide in the center of the room it dominated. A coil of wires at its foot was the sole connection to the machines and computers that formed a semicircle at its base. Beyond them, built obliquely from the ceiling, were the now blank screens. Only one panel on the boards below the screens was active, the master panel to which each ship in action was hooked. If the light which identified the ship went out, the ship had been destroyed. The technician could also tell by the color variation and pulsations the extent, in theory, of damage to any given vessel. At the computers the clerks were still busy. In all the room, no one's eyes stayed long away from the mesmeric quality of the slowly moving masses in the tank.

Guardedly Ferrill indicated Lothar, a green ball in the approximate center of the tank. Above and beyond were Ertoi in blue and Glan's yellow. Below and away from the other three systems was the red of the two Tane planets.

From Ertoi and Glan, lancing downward and bypassing Lothar were the light points of the Alliance ships, speeding to their rendezvous with Lothar's fleet. Beyond Ertoi and Glan, I saw eight tiny points of light at regular intervals; far, far apart. Ferrill said they were the skeletal Perimeter Patrol that would be all Glan would have to defend it from the Mil if they broke through. Ertoi relied still on its sonic barrier.

"Why doesn't Glan have it, too?" I asked, thinking that would have freed eight more ships.

"They never considered it necessary with the protection the Alliance has afforded them up till now."

Speeding out from Lothar and converging from other points around the remaining quadrants of the tank was the fleet, moving not as swiftly as the Alliance ships but as inexorably. From the bottom of the tank, approaching with what I thought appalling comparative speed were the invading lights of the Mil. The alarm of the Councilmen was no longer a verbal fear that Jokan's assurances and Ferrill's amused air could dispel. It took no technician to estimate how near to Lothar that battle would take place. And the Mil's ominous approach was aimed at the equator of the seemingly doomed Tanes.

"Would the Mil land on one of the Tane?" I asked.

Ferrill shook his head in a quick negative response.

"The Mil would never land with such a force approaching them. They could be blown off a planet and our casualties would be light. We overused those tactics a few centuries ago. No. They'll meet Harlan in space. They're pretty contemptuous of us in space, you know. I doubt they'll remain so long."

We watched, as others did, in hypnotized silence as the blinking lights made their almost imperceptible way. Finally, Ferrill touched my arm lightly and we both retired to our sleeping quarters.

CHAPTER SIXTEEN

A GENTLE TICKLING ON MY FEET roused me. The room was lit and I could see Ferrill grinning mischievously as he gave my foot one last brush.

"I used to wake Cherez like that and she'd throw a fit," he grinned. "I thought you'd like to be in on the fun. Harlan's brave gamble is about to start."

I scrambled out of the cot, took time to dash cold water in my eyes and comb back my hair before joining Ferrill. I wouldn't have needed Ferrill's comment to know that the climax was at hand. The entire room watched the screen, some standing on chairs or desks for better views of the all-important spatial tank. The computers were silent. Conversation was limited to terse low whispers. The tension, fear and apprehension in the main room was like a physical blow after the sleeping quarters. Ferrill had paused at the threshold and we both drifted through the watchers until we found Jokan. He was standing behind Stannall and Lesatin. Jokan looked around irritably as I brushed against him to make way for Ferrill. He gave us the sketchiest of acknowledgments before turning back to the tank.

I had to make myself look at the sphere. Its story dried up the saliva in my mouth. I was certain the pounding of my heart would be audible.

Tane had been bypassed. Empty space separated the straggling Lotharian space fleet from the home planet. The blips of light that were our defenders resembled a tiny crystal string of beads thrown casually on a jeweler's velvet around a pendant of twenty-three bright diamonds in random pattern. The beads circumscribed no circle; one end, the Ertoi and Glan contingent being too far out to complete even the roughest circular formation. Ferrill's groan was not noted by anyone.

At first I wondered why the Mil would let themselves

be even so loosely encircled. Then I remembered that the Mil in space would wreak terrible losses, so they could be arrogant about our puny trap. I watched the beads, still loose, but slowly, slowly perfecting their circle. They drifted at the same time with such snail slowness toward Lothar. Ertoi and Glan became stationary, being uppermost to Lothar; below and beyond it, I could see the barely larger blips that were the four Star-class Lothar battlewagons in their major compass-point positions. The pendant moved inexorably and the rear quadrants moved still closer, the uneven beads gradually, gradually settling into a rough circle.

I had been so fascinated with the fleet movement that I had not noticed the movements of the Mil pendant. Once a mass of light, it now began to lose its compactness and to string out into a rough line.

Jokan groaned and twisted his tense body in an unconscious effort to bunch the Mil ships back into their former position. Stannall covered his face for a moment, with a shaking hand. When he turned to Jokan, I was aghast at the exhaustion and hopelessness of his expression.

"That maneuver, doesn't it decrease the effectiveness of the resonant barrage?" he asked, hoping to hear the contrary.

"It depends, sir, it all depends."

"On what?" Stannall demanded fiercely.

"On how much our men can stand of the backlash from the electromagnetos that generate the resonance. If we can saturate the Mil ships with enough force, their belated dispersal means nothing." Jokan clenched his jaws grimly. "I *wish* we had had time to develop effective shielding for the power-bleed. At the moment," he continued in answer to Stannall, "we can be sure of this section being completely paralyzed," and his finger stabbed at the center of the Mil pendant. "Partial disability on either end and, with luck, our normal tactics can take care of the rest."

"If they string out farther?" Stannall dragged the words from his mouth.

"The decrease in total disability is proportional. Individual engagements increase."

Stannall's expression was desperate and his lips, thinned by fatigue to white lines, closed obdurately over his teeth.

We waited. Glances at the time dial were more frequent. It lacked but a few moments of the hour set for the barrage. Jokan was counting off nervously to himself and someone else on the other side of the room counted out loud. I was not the only one to mouth the seconds in concert.

Zero hour!

The tank remained unchanged. I don't know what I expected to happen. How much of a time lag there was between the ships and the tank I didn't know but the next moments or minutes seemed eternities.

A new voice broke the stillness. Glancing up I saw that a patroller was standing before the master panel that checked the condition of the ships. His voice, dispassionate and measured, brought us no consolation.

"No casualties. Two minutes and no casualties. All ships functioning. Three minutes and no casualties."

No casualties, my brain echoed. What an odd war. Bloodless, remotely fought, remotely observed. Would death, too, seem remote to the dying? Fear, however, was not remote. It laid lavish hands on everyone in that room, on everyone, I was sure, on those ships and on the planet of Lothar.

"No casualties," the drone continued.

The intervals between his litany lengthened and suddenly, unable to watch the unchanged picture longer, Stannall whirled on Jokan.

"Nothing has happened. How long does it take?" he cried in tense, strident tones that echoed through the fear-filled room with piercing audibility. Someone started to sob and stopped, choking the sound back.

"The maximum vibrations for the Mil should build in no less than six minutes," Jokan said tonelessly. "The beam is played across the ship for maximum effect. We count on the fact that the Mil cannot initiate evasive tactics at high acceleration speeds as we can. The longer they remain within the effective range of the beam, the quicker the resultant destructive resonance is reached."

Someone was counting the seconds again. Still the formation of the ships, all the ships, remained the same, a circle of beads tightening slowly around the menacing gaggle of Mil ships. The man had counted to ten minutes past the zero hour before a voice, in the anguish of waiting, shrieked for him to stop. The circle of beads tightened, drifting ever upward toward the system of Lothar.

"It isn't working, that's what's wrong," a beefy Councilman snapped, his voice trembling. "That puny electricity doesn't work. Fathor stopped that research. He must have had a reason. They don't work, that's what, and we'll all . . ."

"All ships functioning," the official voice, calm and deliberate, broke in. "No casualties."

"Look, look," someone cried, gesticulating toward the tank.

The string of beads was breaking up, splitting into smaller circles, driving for the ends of the Mil line.

"They're using the suicide ships now. The resonators didn't work at all. We're lost. The Mil will be here," a man beyond Stannall blubbered.

Stannall strode to his side in three swift paces and, although the fellow was younger and heavier, the First Councilman fetched him four sharp cracks across the face and turned defiantly to face the room.

"If the Mil should come, we will be ready with the courage and fortitude which have brought us so far along the road to freedom from their awful raiding. Let no one else forget his valiant heritage."

"One suicide ship casualty," the announcer droned. "All others functioning."

On the tank, a small expanding glow appeared and then one bead blinked out. One light obediently darkened on the master panel. But the tank also told another story. The midsection of the Mil line proceeded unharried by the ships which concentrated their efforts on the ends. The tiniest blips flashed in with unbelievable speed compared with the lumbering efforts of others. The upper end reflected a brief glow and the announcer tallied another casualty.

"They're attacking only the ends," someone cried in dismay. "The rest are coming straight at us."

"NO!" shouted Jokan, his voice ringing with triumph. He sprang to the side of the spatial tank. "The midsection is totally disabled. The resonators did their work. Look, would that big a detachment allow the others to be attacked without firing? See, here, here and here, our positions would be vulnerable to their range and yet there are no casualties. I tell you, that weapon works. It does. It does! And see, there's one of the lead Mil ships going up."

One of the larger Mil lights at the head of the line flared and died. The announcer gave us no death notice for a defender.

"See what Harlan is doing," Jokan continued excitedly. "We have plenty of time to disable the far end. He's tried two passes with the riders to the foremost Mil and is blasting them out of the sky. That means they must be partially disabled. No Mil will set down on Lothar!" His words rang through the big room and set off a cheering, shouting, weeping roar of hysterical relief. Jokan, grinning so broadly his face seemed to split, tears in his eyes, looked around, thrilled at the sight of hope where despair had so long enervated morale.

I, too, was caught up in the emotional backlash, weeping not so much with the relief of salvation as with the knowledge that Harlan would return, in honor and unharmed. The fear of the others did not touch me as deeply, I suppose, because I had not lived with fear of the Mil all my life. Vicariously I was caught up in that joyous hysteria until I noticed Stannall. He was clutching wildly at his chest. His face was gray, his lips blue, his breath shallow, eyes pain-filled and he grabbed wildly at me in his weakness.

Glancing around for someone else to help me, I was even grateful to Monsorlit who must have seen Stannall's seizure from across the room. The physician was fumbling in his belt as he pushed through the milling, shouting, jumping men. He reached us, jammed a hypodermic needle into Stannall's arm and smoothly reinforced my grip around the First Councilman.

Jokan, aware of Stannall's distress, pushed through and lifted Stannall easily into his arms. Bawling for passage, he carried the ailing Councilman to his sleeping room. Monsorlit ordered me to get his instruments from Room 12 and I ran with no respect for dignities.

When I returned with the case, Stannall was pillowed into a sitting position. Although he was sweating profusely, his breath came with less effort. Monsorlit grabbed the bag I opened and seized a stethoscopic device. Jokan was joined by Ferrill now. Monsorlit's examination relieved him, for he gave a barely audible sigh and reached with less haste for his bag. He picked a vial carefully, filled a new needle and administered the medication.

"Good sir," Monsorlit said in such low tones only I could hear, "there are too few of your fiber for us to be deprived of you. This time you will have to listen to me."

He rose from the bedside and, as he turned, I caught the flickering of the only expression I ever saw on Monsorlit's face. It was the more astonishing to me, this combination of fear, relief, worry and compassion, since there was no doubt of Stannall's trenchant disapproval of Monsorlit. The physician glanced at me briefly, his features composed in their usual coldness. He passed me and motioned all of us out to the corridor.

Ferrill and Jokan, instantly the door closed, demanded the diagnosis with impatient concern.

"A heart attack," Monsorlit said dispassionately, replacing his stethoscope with care, rearranging a vial or two precisely before closing the bag. "Natural enough with such intense strain and inadequate rest. I've administered a sedative that should keep him asleep for many hours. He must be kept absolutely quiet for the next weeks and complete bedrest is indicated for the next few months. Or, we shall have to elect a new First Councilman. I believe Cordan is his personal physician. He should attend our

Council Leader immediately. To reassure all of us." Monsorlit permitted himself the vaguest of wry grins at his afterthought.

"But Stannall's presence is . . ." Jokan began, gesturing toward the tank.

". . . is required in his bed and asleep," Monsorlit finished with bland authority. "I do not care what duties he leaves unfinished. There are certainly enough qualified men to make decisions until Harlan returns. Unless, of course, you wish to commit Stannall to the Eternal Flame tomorrow?"

With that, Monsorlit turned on his heel and walked away.

By now the jubilation had subsided sufficiently for the drone of the announcer to be heard. The score of casualties had mounted, but only nine lights were out on the master panel. Two flickered weakly, eight pulsed, but the strength of the light indicated only minor damage. Jokan, after a glance at the picture in the tank, strode across the room to the knot of anxious Councilmen. Stannall's collapse had been noted as well as the exchange between Jokan and Monsorlit.

"I think," commented Ferrill thoughtfully, "that the situation is now under the efficient control of Jokan. Will you join me for some refreshment, Lady Sara?"

"Shouldn't someone stay with Stannall?" I protested.

"Monsorlit seems to have taken that into account," Ferrill said and directed my attention to the brisk figure coming from the farthest sleeping rooms. The woman, a large, efficient-looking person, stopped at Stannall's door. She opened it with a quick practiced gesture and entered. A pair of guards simultaneously took positions on either side of the door.

There was little time for Ferrill and me to refresh ourselves. Food and drink grew cold before we could eat. Ferrill, though no longer Warlord, still had all the knowledge of his former position. He was, furthermore, privy to the confidential matters of the high position and the offices of both Regent and First Councilmen. In this emergency he set aside his affectation of disinterest and made quick, clear decisions, gave orders with an easy authority that controlled the quick-tempered and calmed the hysterical. Messengers crowded around the table, waiting turn. Councilmen opportuned and only Jokan could claim precedence. The little people, too—messengers and technicians—stopped to ask about Stannall or say something, shyly, to Ferrill.

Ferrill remained cool and detached, casual and unconcerned by the rush. At first, he answered the Councilmen's and Jokan's questions with a little self-amused smile. But gradually, I could see the grayness of fatigue conquering the slight color in his face. I urged him anxiously to rest.

"Rest? Not now, Sara. I want to know every detail of the stimulating events. I shall record them in a personal history I shall now have time to write. The firsthand impressions of an ex-Warlord about an emergency and triumph of this magnitude will certainly carry historical weight."

"If you're not careful, the only historical weight you'll carry is a fancy monument," I snapped.

He regarded me with the expression he had used so effectively on Monsorlit, but I was too concerned for him and stared him down. He changed his tactics and reassured me that he knew the limits of his strength.

"I have made no move from this table. I let everyone seek me."

"I thought you didn't care anymore. I thought you were just going to be the bystander," I goaded him.

His eyes flashed angrily. Then he smiled in recognition of my baiting. He reached for my hand and pressed it firmly.

"I *am* still the bystander, shoveling out bystandorial advice by the shipload. But I am the only one who can answer many of these questions in Stannall's absence. Jokan certainly has no practical experience as either Warlord, Regent or First Councilman, and he is all three right now."

I made one of the messengers go for Monsorlit who appeared just as Jokan also reached our table. Jokan did not care for Monsorlit's presence. Ferrill's smile mocked me for my interference.

"Ferrill is exhausted," I said before Ferrill or Jokan could send Monsorlit away.

"Give me a shot of something salutary," Ferrill commanded the physician, proffering his thin, blue-veined arm, daring Monsorlit as well as Jokan and me.

"All of you need stimulants to keep on at this pace," the man observed quietly and issued us five tablets apiece. "An effective compound but harmless," he continued as Jokan eyed the pills dubiously. "One every three hours will be sufficient. I do not recommend taking more than five. That gives you fifteen more hours of peak efficiency. Then no one will have trouble getting you to rest."

He moved off briskly. Ferrill took his pill down quickly and Jokan, shrugging, followed his lead. I waited and then saw Ferrill watching my indecision with such amusement I tossed it down waterless.

"I never really know what to make of him," the ex-Warlord commented to no one in particular.

Jokan uttered a growling sound deep in his throat and then launched into the reason for his coming to the table.

Monsorlit did not underestimate his potion. It did keep us going for the next fifteen hours. I watched Jokan and Ferrill as their eyes brightened, reddened and teared with fatigue, knowing I was no better off. Jokan took to shouting for me if he could not come to us and I became a liaison between Jokan and Ferrill.

As I listened to conversations concerning the resumption of the planet's normal activities, the hurried rearrangements of landing facilities and refueling schedules, I watched the tank. Everyone did. And I, too, did not push the announcer's assessments of the casualties from my conscious hearing. On the tank, I saw the midsection of the Mil fleet continue blindly on its course for nowhere while Lothar picked off additional enemies. I watched as the helpless section was set upon by a double row of our vessels, turned into a new course as Ertoi and Glan pilots penetrated to the control rooms and altered the courses for the naval satellite bases and the one planetary space installation in the southern sea. Landed, decontaminated, the ships would ultimately be refitted and recommissioned into the Alliance force. I saw other Mil ships join this passive group. I saw a Lothar squadron drop down and turn toward the rim of the spatial tank, taking up Perimeter positions until it seemed that the tank was lightly sprinkled with diamond beading on its periphery. I watched as the main body of the fleet turned homeward, catching and passing the convoy of cripples, pushing on toward Lothar. Then I, too, turned my hopeful attention to the screens, waiting for the time when the communication limit was reached and we might have a detailed description of the victory from her triumphant commander.

Of the great navy that had set out to meet the invader, only twelve were not returning, a statistic which brought another wild burst of exultation. Of the twenty-three invaders, once arrogant and feared, nineteen were carefully shepherded toward exile. Never, never, I heard it shouted, had so great a victory been achieved in the annals of recorded history. And, to crown this feat with more glory, fourteen of the fifteen Star-class ships had been taken.

Now we waited, as we had waited for particular moments so often these last violent days, for the screens to reflect the images we wished most to see. So tensely was the first ripple anticipated, a concerted gasp echoed in the room when the picture was abruptly before us, clear and unmuddied.

It was Maxil we saw; a Maxil as changed as only a boy can be who has abruptly survived a brutal initiation to manhood. His voice, harsh with fatigue and physical strain, broke the communication silence. Harlan was nowhere in sight.

"Men and women of Lothar, I bring you victory. I bring home all but twelve of our valiant ships. I bring you news of an offensive weapon against which the Mil have been powerless. The day is not distant when we can reach out and find the home of these vicious marauders and destroy them forever."

But where is Harlan? I whispered to myself.

Maxil paused and licked his lips, glancing off to his right. Then he smiled and continued.

"I am not responsible for this victory. I doubt any of us would have returned today if it had not been for Harlan. He's done the impossible today. He has made the Mil fear *us*. All Lothar must recognize their debt to him."

A cheer, as loud and sincere as it was spontaneous, sprang from the throats of the watchers as Maxil pulled a reluctant Regent to his side.

I could see how tired Harlan was, his shoulders slumped down even as he tried to hold himself erect. His shipsuit was mottled with a white dust, and it was torn at the sleeve. I saw no sign of damage in the control room, but other officers coming and going in the background wore torn or burned tunics as well as bandages. But Harlan was all right.

"I don't see Sir Stannall, my lord," Harlan commented.

Maxil peered out at the crowd and frowned. Jokan stepped forward and formally bowing to the young Warlord, explained the circumstances. Jokan continued to advise what had been done, Maxil and Harlan both questioning and advising further steps.

I don't recall much of what they said. I was content to look at Harlan and know he was safe and coming back. The multiple perils that threatened were dispersing: Gorlot's perfidy, the Mil, and now Stannall was sick. He couldn't resume his deadly questioning so I needn't fear his drive for revenge on Monsorlit. I only had the physician to deal with and Harlan would never let him overwhelm me. A weary exultation filled my tired body. Even the ghastly announcement that Gorlot, chained to the Rock for the Mil as their traditional first victim should they arrive, had been hacked to pieces alive by hysterical Lotharians did not touch me.

The reprieve from fatigue granted by Monsorlit's pellets expired all at once. I was weary to the very marrow of my bones. I turned from the screen that no longer held Harlan. Ferrill had fallen forward across the table, unnoticed by anyone. I touched his hand, fearfully. It was damp with perspiration, but the slow pulse was steady in his wrist. I sat looking at him for a little while, I think. Then it occurred to me that I should get someone to take him to bed, but I didn't have the energy to open my mouth to call. So I put my head down on the table, too.

CHAPTER SEVENTEEN

I DID NOT SEE THE victorious return of Lothar's flagship. Nor did I see the triumphant parade of Maxil and Harlan back to the palace. I did not see Maxil publicly acclaim Fara as his lady from the balcony of his apartment. My presence there might not have been appreciated by the public. I did not see Harlan and that I cared about. I should have given him a proper soldier's welcome. But I was dead to the world and so were Ferrill and Jokan. Monsorlit had threatened the servants with dire vengeance if they did attempt to wake us.

What finally awoke me was, as usual, hunger. What roused me was the unfamiliarity of my surroundings. The dim room appeared to be all wrong to my sleep-dulled faculties. For one thing, the balcony was to the left of my bed instead of to the right. For another, the window hangings were a deep crimson. The furnishings, the heavy chairs and chests, were the wrong shapes and there were enormous shields on the walls, their metallic designs picking up what light there was. A gentle snuffling set me bolt upright in the bed reaching for the light panel in the headboard. The soft glow fell on Harlan's sleeping face and I immediately waved it off. Exhaustion was etched deeply on his face. He had fallen on to bed, still dressed in the torn, creased shipsuit. His right arm dangled in the air above the floor and his right leg was off the bed entirely.

I hoped he had seen me before he fell into unconsciousness, that he at least knew I was here, where I belonged. It worried me that he might have felt I slighted him by not being a part of the welcome he was certainly due.

My eyes accustomed themselves to the dim room and I looked down at the tired warrior. How often I'd looked at his sleeping figure in the asylum, wondering what he was really like. I certainly had had more of his unconscious

company than was necessary. There was so much I
wanted to know about this man. One day, we would both
have to make time to be together when both of us were
awake, in the same room, at the same time.

My hunger could no longer be denied. I eased out of
the bed, a needless caution with Harlan in the depths of
the deepest sleep of exhaustion. He'd wake soon, uncomfortable in that awkward position, I decided. Placing his
arm across his chest, I turned him so that all of his body
was supported by the bed. I removed his boots, loosened
his shipsuit and covered him.

I found the bathroom and discovered that my clothes
had again followed me while I played suite hopscotch
around the palace wing. I dressed quickly and went out
into the next room.

This was a study, deserted but apparently well-used by
Harlan to judge from the clutter of slates and film cans.
As I reached the door in the far wall I heard the subdued
mutter of voices.

"*I* received *my* orders from Harlan himself," an irate
man in patrol uniform was saying to Jokan who had
placed himself between the patroller and the door to the
study.

"Harlan is *not* to be wakened," Jokan was saying
firmly. The Patrolman saw me at the door and tried to
edge around Jokan.

"Lady Sara, is the Regent awake?"

Jokan gave me a quick high-sign.

"No, sir, he is not! Nor could anything wake him. He
is completely dead to the world and will be for some hours
more, I'm sure," I said with a firmness that matched
Jokan's.

"My orders were definite," the poor officer kept insisting desperately.

"I'm sorry, sir," I replied unapologetically. "But I cannot feel that there is any matter so urgent that it needs the
attention of an exhausted man. Surely Jokan here, who is
alternate Regent . . ."

The officer was adamant.

"No, my orders are for the Regent only."

"Well, you may certainly join us while we wait," Jokan suggested amiably. He took the officer by the arm and led him, resisting all the way, to the far side of the living room.

The two Councilmen and Jessl at the breakfast table rose as I approached. Linnana came bustling in from the pantry, wreathed with smiles and looking very well pleased with herself. She greeted me effusively and set my hot cup down in front of me.

"Hungry, Sara?" Jokan said with good-natured raillery.

"I still have several weeks of eating to make up," I replied tartly. "And I don't think I ever will."

"You missed all the excitement," one of the Councilmen said.

"A matter of opinion. The Vaults were exciting enough for one lifetime. I was never so tired in my life as I was last night," I declared.

Jokan exchanged amused glances with Jessl and Linnana giggled.

"You mean the day before yesterday," Jokan corrected me.

I stared at him, suspecting him of teasing. But everyone else was grinning at my disbelief.

"I was very tired," I repeated emphatically, refusing to be annoyed. "No wonder I'm so hungry. I've missed eight meals," I exclaimed suddenly.

Even the thwarted officer joined in the laughter.

"Don't worry. There are films to be seen."

"Then when," I asked with concern, "did Harlan get to bed?"

"Approximately six hours ago," Jokan said with a nasty look at the officer who squirmed on his seat uncomfortably. "He and Maxil got in about sixteen hours ago. The rest of the fleet keeps trailing in." He continued, nodding toward the crisscrossing of plume trails in the sky. "Harlan and Maxil were touched, patted, kissed by everyone in Lothar. I'm surprised the noise didn't wake you."

"Barbarous not to let him rest sooner. He must have

been weaving for lack of sleep," I exclaimed, outraged. "Why wasn't I wakened? I'd've . . ."

"We had our orders about you, too," Jokan laughed, his eyes dancing wickedly. "From Monsorlit."

I hastily covered the initial start his name gave me.

"Did you explain to Harlan why I . . ."

"Several times," Jokan assured me dryly. Jessl snorted his disgust. "He insisted on seeing both you and Ferrill. But he woke *me* up!" Jokan looked so sour I couldn't help laughing.

If I hadn't been so shocked by the fatigue in Harlan's face, I would have taken pity on the officer during the long hours that followed. He sat stolidly, watching the door and waiting. Not all Jokan's cajoling could budge him from his post or elicit the message he brought. We finally gave up.

About noontime, Maxil came in. He looked tired still, the shadows of his grueling experience lurking in his eyes but his step was resilient. He gave me a glad smile and took both my hands in his, squeezing them affectionately.

"We missed you. Harlan was fit to be tied," he said. "Made everyone wait while he checked with Monsorlit about you and Ferrill. Oh, and Stannall, too. Did you know about Fara and me?"

"That's all I heard about the first day in the Vaults," I said.

"Yes, I guess so," and Maxil, although he looked sheepish, did not blush. We had strolled over to the balcony, apart from the others.

"That Harlan's got real nerve," Maxil said quietly, slamming one fist in the palm of the other hand, imitating his hero. "You know, he waited and waited to throw on the resonators until we were so close to Lothar even seasoned spacers were green. And then, those resonators," and Maxil gave his head a respectful shake, drawing his breath in with a hiss. "You don't expect to be able to hear again. And it's not exactly a noise . . . it's a whine inside your skull that jars your teeth loose." His eyes briefly reflected the pain he had endured. "And when it stops . . .

it's like there'll never be any noise again in the world." He shook his head and added with a smile. "But he did it and we'll never have to fear the Mil ever again.

"You know, it's funny how things work out. Gorlot had those installations made on every ship we had in service. But, if he *hadn't* used them during the Tane business, we'd've got every single ship without a casualty of our own. Every time I remember I ate in the same room, breathed the same air as that . . . that unrestored unprintable did, I get sick. *Sick.*"

His choice of adjective had the same effect on me. I tried to fasten my thoughts on Maxil's explosive maturation. For he was no longer an adolescent. He had found himself in his baptism under fire. I think Ferrill was wrong when he felt that Jokan was the only one who showed the true Harlan strain.

"Have you seen Ferrill yet?"

"Oh, yes," Maxil assured me solemnly. "I've just come from there." Then he grinned at me broadly, a touch of the boy showing. "He said you were marvelous, Sara. When Stannall collapsed, when everyone was running around cave-hunting, you were so calm and controlled."

"Ferrill gave you a description of himself, not me," I laughed, nevertheless flattered. I wondered if Ferrill might be indulging in some subtle sarcasm. "He's recovered? He had no business working under such pressure for so long. I was very worried about him."

"No. He's . . . he's . . . Ferrill," Maxil ended lamely as suitable comparison failed him. "Say, what's Talleth doing here? He looks as if he's sitting on . . . something hard."

I tried not to giggle as Maxil changed phrases midsentence.

"He keeps telling us, every hour on the hour, that he has orders to report immediately to the Regent. He has some burning message he'll only give to Harlan. And we won't wake Harlan up."

"You shouldn't," Maxil agreed. "He sent me off not long after we managed to get through the crowds to the palace. I was asleep before I could kiss Fara."

He beckoned to Talleth who, after a quick glance at the study door, rose obediently and came over.

"What's the problem, Talleth?"

"I was given a commission by Regent Harlan," Talleth began patiently. "When I had accomplished it, I was to report directly to Lord Harlan. I've been waiting for five hours and ten minutes, sir."

"When did Harlan get to bed, Sara?"

"Approximately ten hours and ten minutes ago," I replied keeping my face straight.

"He'll be up soon, then," Maxil said easily and, nodding to Talleth, indicated he could resume his post.

I thought Maxil was just saying that, so no one, except Talleth, was more surprised than I when fifteen minutes later, Harlan himself opened the door to the study.

He swept the occupants of the room with a swift glance, smiled briefly at me but held up his hand as I started to come to him. Instead, to my chagrin, he beckoned Talleth into the study and closed the door.

"Close your mouth," Maxil suggested in an aside. "I guess he really did want to see Talleth after all."

Ignoring the slight as best I could, I hastily ordered Linnana to get warm food. Maybe Harlan was annoyed with me because I had been asleep when I should have been there to greet him. Linnana interrupted my nattering by asking what she should order for the Regent's breakfast. I realized I didn't even know what Harlan liked to eat. Certainly the asylum fare was no criterion.

"Plenty of meat, he'll be hungry," I temporized.

Whatever business Talleth had with Harlan, it was brief. The officer exited, saluted Maxil respectfully, glanced at me with a worried frown and left the apartment. Harlan did not appear.

Hot food came up from the kitchens and no sign of him. It was too much for me. Trying to appear casual, I went through the empty study to the bedroom. Just as I entered, he emerged from the bathroom, buckling on a uniform overtunic.

"Harlan, are you . . . displeased with me?"

He gave a little laugh and came over to embrace me,

his face slightly damp, smelling cleanly of soap and fresh linens. "No, you please me tremendously, except when you keep my officers waiting."

He released me quickly, for I was left standing, kissless. He strode over to the big chest to one side of the study door and rummaged through a top drawer, stuffing several objects in his belt pouch.

"I'm hungry," he announced, his smile making his words an intimate reminder.

"It's hot from the kitchen," I assured him as he ushered me out to the living room.

Although he had reassured me verbally that he was not displeased with me, it seemed he was not at ease somehow. As if he held himself from me purposefully. As if there were something between us, separating us. With Jokan and Jessl, Maxil and the two Councilmen as well as the servants, it was impossible for me to pursue the subject of my unrest or set it at ease.

Harlan pulled me to the chair beside him at the table but, as he talked to the others, cheerful, rested, he never once glanced at me. He gave Jessl some instructions about putting their fastest Star-class ship in readiness for a long trip. He all but pushed Jessl through the door to get him started on the assignment.

Once Jessl had left, he turned earnestly to the two Councilmen.

"I appreciate your waiting on me like this, although I had expected to be awake long before this hour," and he shot a humorously accusing glance at me.

"I did it," Jokan interposed, taking full blame.

"I'd've preferred you returned the compliment I paid you when I got in," Harlan said so caustically Jokan looked surprised. "However, Talleth brought me word I hoped against hope he would have. For the first time, we have captured, *intact,* the Mil star maps, complete with primary notations and time symbols."

Jokan and the Councilmen exclaimed excitedly and leaned forward eagerly as Harlan continued.

"I don't say we now have the route to their homeworld. It is impossible to tell whether they were on an outward or inward orbit. The holds were barely half full," he added, dropping his voice and swallowing. I guess I wasn't the only one who looked ill. There was no longer any question in my mind what those holds carried.

"However, I believe it is important for us to retrace their route, starting from the notation that is the Tane group and working backward."

The sound of a planecar right on top of us made me glance up startled. Talleth was at the controls. He secured the craft to the landing balcony and stood waiting.

"I have a quick trip to make, gentlemen, after which I will explain myself in greater detail. If you will excuse me," and Harlan rose.

"You have to go right away?" I murmured, deeply disappointed. I was positive now there was something separating us.

"Will you come with me, Sara?" Harlan asked. There was a quality, a pleading in his voice, that I had never heard before.

"Certainly."

The fact that he wanted my company, coupled with his unsettling look, was not altogether reassuring. But, perhaps during the flight I would have time to get to the bottom of the problem.

This aim was soon thwarted completely when I realized that this plane, fast as it was, was also small. Talleth, stolidly piloting, was no farther away from me than my outstretched arm. This was scarcely the time or place for an important private discussion.

The trouble with public life, I thought bitterly, is that it *is* so damned public. If I had to put up with six years of this while Maxil grew to his majority, I would be a frustrated woman.

Harlan's unaccountable nervousness was obvious in many ways as the trip progressed. He kept up a superficially agreeable conversation, inquiring about the events after the attack, the reactions of the most skeptical Councilmen once the resonators were proved effective.

"Where are we going?" I asked as casually as I could

when our forced conversational gambits were exhausted.

"To Nawland," Harlan said crisply.

"What's that?" I persisted.

I obviously should have known because Talleth jerked his head as if to look at me, but changed his mind and kept facing the instrument panel.

"The Space Research Station," Harlan answered in a tone that brooked no further questions.

But my own terrible worries were more than I could contain, even faced with his unresponsiveness.

"Is Monsorlit there?"

Harlan looked at me, startled. "Of course not. He has absolutely nothing to do with this."

I was too relieved that Monsorlit had not made good the threat he had made in the Vaults. The fleeting impression that Harlan considered Monsorlit a lesser evil than the installation at Nawland did not occur to me until later.

A taut silence settled in the little cabin. The set of Harlan's jaw and the feeling that he had again withdrawn from me were inhibiting to the point that all I felt free to do was stare out the window at the sea.

We were flying swiftly over a long tail of islands in shallow water. In the distance, a smudge across the horizon, loomed the purple shadow of a land mass. Above it, a lance against the darkening evening sky, I saw a rocket blast off. Several miles away was another airborne plane, heading toward our mutual goal.

The sight of a fishing boat, similar to the one Harlan and I had escaped in, sent a stab of pain through me. I blinked back the tears that came to my eyes at the memories that sail evoked. Sitting in silent sorrow, I waited passively for this journey to end.

Space Research Station conjures a picture of purposeful activity, launching pads, half-erected gantries, waiting spaceships. But Talleth circled round the island, away from just such a scene, coming in across a quiet cove to an almost deserted strip of slab rock and sand. Two enormous hulls, all their airlocks open like terrible wounds to the setting sun, rested untended on the strip. A smaller rocket was parked to one side of the giant ship Talleth hovered near. Both he and Harlan peered out their side of the plane, searching for something. I noticed that Talleth's face had a greenish tinge and he was sweating profusely.

Then I noticed there were huge tubes, several feet in diameter, plugging the entrances to three of the locks. A variety of equipment, tubing and wires, was carefully stacked against the curve of the huge ship's hull, half obscured by shadow.

"Number Three," Harlan muttered savagely.

Wordlessly Talleth guided the plane down the length of the ship to an open lock, tubeless, in which stood three tall Ertoi figures, one beckoning to us.

Talleth set the plane down, the sweat pouring off his face. It hadn't seemed that the plane required that much effort to fly and the temperature was mild.

"I must ask you to come, Sara," Harlan said in a terse, hard voice. Glancing at him, I was startled to see he, too, was sweating and constantly swallowing. He opened the plane door. An awful smell overwhelmed us and I coughed wildly to clear my lungs of the stench.

I heard Talleth groan, but Harlan had a hand under my elbow and was urging me out onto the sand.

"What's that stink?" I asked, covering my nose and mouth with a fold of my tunic.

Harlan didn't answer. His face showed great distress. Relentlessly he guided me quickly up the rampway to the open lock. The three Ertois moved quietly aside to let us enter.

"This way," one of them thrummed in an incredibly deep voice.

Harlan didn't answer and now I felt his hand trembling even as his fingers took a firmer grip on my elbow. Now, I was scared, too.

"We have put samples in the nearest chamber," our guide boomed hollowly, his voice echoing and echoing down the long dim corridor. "The others have been disintegrated."

The Ertoi stopped by an oddly shaped orifice and nodded his head gravely to Harlan.

Harlan looked ghastly, the sweat pouring down his face, his jaw muscles working furiously as he swallowed. He gave every indication of someone about to be violently ill and mastering the compulsion by sheer willpower.

The moment I stepped through that orifice a scream tore from me. Only because the Ertoi and Harlan were holding me fast did I stay on my feet. I knew why Harlan looked ill. I knew what that smell was. I knew where I was. I was on a Mil ship and I had been in such a room before. I had been in such a room and what I had seen there had sent my mind reeling into the deepest shock.

"They do not look like *you,* the Ertoi say," Harlan managed to say between his teeth. "I have to make you look."

He and the Ertoi half carried me to the long high frame where several sheeted mounds lay still. One of the other Ertoi very carefully pulled back the top of the sheets and the first face was visible to me.

I didn't want to look down. But I had to. With that dread fascination horrible accidents have for you. No matter how ghastly, you have to look and assure yourself it is just as bad or worse than you have already imagined. He was Chinese or at least some Oriental ... his race didn't matter beyond the fact that he had once lived on my planet. I was propelled to the next victim and this was infinitely worse. Because it was a blond girl with the fresh misty complexion of an Englishwoman. Her hair had been shorn off close to her scalp and her face was contorted in the horrible rictus of death. There was no skin on her neck, only raw red flesh, the muscles and neck tendons exposed. I gave the covering a twitch and saw, as I instinctively knew I should but nevertheless had to confirm, that all skin had been flayed from her body. Skin, golden skin, my new golden skin. I, too, had once been flayed and ... restored with golden skin. How much skin can a human lose and live? I stood swaying, my eyes unable to leave her face until I spun away to retch in deep terrible spasms.

I knew it was Harlan who picked me up and carried me out of that charnel place, I felt skin not scales under my hands as I struck out wildly, intent only on inflicting pain on him who had led me, all unwitting, back into horror. I must have acted like a madwoman, shrieking, flailing with arms and legs. Then the pressure around me and in me was relieved as I felt the tart freshness of uncontaminated air around me and the smell was gone from my nose and throat and lungs. I was conscious of the sound of surf, the unlimited sky above me and then a sharp prick in my arm.

A scaly hand thrust an aromatic under my nose, but it only caused my stomach to heave again.

A hand, gentle for all it was scaly and hard, held my head as I vomited, stroking my streaming wet hair back from my face.

As the convulsive dry retching subsided, I became aware that I was propped against the scaly leg of one of the Ertoi. Another Ertoi was shielding my face from the brilliant sunset, his saurian face kind and compassionate as he bathed my face and hands.

Beyond my line of vision, I could hear someone else being violently ill and the thrumming voice of the third Ertoi talking quietly.

I don't know how long it took before we recovered from the experience but it was already full dark when Harlan came over to where I lay, still propped against the patient Ertoi, too weak and spent to move.

"Are they people from your planet, Sara?" Harlan asked with sad weariness.

"Yes."

And I knew why he had subjected me to that horror. I knew, too, what incredible courage it must have taken him to accompany me, knowing what he would see, knowing what he must put me through, and unwilling, despite the cost to himself, to let me go to that little death alone.

"You may proceed with orders, Ssla," Harlan murmured.

One Ertoi saluted Harlan and then me and went back

to the ship. In a minute or so I heard the chirropp, chirropp of the planecar.

Harlan managed to get into the plane himself, but the two Ertoi had to lift me in. Harlan held me in his lap, my head against his chest, both of us too exhausted to move.

Talleth took off at top speed. He, too, had had more of that stretch of Nawland than he could endure.

Whatever injection had been given me, the lassitude it produced spread through my body. Although I feared for a sleep that might be punctuated with the nightmare of revived terrors, I felt myself slipping without volition into the black velvet well of unconsciousness.

The first thought that crossed my mind on wakening was that it wasn't hunger that roused me. It was a soft light, diffused on the wall above the bed. I turned my head to see Harlan, propped up, writing quietly but quickly on a thin metal slate. It was the slip of the stylus across the metal that had penetrated my sleep.

At my movement, Harlan turned, his expression anxious and hopeful, changing quickly to a hesitant smile as our eyes met.

"You were so still. So deeply asleep ..." he said in a low voice.

"No, I'm all right," I assured him, giving his hand a reassuring pat. He caught my hand, squeezing so tightly I gave a little cry.

He put down his writing and turned on his side toward me, his eyes still concerned.

"They have a saying on Earth," I began, trying to lighten his mood, "the criminal always returns to the scene of the crime. Then the law catches him. In this case, it was the victim who returned."

Harlan groaned and dropped his head down to the bed, hiding his face from me.

"Frankly," I continued, around the tightness in my throat, "I think it did the victim good. By all rights, I should have had horrible nightmares and I didn't."

Harlan grabbed me by the shoulders, shaking me, his face twisted with emotion.

"How can you forgive me? How can you ever forget what I have done to you? Forcing you to face that unspeakable horror?"

"Harlan," I said, *"You* went with me. It must have been ten times worse for *you*."

He stared at me blankly, as if I had lost my mind.

"You're incredible. It must have been ten times worse for me?" he repeated, shaking his head in disbelief at my words. "For me? For ME!" He gave an explosive snort of laughter and then hugged me so fiercely I cried out. "I'll never understand you. Never. Never." And he began to laugh, rocking me back and forth in his arms, laughing, I realized, in sheer relief.

"Well, it wasn't very funny," I reminded him, nonplussed at his reaction.

"No, not funny at all," and Harlan continued to laugh, softer now, with silly tears coming to his eyes.

The strained look of worry had lifted from his face when he held me off a little to look at me. His eyes and mouth held traces of his laughter, but his look was intensely proud and possessive.

He brushed my hair back from my forehead tenderly and settled me against him, my head on his chest.

"I have several things to tell you, Sara," he began in a more normal voice. "One, I was honestly afraid you would wake mad or hating me. No, don't interrupt," and he placed a finger on my lips. "I never expected you to understand why I had to subject you to that ordeal. I said be quiet," and his voice was stern, more like himself. "I had only a short time to get you there for the identification. If you remember, I told Jokan and the two Councilmen that we had discovered undamaged star maps from which we could retrace the routes of the Mil. From certain procedures we know they follow," and he swallowed suddenly, "Ssla is of the opinion that their last touchdown was at the planet from which those people came." He held me tightly as I inadvertently began to tremble again.

I took several deep breaths and nodded at him to continue, to ignore my reactions.

"The Star-class I ordered Jessl to refit will carry Jokan

and Talleth to your own world with such help as we can give." He paused and then added in a low voice, "I was going to suggest that you return with them."

"You were going to," I pushed away from his chest so I could see his face.

"I don't want you to leave, but I felt, in view of what happened yesterday, I owed you the choice. There may be someone on your world you would prefer to be with."

I turned in his arms, looking him squarely in the face. His expression was grave but gave me no indication of his thoughts.

"Are you trying to get rid of me?" I asked, amazed at the hoarseness of my own voice. "I've made a pest of myself, I know. First I tag along on that escape. You could have got away much faster by yourself."

"But I don't sail."

"And you should have left me at Gartly's. That would have made much more sense."

"True. But you'd not have encountered Maxil and got into the palace."

"Where I caused Ferrill to collapse completely."

"Which meant Council automatically convened, exactly what I hoped to effect."

"But I angered Stannall so."

"And got yourself into an untenable position as Maxil's woman." I saw a flare of anger in his eyes.

"I got myself involved with everyone!" I said, sunk in miserable reflection.

"Causing Harlan to complicate his own life unnecessarily by claiming you before anyone else dared."

"I'll unclaim you any time you want," I said wildly in my dejection.

"Do you really think I'd let you?" Harlan laughed, half frowning, half smiling. "I haven't known a moment's peace since you half starved me in that asylum. For the sake of the clan mothers, *do* you love me, Sara?"

"Yes, of course. Isn't that obvious?" I gasped, astonished. "I've been madly in love with you since you propositioned me on the boat."

His face relaxed into such an expression of tenderness and entreaty I thought my heart would stop.

"Love me, Sara!" he commanded softly. His hungry mouth claimed mine in a giving and taking that was complete fulfillment for us both, a release from the uncertainties and terrors of the past few days and a promise of richness and peace to come.

CHAPTER EIGHTEEN

"I HATE TO WAKE YOU, SARA, but Jokan's pounding at the door," said Harlan's voice in my ear. I felt a feather kiss on my eyes. I stretched with delicious languor as Harlan continued, "and I want him in here where we can be private."

"Well," I prompted agreeably.

Harlan, standing at the side of the bed, looked down at me quizzically.

"You have nothing on, dear my lady, and while he *is* my brother . . ." and Harlan threw my robe in my face. "Put it on. He's got to keep his mind on what you're *saying*." Harlan laughed at the face I made at him.

I drew the robe on and accepted the hot drink Harlan handed me before he called Jokan in.

"You *want* me in here?" Jokan asked pointedly, glaring at me. I learned later that such intimacy was unusual in Lothar where men were extremely possessive of their ladies.

Harlan indicated Jokan should close the door. Shrugging, Jokan approached the bed and took the chair Harlan pointed to.

"Well?" Jokan asked helpfully, looking from one to the other of us.

"Ssla discovered that the latest Mil victims," Harlan began quietly, sitting down on the edge of the bed beside me, one arm loosely on my shoulders, "are people very similar to us. From certain indications," I noticed Jokan also swallowed rapidly, wiped his forehead nervously, "the last planet was not far away. I want you, with Talleth as captain, to take the Star-class command ship and retrace that route, establish relations with these people and give them whatever scientific and military experience we have to share. Provided," and Harlan held up his hand, "they

227

will agree to joining forces with us to track the Mil to their lair and destroy them."

Jokan snorted, shaking his head at the orders his brother had given him.

"Just orbit in, in a ship no different from the ones raiding them, land in the midst of the poor barbarians with their spears or swords and say, look here, *I'm* friendly."

I was conscious of Harlan's hesitation.

"Use one of the smaller rockets," I suggested and Harlan's hand pressed my arm in approval. "You'll need it to get past the satellites and to take evasive action against the nuclear missiles that, I assure you, will be launched."

"To get past what?" Jokan asked, blinking in surprise.

"The planet in question has atomic energy, has landed robot ships on the moon and orbited its nearest space neighbors."

Jokan glanced, wide-eyed, at Harlan for confirmation. Then turned his incredulous blue eyes to stare at me.

"Oh, and we already have electrical power in quantities. So once you explain the Ertoi defense mechanisms, I'm sure they can be put in place very quickly. If someone hasn't worked out an even better defense already."

Jokan made an attempt to rise from his chair and then sat back, stunned.

"I came from that planet, Jokan."

A look of horror replaced the surprise in Jokan's face and he turned to his brother with an angry accusation. At first all I could think was he was revolted by the natural conclusion that I was a restoree.

"You took Sara *with* you to Nawland yesterday?" he rasped out, his eyes flashing.

Harlan nodded slowly.

"I had to identify the victims," I said hurriedly, taut with strain for his reaction.

"But you ... you're ... not ..." and Jokan stared at me fixedly.

"Yes," I said slowly, because Jokan's good opinion mattered. "I am a restoree."

"Sara!" Harlan snapped, anxiously.

"No," I countered, watching Jokan's face as he struggled with his emotional reactions. "I think Jokan should know. I don't like to deceive *him*."

Jokan continued to scrutinize me, not masking traces of revulsion because he had them subdued quickly. He looked at me with great interest and finally, rubbing his hands slowly up and down his thighs, he began to smile at me.

"While I went into deep shock," I continued hastily, "not from restoration, but from . . . what I saw, I came out of it gradually. *That's* how I met Harlan. I must have been taken to Monsorlit's Mental Defectives Clinic sometime during the early part of the Tane wars when a Mil ship was disabled, either on Tane or in space. I guess Gorlot's people thought me a Tane colonist. At any rate, there I was. When I overheard Monsorlit and Gleto talking, I realized Harlan had been drugged. And, well," I ended lamely, "you know what started happening then."

Jokan expelled all the air from his lungs in a deep sigh. He began to relax, nodding his head slowly up and down.

"Well," he said briskly, slapping his thighs, "that explains a great many things, doesn't it?"

"It should," Harlan agreed, a faint smile on his lips. I could feel he was still tensely waiting for something.

"It's very reassuring to learn, however, that your people are *not* hiding in caves," Jokan remarked in a completely different tone of voice. He rose, drawing a slate out of his belt pouch, and sitting down on the bed beside me, asked if I could draw a map of my world.

The tension left Harlan's body and I realized he had been waiting, hoping that Jokan would do something of this order, proving that my restoration did not render me physically revolting in his eyes. That he had hoped Jokan, too, could put aside the conditioned reaction toward a restoree.

"I'll be glad when you bring back paper," I muttered, struggling awkwardly with a stylus.

"What's that?" Jokan asked, sharply inquisitive.

"It is made of wood pulp combined with rags, pressed flat and thin. It can be made quickly and cheaply and is much easier to write on."

"Wood pulp, rags?" Jokan repeated. "Doesn't seem very durable. I've been using this pocket slate for years. Can you use the same piece of . . . what did you call it . . . paper . . . for years?"

"Well, no," I demurred, "but you people are backward in a lot of other things."

Both Harlan and Jokan rose up in concerted protest.

"Just because you have space travel—which you inherited, you didn't develop it—don't go looking down your noses at my world. We had to start from scratch to get off our planet. There are plenty of things on Lothar where it'd be better if you started all over again with a clean slate." I stopped, bemused by my pun. "You see," I told Jokan archly, "we gave up slates a century ago."

"All right, all right," Harlan chuckled. "Draw."

I had the general outlines sketched in when a vagrant thought came back to me.

"You know, getting you on Earth is going to be a problem," I said with concern. "You're right in that you can't just touch down. Particularly not in a Mil-design ship. You see, we have a radar network that would spot you miles up and while I don't know what the Mil may have done to the internal politics of Earth, you're sure to meet a barrage of nuclear missiles. And a Star-class is just too big to miss."

"The rider ships are not Mil-designed," Jokan suggested.

"That doesn't mean they won't be shot at."

"What kind of communication systems does your planet have? They must have some if they are experimenting in space flight," Harlan put in.

"Telstar!" I cried with sudden inspiration. "Why you'd reach every country in the world!" Then I got deflated just as quickly. "No, I wouldn't even know how you could jam it or interpose your broadcast on it."

"What is it?" Jokan prompted hopefully.

I explained as best I could and Jokan beamed at me patronizingly.

"We may still be using slate, dear sister, but in space we are completely at home. It's a simple matter to locate this Telstar of yours on *our* equipment, well out of the range of your radar screens and defensive missiles. Interfere and use its transmission for our purposes. That's an excellent idea."

"Fine," I agreed tartly, "I grant you can do it. Then what?" I demanded acidly. "No one *there* speaks Lotharian."

I couldn't help laughing at the expression on their faces.

"Now, get me a tape recorder and I will introduce you. I speak enough of our languages to get across what I mean. The point is to get you *down* to Earth and let the linguists take over from there."

"Good," Harlan put in, his face echoing his prideful pleasure in possessing me. "Sara has a curious habit of supplying our need. Did you know she can sail boats?"

"I believe you've mentioned that, Harlan," Jokan remarked with dry testiness. It was my first indication, however, that Harlan had ever mentioned me to anyone. He had seemed so concerned I shouldn't arouse any attention at all.

"You can see why she's been so important," Harlan commented.

"Because she can sail?" Jokan retorted with an innocent look.

"I'm surprised," Harlan continued, ignoring his brother, "it hasn't come up in conversation so far this morning," and he regarded me suspiciously, "but I'm hungry. And I'm going to break my fast."

"Why didn't someone say breakfast was ready?" I exclaimed sitting straight up.

Jokan jumped to his feet. "We'll all work better after eating. Less snarling at each other." And he grinned boyishly at both his brother and me.

"Jo," and Harlan stopped his brother with a hand on his shoulder, "do I need to caution you about revealing Sara's . . ."

Jokan shook his head solemnly from side to side.

"She's just infernally lucky it was you," he commented. "But I'd suggest that you in your official capacity as Regent, redirect Stannall's campaign to put Monsorlit on the Rock as a collaborator. Sara could be implicated."

"Yes, the day the Mil invaded, Stannall was trying to get me to accuse Monsorlit," I added, and fear of the cold physician, never far from my consciousness, returned. If Jokan had also noted Stannall's preoccupation, I had not misinterpreted my danger.

Harlan put an arm around my waist comfortingly. "I also know Monsorlit and, despite everything I've heard, I don't think Sara has anything to worry about from him."

"Well, I'd rather find a deep cave I didn't need than not have one when I did," Jokan remarked pointedly and, turning on his heel, started for the main room.

Harlan gave me another reassuring hug before we joined him.

There were just the three of us at breakfast this morning. A very unusual occurrence in itself, for breakfast was the hour of the patronage seekers or intense political conferences. The intimacy we three shared was therefore an unusual and unexpected respite. Because of Linnana and Harlan's servant, Shagret, we couldn't talk about Jokan's mission. And, as soon as breakfast was over, the communicator lit up. Harlan was called to meet the Councilmen in charge of Jokan's mission, so he left for his offices in the administration wing to get the necessary clearances.

Jokan and I retired to the study with closed doors and I taped a message that he would, he assured me, be able to transmit over Telstar. I started to give him a brief summary of our world history and decided it was useless to predispose him. The menace of the raiding Mil might well have consolidated and changed everything. Instead I spent the morning giving him some basic English phrases and such terms as he might need to effect a safe landing. I suggested that Cape Kennedy or the new Dallas Space Center would be able to accommodate the huge Star-class ship. I showed him these centers on my rough map, sighing at such inadequate cartography.

It was as if a cork had been pulled out of me that had damned up my Earth past. I talked and talked while Jokan listened, directing me occasionally with questions about his own areas of interest. My work as a librarian in a huge advertising agency had forced me to acquaint myself with a broad index of references, so I had a thin understanding of many facets of industry and technology. But I was painfully lacking in the details he needed or wanted so that he groaned over the tantalizing snips and snatches I held out to him. I talked until I was hoarse. Then Jokan covered up his slates and announced he was going to see what progress Harlan was making in ramming through the expedition.

Jokan was able to leave two days later, a big coup for Harlan who had indeed rammed the clearance through any opposition in Council. He attributed his success to the fact that Lesatin, thoroughly shaken by the Tane disaster and the Mil penetration, was more than willing, as Acting First Councilman, to expand the Alliance. Stannall, Harlan remarked privately to me, would have delayed until he "had given the matter mature consideration."

"However," Harlan said with a grimace, "I did have to agree to take a committee of Councilmen to the Tanes to see firsthand what has happened there." He covered my hands with his, smiling ruefully. "I'd take you along if I could . . ."

"I'm all right. How long will you be gone?"

"Two, three days, depending on how much convincing they take. And one of them is Estoder."

"I remember him from the Regency debate," I said sourly.

"So do I," Harlan remarked in a thoughtful way.

So he left and the first day I occupied myself with the mechanics of getting my Council grant in order. The much bemedaled slate Stannall had given me the day of the Mil invasion turned out to have considerably more value to me personally than a mere official propitiation. Harlan had read it to me and explained that I had been given a lifetime income from three iron-producing shafts in Jurasse. Someday I would have to inspect these but in the meantime this income was a tidy sum.

"It's enough for you to be comfortably placed if you were still unclaimed," Harlan explained, then his eyes twinkled wickedly. "It also provides that, if you die while you are unclaimed, the income devolves to your issue until they reach their majority."

I glared at him. I had a lot to figure out about the complicated marital and extramarital and post-, pre-, and ante-marital mores of this world where women are expected to produce children and no one asks who is the father.

"However, you are very much claimed and I will provide for your issue, making certain it is all mine."

I held him off for he started to wrestle me and I didn't want to be diverted quite yet from this subject.

"Are you rich, Harlan?"

"Yes, I guess so," he said. "I have the family holdings, of course, as my mother is dead. There are the prerogatives and privileges of my position. I haven't used much of my income and neither has Jokan. I had intended," and he grinned one-sidedly at me, "to finance a private expedition. However, my lady Sara," and his smile broadened, "as usual, chose to come from a very interesting planet so Lothar is the outfitter."

"Then, with that settled, I'll go out tomorrow and spend it all on my back," I declared.

"I like your back the way it is right now," Harlan murmured and he started to make love. A thrifty man, Harlan.

At any rate, while Harlan was on his way to Tane, I took my slate to his estate agent. This gentleman, one Lorith, was very polite and helpful. I was extremely pleased with myself that I made no blunders in our interview over matters I should have understood. One thing, however, I decided I must get Harlan to do immediately on his return from Tane was to teach me how to write at least my own name. Lorith would start the proceedings to secure the grant, but there would be many things for my signature in a few days.

Consequently I was not in the least apprehensive the next morning when Lesatin asked me to attend an informal meeting in his chambers.

I had not expected, considering the wording of his invitation, to see the large committee room filled with Councilmen, including four of the Elder Seven and a woman and seven doctors, by their overdress. I was also surprised to see Ferrill enter. He nodded to me and sat beside me at one end of the large room.

Lesatin was scanning the faces of the assembled when Monsorlit entered. I glanced, apprehensive for the first time, at Ferrill. He smiled noncommittally and I settled back, reassured. As far as I could tell, Monsorlit did not so much as glance in my direction. The woman, however, constantly looked at me.

"We are met today to assess accusations made against Physician Monsorlit," Lesatin began in a formal opening of the session. "These charges include complicity with the archtraitor Gorlot in the genocide of the Tanes; furnishing drugs capable of inhibiting and demoralizing certain officials in our government and . . ." Lesatin glanced at his note slate, "illicit surgery."

I pulled at Ferrill's arm nervously. Illicit surgery meant restoration. Monsorlit was unruffled by these charges and Ferrill only patted my hand.

Lesatin first called various hospital officials and technicians who had been in charge of the victims taken off Tane. They testified that the early wounded to arrive at the hospital were invariably in some stage of paralytic cerolosis. Cerol, in unadulterated form, could produce total paralysis of the body and its functions, resulting in death. Complete and immediate blood transfusions would lessen its deadly effects, but too often brain and nerve centers were affected. Monsorlit had developed a series of cold and hot baths as shock treatments, a radical new approach in Lotharian medical practice, to rouse the sluggish, cerolized areas. Two physicians who testified did not entirely approve of such a rigorous course of treatment although they admitted Monsorlit's techniques effected partial cures that were considered miracles. Patients were able to do for themselves, perform simple duties and relieve society of the burden of their care.

Yes, it had been Monsorlit's idea to place a hospital ship so near the Tane planets for prompter care of the injured. No, they could not say that any of the men appeared to have been restored. Of course, at that time, no one looked for such evidence because no one had realized that the Mil were in any way involved. Yes, they had heard Monsorlit use the expression "repossessed" often. One surgeon had called him to account because of the word's unfortunate similarity with the unpopular practice of restoration. Monsorlit had replied that the men were actually repossessed, repossessed of their faculties disabled by cerol.

Had Monsorlit practiced any total restorations since the edict against it? Yes, two operations had been performed with official sanction on burn victims in a satellite yard fire. What were the results? A reconstruction so perfect as to defy detection.

I found myself unconsciously stroking one wrist and hastily clasped my hands firmly together. Looking up, I was aware of Monsorlit's eyes on me. He had caught my gesture and smiled slightly.

I knew then that he had merely bided his time. That I had been foolish to think myself immune. I wondered if he had planned this trial to coincide with Harlan's absence. I hoped desperately that someone else beside myself could incriminate him; that his own preference for life would keep him from disclosing my restoration.

Lesatin continued his investigation with further questions about the illegal restoration.

Was it possible that total restoration could be detected? Only by a check of cell coding within a month of restoration and, even so, there would still be room for doubt.

Lesatin asked for an explanation of cell coding. It was so long and technically detailed I paid no attention.

"I fail to understand its application to restoration," Lesatin prompted patiently.

Before restorations had been ruled illegal twenty-five years ago, intensive research had tried to perfect ways in which a total body graft could be undetected. It had been felt that the unsightly scars at wrist, ankle and neckline contributed to the revulsion caused by restorees. A high fever was induced in the patient by a virus injection for the purpose of changing the cell coding of the body so that it would accept new skin from any donor. The new skin would bond properly, assimilating and overgrowing what original epidermis remained, leaving undetectable the restoration.

Well, that explained the golden tinge to my skin, I thought. I'd wondered how they'd accomplished that.

In cases of plastic surgery, this technique was often applied with detection-defying results.

I managed to keep my hand from my nose.

Lesatin continued doggedly. Was it possible for any of the so-called Tane wounded to have been restorees? Possible, but not probable, for the men admitted to the War Hospital had been unquestionably suffering from acute cerolosis. Most were now able to take care of themselves and were employed in routine jobs. By common definition, they could not be restorees, as it was well known that a restoree was incapable of any independent action.

Crewmen on the hospital ship that Monsorlit had sent out were questioned. They gave detailed descriptions of cases they had handled. They confirmed in every way the information already given.

Lesatin paused and then asked several men how long they had worked for Monsorlit. They had, without exception, been trained by the physician, had served him since their certification and were, admittedly and vehemently, loyal to him. Lesatin dismissed them, having made a point.

From Lesatin's questioning and bland manner there was no indication whether he was out to clear Monsorlit or convict him. But I knew clearly what I would do. I would speak out against Monsorlit. I would tell them he had perfected the drug that had been used on Harlan and the others. I would tell them all I knew and remove

Monsorlit from a position in which he could threaten and terrify me.

Lesatin issued an order I didn't overhear and the side door opened to admit a chained, shrunken, groveling Gleto, flanked by two strong guards.

Lesatin turned to Monsorlit with an apologetic gesture.

"This is one of your accusers, physician," he said. "Gleto has sworn that you developed the drug, cerol, into several compounds which were used to depress Harlan, Japer, Lamar, Sosit, to name only a few. That you were completely aware of the perfidy against the Tane race and knew that the supposed casualties you handled in your hospital were victims of the skirmishes with the Mil ships. That you have actually performed illegal restorations to cover evidences of Gorlot's treachery."

Lesatin smiled deprecatingly and he was joined by the four Elders who were plainly telling Monsorlit that the source of these accusations was very suspect.

"Gleto has also gone on to insist that your personal fortune has swelled to enormous proportions. That you have secretly continued your abominable research on human beings."

Monsorlit nodded calmly. It was well known that Gleto's personal fortune had also swelled to enormous proportions. The physician arose and presented a thick pile of slates to the first Councilman at the table.

"Sealed and documented records of all my personal financial affairs," he said. "I beg pardon for such a bulky package but my income is heavily involved with my experimental work at the Mental Clinic."

Lesatin acknowledged this and motioned the Councilmen to examine the slates.

"As to the secret and abominable research on humans," Monsorlit continued, addressing the Councillors, "my colleagues will tell you that some of my work is done in secret, behind closed doors and the results are in locked files. That is the only way to protect the privacy of our patients, some of whom are well placed in life, despite their inner uncertainties. Yes, the research we have been conducting lately might once have been called abominable, but the results have been a return to health for many. Very often a medicine tastes abominably, but that does not mean its efficacy is affected."

He spoke so glibly, his explanations so pat, yet nothing he had said sounded rehearsed or insincere.

"As to my developing cerol compounds, I could scarcely deny so well publicized a fact," and Monsorlit smiled pleasantly. "My laboratories have been aware of its effectiveness ... if properly and abstemiously used ... in restraining mental cases, in the stimulation of certain muscular centers, in ... ways too numerous to list. It is a remarkably versatile base for a wide range of uses. It will be some time before we reach the end of its potentialities.

"But, as the man who invented our slates cannot control what we, centuries later, write upon them, I cannot control the uses to which the discoveries in our laboratories have been put," and with a shrug Monsorlit resumed his seat.

Lesatin exchanged low comments with several of the Councillors.

"Did you, physician, at any time suspect you were being used by Gorlot to cover up his treachery against the Tane?"

That to me was the silliest question yet. But Monsorlit considered it gravely before answering.

"I am not a politician, gentlemen, but a serious scientist. It was my duty under Regent Gorlot to perform such services as he required of me in my capacity as Head Physician of the War Hospital. If I had any doubts as to the authenticity of the afflictions, I had little time to pursue them due to the extreme pressure of work and the speed with which it is necessary to treat acute cerolosis."

"Does not acute cerolosis parallel the symptoms of restoration madness in so far as the mental processes of the patient are concerned?" snapped Lesatin.

I gasped and so did others at the sting of the question.

But it reassured me that Lesatin must be after Monsorlit.

Monsorlit pondered this question calmly.

"Yes, it does," he said deliberately, still in thought. "There is an absolute paralysis of mental centers, sluggish reactions, no independent action. But, as you gentlemen are aware, the shock treatments we have used have brought the patients back to as normal a pursuit of life as possible, considering the irreparable damage done by the cerol in some cases."

There was an unfinished quality to his statement that reached me if no one else.

"You are noted for your skill in restoration, Physician Monsorlit," Lesatin continued. Monsorlit accepted the implied compliment as his just due. "Are there other surgeons today capable of such technical perfection?"

"If you mean partial restorations due to common accidents, yes. My techniques, as published in the Medical Library, are effective for partial as well as complete restorations. I could name dozens of surgeons capable of performing undetectable restorations. Partial ones, of course."

"Could Physician Trenor perform undetectable restoration?"

Everyone waited for Monsorlit's reply and again I wondered if Lesatin were for or against Monsorlit.

"It is entirely possible although I have never observed the physician in question in the operating arena."

Had it been Trenor all along and not Monsorlit? Had I been mistaken? No, no, that wasn't possible. Something vital assured me of that.

"Thank you, physician." Lesatin consulted his slate. "May I call the Lady Sara?"

I stood up nervously.

"You were Lord Harlan's attendant during his ... stay at the asylum, weren't you?"

I confirmed this.

"Monsorlit was Harlan's physician, I believe," and Lesatin looked first at Monsorlit, who confirmed this and then at me. "Did he attend Harlan at the sanitarium?"

"Yes."

Lesatin knew this, for he was referring to slates he must have made during the inquiry Stannall conducted.

"Did you ever have occasion to suspect Harlan was being mistreated? Drugged into insensibility, rather than helped to regain his sanity?"

"Yes, I did."

"What aroused your suspicions?"

"A conversation between Gleto and ... Monsorlit," I announced, looking accusingly at the physician who merely watched.

"Really?" Lesatin appeared sincerely surprised. "Can you remember this conversation?"

"Yes, I most certainly can. Gleto had called Monsorlit to examine Harlan because he was afraid Harlan would revive from the drug."

"The drug was named?"

"Yes. Cerol. Monsorlit said that there was no need to increase the dosage. He told Gleto to have a weekly absorption rate taken and that would give an indication when more would be needed. Gleto said he didn't have the personnel and Monsorlit offered to send him a repossessed technician who could perform the test on Harlan. Monsorlit also said that Gleto had better do the same for the nine men who were Trenor's patients." My story came out in a rush because I was afraid of being interrupted and because I wanted desperately to say it before I lost my nerve.

Lesatin turned with anxious concern to the Councilmen. They whispered agitatedly among themselves.

"Why didn't you bring this conversation to light in the earlier investigation?" I was asked.

"I never got the chance. The Mil came," I defended myself.

Monsorlit's voice asked for the right to question me and permission was given him.

"How did you obtain the position as Harlan's attendant?" he asked me pleasantly.

"I was placed there from the Mental Clinic."

"Oh. You'd been a patient there?"

Watching every muscle in his controlled face, I nodded.

"How long were you a patient at the Clinic?"

"I don't remember exactly."

"Accuracy to the minute is not required. A rough estimate is all that is necessary."

"Two months," I blurted out because that number came to my mind first. It was wrong. I could see that in the gleam in Monsorlit's eyes. He drew out another bundle of slates and passed them to Lesatin.

"The Councilmen will see the documented record indicates a stay of over five months."

He's covered up here, too. All I have to do is not get rattled. He can't beat me. I'm right and he's wrong. He's dangerous. They've got to believe *me*.

"Lady Jena," and Monsorlit turned to the other woman in the room, a gray-haired, gentle-faced lady, "was the ward nurse in Lady Sara's early days with us."

"I was indeed, poor thing."

"Describe her condition."

"Sir, she couldn't speak at all. She didn't seem to understand anything. They're like that sometimes, poor dears. Especially the civilians who came to us from Tane. But it took her longer to understand even the simplest things. Her early achievement tests are just too low to be possible. I have included them in the records."

Lesatin hemmed and cleared his throat, looking at me with an expression close to anger and resentment. I saw that I had been wrong. Lesatin really wanted to clear Monsorlit and here was my incriminating testimony to confuse the issues already settled in his mind.

"The Lady Sara seems quite able to make herself understood now," one of the Elders pointed out dryly.

"Notice, however," Monsorlit said smoothly, "that odd labial twist. Notice the aspiration of the hard consonants, as if there were difficulty in controlling the speech centers."

"A personal quirk?" asked my champion.

"Possibly," Monsorlit admitted, but there was no conviction in his voice. "Lady Sara," and he spaced his syllables oddly, "what is the capital of Ertoi?"

"I don't know," I replied quickly. "Do you?" and I directed my question to one of the Councilmen. He blinked at me for my insolence.

Monsorlit laughed. "They can be very shrewd."

"Sir," Lesatin began angrily, "your line of questioning is irrelevant and offensive. Lady Sara's contribution to Lothar is great and you must be careful of your aspersions."

"She isn't careful of hers," Monsorlit answered tolerantly. "They often aren't tactful. But she is very beautiful, isn't she?" he added kindly.

I held my breath. He couldn't be going to . . .

"She has only to smile," Monsorlit continued, "and be admired. Beautiful women know that intelligence is not required of them and conduct themselves accordingly. However, the fact remains that the Lady Sara was a patient in the Mental Defectives Clinic and she *fails* to remember how long. She does not know the capital of Ertoi and there isn't one. Here, Lady Sara, write me a few lines. Write your name. Even beautiful women who have attended our Mental Clinic can write."

Monsorlit thrust a slate and stylus at me.

"I protest this preposterous treatment," I cried.

"That's a good sentence to write, isn't it?"

The slate was put in my hands. I didn't know what to do. Lesatin and the others were waiting with increasing impatience. It was such a simple thing and I couldn't do it.

"I cannot write," I said finally.

"Of course not," Monsorlit said, turning to the Councillors. "Her records show that she was incapable of learning anything except the most routine duties. How to dress herself neatly, keep clean, act cooperatively. That's why she was in a mental-home attendant's position. She can learn anything by rote. *Anything*."

"You certainly cannot insist that Lady Sara has responded to rote lessons today?" my champion asked.

"Not entirely. I most gladly admit she has improved

tremendously since she left the Clinic. She shows more promise of complete recovery than those records indicate possible. She must be allowed every opportunity to grow toward complete mental health, to restore her lost knowledge. I suggest, Councilman Lesatin, that she be returned to my Clinic to complete a recovery so auspicious."

Someone must contradict this diabolical man. I turned anxiously toward Ferrill and saw to my horror that his seat was empty. How could he leave me? Now, when I needed a friend most? I burst into tears and tried to draw back from Monsorlit as he placed a proprietary arm around my shoulders and began to lead me from the room. I resisted, but the man was unbelievably strong. He led me out a side door into a small anteroom while, in the chamber behind, the Councilmen burst into angry questions and discussion.

"You should have come of your own accord. I did not wish so public a humiliation for you," Monsorlit chided.

"You *know* I'm no defective. Harlan will be back and you'll be sorry."

"Threats. Threats. Harlan can return when he wishes, but you will go back to the Clinic and stay until my treatments bring about a full recovery."

"No! I am recovered. I don't need more treatment."

"You do. One day I'll have a complete success with my technique of restoration," and his eyes were fixed at a point above my head, "mind and body. There will be no mental blocks such as you have in the memory synapses. It will be a complete cure."

I stared at him. He didn't know either. I had always assumed he did. He thought I was a Lotharian and just didn't remember. He really believed I had been a colonist on Tane when the first Mil attack came. He had collaborated with Gorlot so he could prove, to himself if to no one else, that restoration itself did not cause the mental deterioration.

"You're mad," I cried. "And you're wrong."

The door opened wider and Lesatin and several other Councilmen entered.

"The charges against you are dismissed, Monsorlit," he said gravely. "And you have our permission to take this ... girl with you. For all our sakes I hope you do effect a complete cure for her."

"It's a pity she had been so closely connected with the young Warlord. I wondered why Harlan tolerated her."

"Harlan has always liked a pretty face. Look at Maritha. And then, too, Harlan is probably grateful."

"No, no, no," I shouted at their pitiless faces. "That isn't it!"

Monsorlit took my arm in one steel-fingered hand.

"She's done remarkably well considering her early ineptitude," he said. "I can't imagine who could have turned her against me."

"No one," I shrieked at him, trying to twist free. "I'm not defective. I can't write Lotharian because I don't even come from this planet. I came from Earth, the place those corpses on the Star-class Mil ship came from, the planet Jokan has gone to find. I'm not from Lothar. I'm from Earth," I screamed desperately, for Monsorlit was fumbling in his belt pouch and I knew what he was seeking.

"What's this about Jokan's expedition?" "Another planet?" "Who's been babbling?" The Councilmen all asked at once.

"Delusions," Monsorlit reassured them, smiling at me as he got the needle out of his pouch.

"On the contrary," a new voice said from the hall doorway. Ferrill pushed through. "On the contrary, she is telling the truth. And here is a slate, written by Harlan before he left for the Battle of Tane. It is addressed to me. Lesatin, I suggest you read it to everyone. You see, in this corner is the date, hard and fast."

Monsorlit dropped my hand as if it burned him. Even he looked his incredulous surprise at Ferrill's news. I ran to the ex-Warlord, weeping with relief, clinging to him. He put an arm around me with awkward but very reassuring gentleness.

Lesatin mumbled the phrases Harlan had written and the others peered over his shoulder. When they had read, they stared at me in complete confusion.

"How did you get here?" Lesatin roused himself to ask.

"Evidently on a Mil ship," I said cautiously. "I ... don't really know. I was in shock. I'm here. I'm me. I'm not mentally ill."

"But those tests we were shown? Jena is a very reliable person. A woman of her background and breeding would have no reason to fabricate lies," Lesatin stopped.

"The tests were undoubtedly accurate," Ferrill suggested sensibly. "I doubt any of you could understand her language so how could you expect her to understand ours ... particularly after having been so nearly ... skinned alive."

Monsorlit's eyes blazed as if I had suddenly changed into another person.

"How did she get here?" Lesatin repeated, dumbfounded.

"She was brought into my base hospital along with several other cases," Monsorlit interjected smoothly, but there was a curious look of triumph in his face. "I assumed at the time she was one of the colonists who had been attacked by the Tane. There was no reason to suppose otherwise at the time. We know that Gorlot had several brushes with loaded Mil ships. Some were disabled. Undoubtedly she was on one of them."

"In what condition was she brought to you?" demanded Lesatin with fierce urgency. I clutched at Ferrill for support.

"In a state of complete shock."

"No, no. Physically," demanded the Councilman.

Monsorlit looked at Lesatin with surprise, then back at me as if comparing two pictures in his mind. "Why, much the same as she is now," he replied unhurriedly. "Much the same."

"Could she have been restored?" my old champion demanded, bluntly.

Monsorlit pursed his lips. "How could she have been? She is as rational as any of us," and to my amazement he smiled at me.

"A few moments ago, you assured us she was mentally incompetent," Lesatin reminded him, eyes narrowing.

I could see that Lesatin was not entirely sure my comments were rote lessons.

"My remarks on her apparent defectiveness are still valid," Monsorlit pointed out. "She does not read or write Lotharian. She does not know simple facts our children do. She still talks with an odd accent. But she does not know how long she was at my clinic. She most assuredly had the violent nightmares such as were recorded. She most certainly was incapable of anything but the simplest, most routine tasks. She has been in deep shock and by some miracle has survived and regained complete mental control. *When* she gained it, I do not know." He stressed the conjunction deliberately. "Therefore I can clinically doubt her recollections of a conversation such as she reported here today."

He paused to see the effect of his words. I was about to contradict him, but Ferrill shook me quickly and silenced me with a glance.

"But, gentlemen," and his voice rose above the interruptions of the others, "she presents an incontrovertible proof that I have tried for years to have recognized. That it is the capture by the Mil, not the restoration, that produces deep shock. We have completely restored burn victims and they did not go into shock. It has been our own fears that kill us. She never heard of the Mil. She went into deep shock, true, but she has recovered. I believe that any Mil victim can recover, if properly treated. Restoration has nothing to do with it. Can you realize that?" he demanded triumphantly. "*There* is your proof."

I sagged wearily against Ferrill at the end of my strength.

"As you can see by that slate," Ferrill drawled, "Harlan, our beloved Regent, has entrusted the Lady Sara to my care. She needs it right now. You will excuse us," and he led me from that room.

I remember hearing Monsorlit's voice rising above the arguments of the others as the door closed. I had been forgotten and I was glad.

CHAPTER NINETEEN

FERRILL MARSHALED ME DOWN the halls and back to my apartment without stopping for anyone.

He called Linnana to bring a stiff drink and then propelled me to my bed. He propped me up, covering me with a shaggy blanket, took the drink from a startled Linnana and shooed her out of the room.

I gulped at the stimulant gratefully, disregarding the raw bite on my throat.

"Don't leave me, Ferrill," I whispered as he turned from the bed.

"My dear aunt, not even a surprise attack by the Mil could stir me from my post," he said with complete sincerity. He brought a chair to the bedside and settled himself comfortably.

"My curiosity is boundless and you won't get rid of me until I hear everything I want to know about your fascinating recent past. Really, Sara, I consider it immensely rude of you not to have relieved my tedium these past days with this exciting disclosure. A planet, full, I hope, of other enticing females? My, my! Jokan will have fun. I do hope he returns with another extraplanetary aunt. They're much more alluring than the homegrown variety."

His absurd raillery was more effective than any tenderly delivered conciliations. The drink diffused its heartening warmth and it was ridiculous to think events would not turn my way with Ferrill putting them into their proper perspective.

The door exploded inward and I cried out, trembling all over even after I saw it was only Jessl.

"Who's been knocking caves down?" Jessl demanded, glaring fiercely at me.

"Easy," snapped Ferrill, holding up a warning hand, his eyes flashing authoritatively. "If you've come storming in here, you know as much as you should."

"The Councilmen are in panic. I thought we were to leave Monsorlit alone. And I thought news of that new planet was to be strictly confidential. What on earth possessed you . . ."

"Hold your tongue, Jessl," Ferrill ordered with such force in his tone that Jessl eyed the ex-Warlord in respectful silence. "Sit down." Jessl complied.

"Now," Ferrill continued more calmly. "Sara has had good cause to be frightened of Monsorlit. Harlan, in his infinite wisdom, chose to ignore it and none of us had the facts to understand her concern. During the Alert, Monsorlit threatened her that she must return to the Clinic," Jessl started to interrupt, staring at me suspiciously. Ferrill held up an imperious hand, his eyes flashing, his pose of bored bystander forgotten. "Don't interrupt *me!* That's better.

"Even if she weren't Harlan's lady, that establishment has little to recommend it to the healthy-minded. Consequently Sara found herself placed in an untenable position at the meeting. I had no chance to warn her what it was all about because I only found out by accident Lesatin had scheduled the hearing today. I was under the impression Harlan was to preside. You are, I believe, aware of the terrible strain Sara has been under," and Ferrill's face was stern. "I sympathize with her completely. I doubt I could have maintained such control were I in a similar position, struggling to survive on her planet."

"Then what Lesatin was saying . . ." Jessl stared at me anew, "you *are* from another planet?"

I nodded.

"Then what . . . they say about Monsorlit doing restorations," Jessl began in a hoarse voice, his attention riveted to my face.

". . . is nonsense," Ferrill said in an airy voice not echoed by the tense expression on his face. "Her planet is so close to the Tanes that she hadn't so much as a mark on her. She was, understandably so, in deep shock. Monsorlit's team discovered her and assumed she was a Tane civilian casualty. She was processed along with others through the Clinic and ended, so fortuitously as far as Lothar is concerned, as Harlan's attendant."

Ferrill's easy explanation gradually reassured Jessl who began to untense and ceased looking as if he wished he were anywhere but in the same room with me.

"But, if she were never a mental defective, then her testimony about Monsorlit's complicity is valid," Jessl said.

Ferrill shook his head in exasperation. "It is useless and wasteful to implicate Monsorlit. No one, except Stannall or Gleto, really wants to indict him. He's done too much among the little people of our world. And just as much for the rich who might want a new face. He is too well established in people's sympathies. His entire hospital staff worships the ground he touches. No real evidence can be found against him. Except Sara's testimony. And because she cannot establish when she came out of shock, Monsorlit has cleverly convinced the session that her recollection of a conversation in her recovery period is probably faulty."

"But I can establish the moment I recovered," I contradicted. "It was the day you visited Harlan with Gorlot and four other men. We were all walking in the gardens and you said 'Harlan, to see you this way.' Gorlot told you you had to keep your mind clear for the evening's work and you told him he could control your decisions but not your heart."

"You were sane then and didn't speak out?" cried Ferrill stunned.

"That was the day everything cleared up. Before it had all been so confused. But I didn't know where I was or what I was doing so I just kept quiet."

"Continue to do so," Ferrill suggested with authority.

"But," and I had another horrible thought, "if the Councilmen now know I'm from another planet, won't they wonder about restoration?"

Ferrill shrugged this suggestion off.

"Why should they? Monsorlit has testified you weren't and he should know."

"Loyalty? Statesmanship—better to say I wasn't, even though I was, from top to toe, a restoree?" I said.

"I feel certain," said Ferrill firmly, "that the incident is closed. Council has something of great moment to concern itself with . . . preparations to attack the homeworld of the Mil itself."

Jessl rose slowly, nodding his agreement with Ferrill's pronouncement.

"My apologies, Lady Sara, but I was deeply concerned," he said. He bowed respectfully to Ferrill and left.

Ferrill waited till he heard the outer door close. Then he got to his feet, smiling broadly.

"Yes, my dear Aunt Sara, Council is going to be very busy. They'll leave you alone and Monsorlit alone."

"You're sure Monsorlit will leave me alone? That I won't have to go back to that ghastly Clinic of his to prove anything more to him?"

"Yes, Sara, I'm sure. You don't have to fear Monsorlit anymore," and Ferrill grinned with his secret knowledge. "Don't you realize why?"

"No."

"The only reason he wanted you back was he thought he had failed in a complete recovery. Now that he knows you have all your old memories, now that he has proved to himself that capture by the Mil does not, in itself, produce insanity unless the victim has been taught to expect it, he doesn't need you anymore. Your case is closed as far as he's concerned. So," and he shrugged his thin shoulders, "you have nothing to fear from Monsorlit."

I stared at Ferrill as the logic of his argument dispelled the last vestiges of my apprehension. He was quite right. Monsorlit had proved his point. I didn't have to worry about returning to the Clinic. Or about my restoration.

Ferrill had pulled the draperies back from the window. The Young Moon, the faster nearer satellite, was rising in the early afternoon sky, a ghostly globe on the green horizon.

"Ironic, isn't it, Sara?" he commented into the companionable silence that had fallen. "We've finally dispersed the last shadow of our fears of the invincibility of the Mil. We can stand free of any subconscious taint of sacrilege after two thousand years at war with ourselves and our old gods. Our weapons can paralyze their strong armadas. Our science is conquering superstition and releasing the last captives from the thrall of the Mil just when no Lotharian will ever have to fear being captured. Our envoy speeds to bring us a new ally."

He looked out over the city. I threw off the blanket and joined him.

"One of my planet's great statesmen said, at a very crucial time in our history, that the only thing we need to fear is fear itself."

Ferrill looked around, pointing a finger at me.

" 'The only thing we need to fear is fear itself.' I like the sense of that. It is very sensible, you realize from your own recent experience with fear." Then he laughed, mockingly. "Of course, it doesn't make allowances for cowards like myself."

"Ferrill," I said angrily, "don't give me that nonsense about being a bad Warlord and you're glad Maxil's got it now because . . ."

"But I am glad," Ferrill objected strenuously. "Something I can't seem to convince you, Maxil, Harlan, everyone . . . except Jokan who understands completely . . ." and he broke off. He snorted, annoyed he had risen to my baiting.

He laughed and, taking my hand, led me from the balcony.

"It's going to be an exciting era for both our planets, Sara, and I'm going to be a part of it . . . even a bystander can enjoy that much. But right now," and his eyes danced as he waggled his finger at me, "I'm afraid," he chuckled, "I'm afraid I'm hungry. Aren't you?"

I burst out laughing, dispelling the last shadows of my weeks of fearful doubts and uncertainties.

"Have you *ever* known me when I wasn't?"

DEL REY SCIENCE FICTION CLASSICS FROM BALLANTINE BOOKS

DEL REY *Catch a Rising Star!*